# ADIRONDACK PROUD

# Adirondack Proud

---

## BOOK 2

Gail Huntley

Published by
Tweed River Publishing

Cover Photos: Louisa Wright and Charles Robinson
Cover photography: James Swedberg
*Front cover background: Robinson Sawmill chute, Long Lake, NY*

Also, you will need price for book. It is $18.00

ISBN 978-1-7367661-0-1
Library of Congress Control number 2021904668

Printed in the United States of America

Other books by Gail Huntley

Blunt Force Winds
Conquering the Wild
Long Lake, Adirondack Heartland
So Proudly They Hailed, Book 1

*Dedicated to Jeanie Cooney Lyman*

*We spent hours talking about Long Lake history. You were my cemetery detective and secured the names of soldiers from Long Lake who were in the wars. We shared a joy and excitement about history, whether in the past or happening now. We were friends, roommates, and sober mates together bouncing along this road called Life. I will see you on the other side, my friend.*

# TABLE OF CONTENTS

Introduction · · · · · · · · · · · · · · · · · · · · · · · · · · · · · · xi
Historical Background · · · · · · · · · · · · · · · · · · · · · · · xiii

1  Long Lake, New York, 1845 · · · · · · · · · · · · · · · · · 1
2  Rossie, New York · · · · · · · · · · · · · · · · · · · · · 15
3  The Journey Home · · · · · · · · · · · · · · · · · · · · 21
4  Two Old Thieves · · · · · · · · · · · · · · · · · · · · · 27
5  Stagecoach to Newcomb · · · · · · · · · · · · · · · · · · 35
6  Town Meetings, Memories, and Sugaring · · · · · · · · 42
7  When He was Bad, He was Horrid, Epitaph · · · · · · 51
8  Fireside Chat · · · · · · · · · · · · · · · · · · · · · · · · 59
9  Revenge · · · · · · · · · · · · · · · · · · · · · · · · · · · · 67
10  Finding Wright Rule · · · · · · · · · · · · · · · · · · · 73
11  The Ingenuity of Uncle Wright · · · · · · · · · · · · · 79
12  The Last Panther, as told by Mitchel Sabattis · · · · · 91
13  Sobriety · · · · · · · · · · · · · · · · · · · · · · · · · · · 97
14  The First Church · · · · · · · · · · · · · · · · · · · · · 109
15  Down the Rabbit Hole · · · · · · · · · · · · · · · · · · 116
16  Michael Wright and Eliza Martin · · · · · · · · · · · 123
17  Midnight Madness · · · · · · · · · · · · · · · · · · · · 127
18  Seasons Come and Seasons Go · · · · · · · · · · · · · 132

19   The "Homecoming" · · · · · · · · · · · · · · · · · · · 141
20   The Gathering · · · · · · · · · · · · · · · · · · · · · 152
21   The Abenaki, The Politician, and The
     Congressman · · · · · · · · · · · · · · · · · · · · · 157
22   Big Brook Village · · · · · · · · · · · · · · · · · · · 164
23   Those in Need · · · · · · · · · · · · · · · · · · · · · 178
24   A Life for a Life · · · · · · · · · · · · · · · · · · · · 186
25   Last Days at the Logging Camp · · · · · · · · · · · · 198
26   The Last Hunt · · · · · · · · · · · · · · · · · · · · · 204
27   A New Rice; Another Move · · · · · · · · · · · · · · · 212
28   The Winter of 1880 · · · · · · · · · · · · · · · · · · · 223
29   The Visit · · · · · · · · · · · · · · · · · · · · · · · · 229
30   Hotels, Bridges, and Homecoming · · · · · · · · · · · 239
31   Fire and the Buttercup · · · · · · · · · · · · · · · · · 255
32   Duncan Dodds and Leafie Wright · · · · · · · · · · · 263
33   Clouds on the Horizon · · · · · · · · · · · · · · · · · 275
34   The Scourge · · · · · · · · · · · · · · · · · · · · · · 283
35   The Wedding · · · · · · · · · · · · · · · · · · · · · · 295
36   Smoke on the Horizon · · · · · · · · · · · · · · · · · 303
37   Freedom · · · · · · · · · · · · · · · · · · · · · · · · 317

     Acknowledgments · · · · · · · · · · · · · · · · · · · 325
     References · · · · · · · · · · · · · · · · · · · · · · · 327
     Background Note · · · · · · · · · · · · · · · · · · · 331

# INTRODUCTION

WE BEGIN ON the west bank of Long Lake, New York, where Jenny Dodds Scott and her husband John have lived since arriving sixteen years earlier. Book One of *The Proud Series,* centers on Long Lake, Newcomb, and Rossie, New York, with the Dodds family joining their famous uncle who fled Scotland carrying a charge of horse thievery. Soon, the oldest daughter and her husband travel to the Adirondacks. The first book, *So Proudly They Hailed,* follows their travels, exploits, and tragedies as they join the first pioneers of Newcomb and Long Lake, two emerging towns in the Adirondacks. *Adirondack Proud* continues the journeys of these settlers, their children, and grandchildren. Since these are real people, and many men and women of that time shared names, it can be difficult to distinguish between father, son, mother, and daughter. Therefore, I have included three family trees. Though the names, places, and events are true, some stories and dialogue are added, depicting what might have occurred during this time and place in history.

# HISTORICAL BACKGROUND

THE PROUD SERIES begins in St. Boswell, Scotland, in 1816 during the Industrial Revolution. My ancestors, the Doddses, were poor tenant farmers who worked for Laird Baccleuch, who owned most of the middle of Scotland called the Borders. His land bordered the property of the famous author, Sir Walter Scott, fifteen miles southeast of Edinburg in one of the most violent areas of Scotland from the 14th through the 16th century. England and Scotland continuously battled over this border territory. Though the invasions ceased, the animosity between the Catholics and Protestants continued, as I depicted in *So Proudly They Hailed.*

My ancestor, George Dalzell, who was a maritime lawyer, kept a detailed journal of his family's journey from Scotland starting in 1819 and continuing through the 1900s. Before George died, he passed the journal on to my father. In the journal, he meticulously documented the lives of our family, the Doddses, and others who were forced to make the treacherous journey to the colonies. George and Helen Dodds and their five children boarded a ship and set sail for Newfoundland dreaming of owning land. They traveled down the St. Lawrence River and settled near its banks in Rossie, New York, where Helen's Uncle Wright Rule and several other Scottish families had already made their homes.

Later, several family members made their way into the Adirondack Mountains of New York, settling in Chestertown, Newcomb, and Long Lake. There they met up with the first settlers of these towns. Long Lake began with a summer visitor, Anthony Theophilus, who vacationed at the northwest end of the lake. The first permanent settler, Joel Plumley, came in 1833 and settled on the south end of the lake. There he met Peter and Mitchel Sabattis, Native Americans who hunted this area. Soon, others followed the wagon trail from Newcomb to Long Lake, and the settlement began.

## The Families

## The Rice Family
## Long Lake, New York

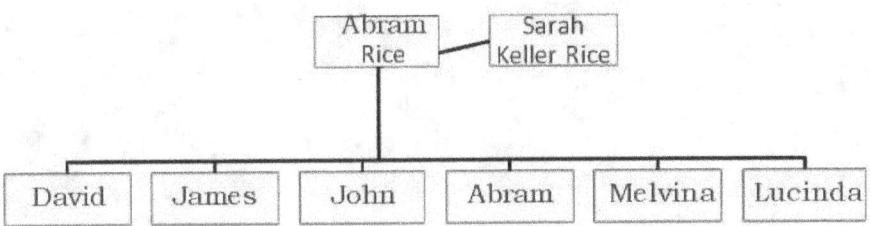

# The Dodds Family
## Rossie, Hammond, Waddington, Newcomb, Long Lake, New York

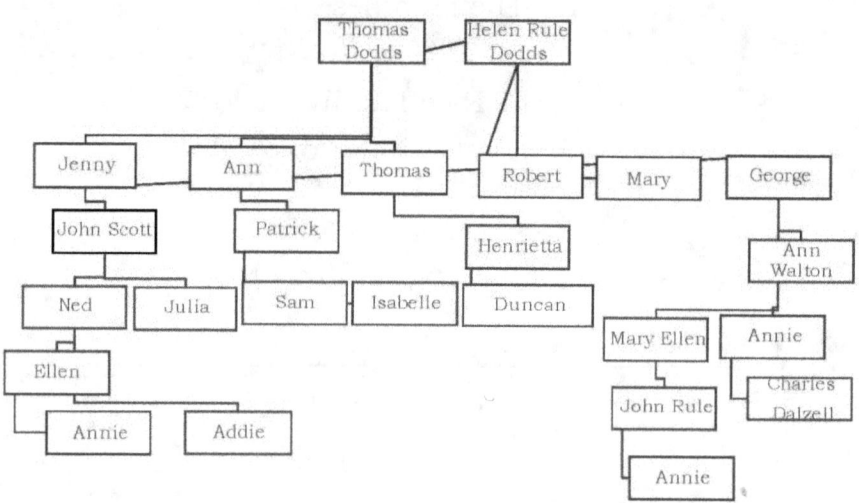

## Wright and Huntley Family
## Crary Mills and Waddington, New York

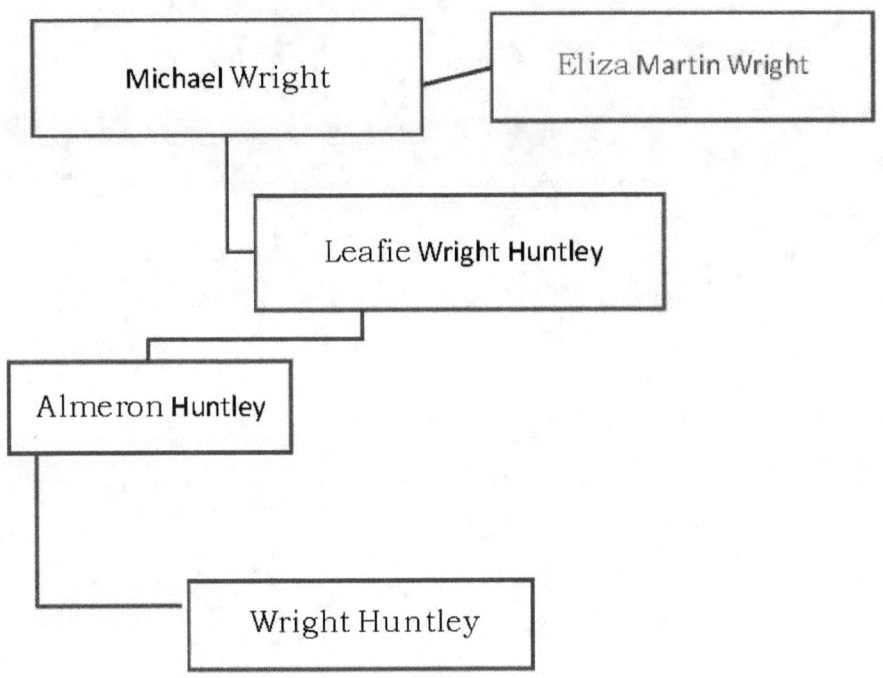

# 1

## LONG LAKE, NEW YORK, 1845

JENNY SCOTT STEPPED onto the worn wooden porch of her log cabin nestled deep in the Adirondack forest. The sun woke, its rays illuminating the tops of the surrounding balsam trees, their fragrance riding the morning breeze that Jenny breathed in as she glanced toward the thick line of red spruce. There he was again. That giant interloper that slipped out into the night ravaging their young garden. Jenny caught only a shadowy glimpse of the creature as it slithered away behind a giant white pine. She jumped off the porch, running around back where her husband, John, was stacking wood.

"Did you see it?" Jenny yelled as she ran along the side of the cabin.

"See what?" John looked up; his blonde hair stuck to his sweat-drenched temples.

"The panther, John; I saw it, and it's a panther." It was April, and every morning for the last two weeks they had planted, and every night something was eating the seeds. They suspected rabbits, a fox, even a bear, not a panther, but it had been a long, cold winter that left hunger in its wake.

"Are you sure, Jen?" John buried the ax in the stump and began walking over to her. Jenny watched him. His gait was a little slower now; his shoulders a little more bent over than the day he had crossed Lake Champlain into the great mountains of New York. Several years and four children later, Jenny still adored the man coming toward her. Their oldest son, Ned, was grown and had been raised a Scott even though he started his life as Ned Walton. When he was old enough to know the story, Jenny told Ned how she had become pregnant by John Scott before leaving Scotland. Fergus Walton knew the truth and married Jenny, giving Ned his last name. Ned never knew his stepfather as he was a baby when Fergus was killed, but he was grateful that such an honorable man had been in his life. Now, Ned was married with a family of his own. He had become a news-paper man and moved to Moira, New York, to work. He had married and had two daughters, Annie and Addie.

Julia, Jenny, and John's daughter, was now a young lady; their second son, Patrick, ten, and his younger sister, Catherine, eight.

She looked at him and with hands on her hips replied, "Yes, I'm sure, John; I know what a panther looks like. Come on; it went through here." He grabbed his rifle and followed Jenny to where she had last seen the panther.

Though these animals were disappearing, Jenny had seen them alive and dead. They were mostly black and smaller than bears, with cats' faces and frightening eyes. Oh, yes, Jenny knew.

One night she had gone to get clothes off the line and saw the inverted leaves on the trees and the magnificent silence that heads a woodland storm. She had quickly unpinned the white muslin sheet, bent over to put the pins in her basket, and heard a low growl. She had snapped up, turned, and stared into the dark forest. She could not see the bear but knew it was close. Bears didn't worry her. They rambled all around the cabin and ran off at the sound of a human. "Get out," she had shouted, "off with you." She had turned and begun to unhook the pins to the next sheet. The sheet corner came loose and draped down in her hands, and she found herself staring not into bear eyes, but yellow eyes. Not eight feet from her, perched on the branch of the massive red spruce, sat a black panther staring straight at her. She screamed, dropped the sheet, and ran into the cabin. By the time John came out with the gun, the animal was gone. From that night on, Jenny made noise when she came out in the night, and she had not seen one since, though they had seen tracks where the animal had come within several feet of the house.

John looked at the trail the animal had taken. There were no tracks, just broken limbs and black hair stuck to one of the thin branches of a budding birch tree. "I am going after it. It got way too close this time."

"Wait!" Jenny cried, "Let's get Jeremiah Plumley or Mitchel Sabattis to go with you."

"Why?" He stared at her. Jenny lowered her head. John didn't see any reason he would need another man with him to kill a cat, but Jenny knew that John was not a skilled marksman. Though they had lived here many years and John and even Jenny hunted, they were not raised in these woods. She always worried when he was out hunting by himself. Another sound of crackling leaves awfully close prompted John to yell, "Jenny, get in the house, now!" He turned his head for a second, watching her. Then he saw little Catherine running out the door. "Get her back in the house!" Jenny ran, scooped her up, and stood in the doorway.

Once again John sighted his rifle into the path that ran beside the white pine where he had heard the noise. He found himself staring straight into the face of Lysander Hall.

"Whoa, Whoa. Hey, it's me, John!" Lysander shouted, raising his hands in surrender.

"By God, man, you scared the hell out of me. Blimey, I darn near shot you."

"I'd say so, but, blimey, you didn't!" Lysander always made fun of his friend's Scottish accent. John had become used to it. "What are you really pointing that big gun at?"

"Panther."

"Panther. You sure? I thought they were all gone." "Jenny saw it, and I heard Bill Austin got one this year." "Right, but I'd also heard that was the last one in these parts."

"Apparently not."

Lysander turned and faced north, "You know, the Kelloggs said they have been having a problem the past few nights with something stealing their seedlings. Wow, that is unusual for a cat to eat young plants. Must be a hungry one. Better be careful. I can go with you." This was not an offer John would turn down. Lysander was the second best shot in town.

"Hell, yes; I'll take your help." Lysander was as young and wild as any animal in the wood, a hunter, and a friend. Wasting no time, John Scott and Lysander Hall headed into the woods that led down to the northwest shore of Long Lake.

Lysander Hall was well known for his tales about most anything anyone wanted to bring up to him. If it was fishing, then he had a story about the big fish devouring the bigger fish and how it ended up on his line and in his stomach. If it was about the weather, then he had the story about how he was up the lake at the outlet paddling home (about two miles) when the fall freeze-up began, and he had to walk the last stretch of his path on the ice, dragging his canoe behind him because it froze so fast all around him. His school-teacher uncle, Lyman Mix, just shook his head and walked away when asked about his nephew's stories and if they were true.

The two men followed the tracks south toward Dave Keller's. Coming around the last bend, they saw the top of the large Keller barn. "I don't like the idea that that animal is coming so close to us," John said. "The Rice kids will be running around those woods, and if that cat is this hungry...." A scream rang through the mountain air. The two men started running up the hill. Another scream. This time they knew it was a child. The two men flew through the woods kicking through the witch hobble as its vines threatened to wrap around their boots. A gray squirrel scurried out of their path. Finally, they reached the clearing to the Keller farm where they saw nine-year-old Melvina Rice, David Keller's granddaughter, standing on a log next to the well staring at the ground below her. Their eyes shifted as they saw someone come racing out of the barn toward the well.

"It's her dad Abram," whispered Lysander. As the two men raced up the hill toward the raven-haired screaming girl, Abram Rice raced down the hill, shotgun in hand, veering past the sheep as they grazed on the grass, unaware of the danger around them.

"Lysander!" John shouted and pointed at the object of the girl's screams. A large black panther was crouched less than fifteen feet from the girl and was inching toward its prey. Melvina had edged as far up the log as she could get. Abram was now within ten feet of the animal. Lysander and John were still too far to shoot. Abram shouted, "Go on, get out of here!" and shoved the gun into his shoulder. The magnificent animal stopped long enough to turn its head in Abram's direction, but Melvina's crying made the animal turn back to his prey. Just as the panther pounced, Abram pulled the trigger. The panther crashed to the ground, his claws within a yard of Melvina. Silence spread. Everyone stopped, watching, waiting to make sure the panther was dead. It did not move. Abram ran to his daughter, took her in his arms, and hugged her.

"Daddy, Daddy. I was so scared, but you killed it!"

"I know, me too," Abram cooed as he gathered his daughter in his arms and looked at John and Lysander. "It's okay, now, honey; the men killed it. He pointed to the men and yelled out, 'thank you.'" Sarah Rice and her five-year- old son, James, had heard the screams and run out onto the porch. Sarah had three-year-old John in her arms.

Lysander and John ran forward. "Is she okay?" John shouted. "Yes, just very scared. Thank you. Which one of you shot it?" "Huh?" Lysander uttered. "You killed it."

"No, I didn't," Abram replied, "my gun jammed. One of you must have shot it."

"No, we weren't close enough to get a shot," John replied. "Then who?" Abram stood up, keeping Melvina in his arms.

"Her," Sarah said, as she pointed to her sister coming up the south side of the hill. They looked at Mary Ann Keller walking slowly and steadily toward the gathering, her black pigtails jutting out from a worn-out hat that had been her father's.

"No, no way. She was so far away I couldn't even see her," Abram replied. Everyone knew that Mary Ann Keller was a crack shot, but this was too far even for her. Finally, she came within speaking distance of the group. "I got him, right?"

They all stared at her with their mouths hanging open.

"Well, is it dead?"

They all nodded, still speechless until Melvina finally spoke haltingly. "Oh, Aunt Mary Ann, thank you, thank you so much."

"You are welcome, little one," she said as she looked over at the large black mass that lay in front of the well.

"But where were you?" Sarah asked.

"I was down checking the maple trees to see which ones are ready for tapping this spring when I heard screams, so I came running. Shot it with my new rifle." She lifted it up. They all looked at each other and continued thanking Mary Ann. Abram still had Melvina in his arms. He could not let go of her yet. John was squirming in her mother's arms, so she put her down. He moved behind Sarah peeking out behind her dress at the monster. Sarah and Mary Ann had turned to go back to the house, inviting the men for tea when out of the corner of his eye, John thought he saw the panther's chest move. He fisted Lysander in the arm.

"Hey, I think it's still breathing."

The men looked at the panther, but it lay unmoving. "Nah. No, he's not. Look," Lysander replied as he walked up and kicked the animal. It did not move. "See, it's dead. You are just imagining the worst."

"I'm not seeing things, I tell ya, and I'm not taking my sights off that thing until everyone is safe away from it." He walked away from the family to the other side of the panther, determined to watch it for a few more minutes. "Abram, get away from that well with her!" John shouted. It was then that Abram saw a slight movement behind him. Before he had a chance to drop Melvina and grab his knife, before he had time to shout, before he could move, that huge black hulk rose from the dead and was staring straight at Abram and Melvina. Abram couldn't believe his eyes.

"Daddy, it's looking at us!" screamed Melvina, squirming and trying to get down. Abram held his daughter tight. He knew they did not have a chance. This was a panther. If Abram moved, it would attack. If he didn't move, it would attack, and now that it was wounded, it would kill this human in front of it, hungry or not.

John Scott watched in horror as the massive black animal rose to its feet, head down, glaring at the young girl and her father. Dang, his gun was leaning against the beech tree. He had just set it there. Lysander lifted his gun to his shoulder, looked over the sight of his gun, and was horrified at what he saw. Baby John Scott was toddling toward the panther with his hand out intending to pet it. "Abram," he shouted, "it's the baby." Abram turned and saw John steadily walking to the animal saying, "Doggy." The panther had risen on his front paws. John Scott saw it too. He pulled out his hunting knife and jumped on the back of the animal, plunging the knife deep into the neck.

Abram grabbed his son, scooping him up with his other arm. The animal roared as it and John Scott both went down. By now Lysander had his gun on the animal's head, but this time it stayed down. They were all silent for a moment. John did not move. Lysander walked over and knelt, looking at John, who still lay on top of the dead animal. "John, John," he shouted as he grabbed his arm, "you okay?"

"Jolly right, I am, but sure lucky that beast was already near dead, or I am sure it would have knocked me off its back like a pesky fly." Everyone took a breath.

Melvina screamed, "Daddy, they killed it again! They killed it again!"

Lysander kicked the animal, making sure it was down, and then slit its throat. "It's dead now."

Abram loosened his hold on Melvina, put John in her arms, and told her to go inside. He turned and put his hand out. The three men shook hands.

"Thanks, guys. I should have checked to make sure. Thought Mary Ann got him square."

"We did too," John was breathless. "Couldn't believe my eyes when I saw him getting back up." "You men take the fur." "No," both said in unison.

"It is Mary Ann's panther." They all looked at Mary Ann.

"We can drag it out to the barn and see if Ma wants a rug for the house. We'll cut up the meat. Dad will take care of it." By this time, David Keller Sr. and Christine Keller had joined them. Sarah and Abram lived with David and Christine in the Keller house.

"We'll have you over for dinner. How does that sound?" Christine Keller remarked as she looked at Lysander and John.

"Sounds like a good plan to me," John replied looking at Lysander who was nodding.

By this time, Abram's oldest boy, David, had come from the barn and was staring at the panther with eyes as big as paw prints.

Sarah Keller Rice, coming out of shock on the porch, began running to Melvina and John crying to Abram that she thought John was behind her. She had not seen him toddle around her on the porch. She hugged them both and sobbed, "Melvina, are you hurt, sweetheart?"

"No, mamma, but I sure was scared." Sarah held them tight.

"I would have shot it if I had gotten here first," young David Rice piped up sticking his chin out defiantly.

"Me too," cried his brother James puffing out his chest.

"Better not try and shoot one of these, son." Abram chided. He looked down at the boy thinking, I'm glad it was Melvina not James who was targeted by the panther; that boy's defiant nature would have had him running right up to the animal challenging him to a fight.

David Rice looked up at his Grandpa Keller and said, "Grandpa, you know, I would have shot that cat if I had a gun."

"I bet you would have, David." Dave reached down and ruffled his namesake's hair. "Abram, I been telling you, it is past time that boy should be handling a gun."

"Ya, I know. I know. Just ain't had time."

"Uh huh. Well, tomorrow, son, we will shoot. I'll bring my gun."

"Ok, thanks Grandpa." David looked over defiantly at his father. Sarah did not miss this interaction between father and son.

"Well then, thank you again, Lysander and John. Please come in for a bit and rest."

"I have fresh biscuits ready," Sarah interjected.

"Won't you take at least the hide?' Abram asked.

"No, Abram, we would have to haul it all the way back, and it is right here. Please just take it."

"Ok," Christina Keller interjected.

"Lysander, John, please do come for supper Wednesday night. Bring Jenny, Rachel, and the kids." Lysander and Rachel had no children, but Jenny Scott's daughter, Catherine, and Melvina were best friends.

"Okay, we will do that. Thank you." There was no thank you for Mary Ann Keller; no special dinner; no release of chores. Only one person singled her out and told her how grateful he was and how special she was. That man was her brother-in-law, Abram Rice. Later, he chastised Sarah for putting John down when there was so much danger.

"But I didn't see him until it was too late, Abram."

"I know," he snapped back, picking up the toddler. "Sarah, sometimes I wonder what you are thinking. It seems to me no one else would stand there oblivious while her child runs toward a panther. It was all I could do to protect Melvina, and there you were standing on the porch seeing what was happening and letting him run loose."

"For God's sake, Abram, I didn't do it on purpose. I had no idea what was going on. I heard a ruckus and came out. He wanted to get down. I thought the animal was dead, so I let him down."

"Then he ran, and you didn't get him."

"Abram, it is so easy for you to judge. You don't have them with you all day and another on the way. Sarah patted her bulging stomach. You just get to hold them and then give them back to me. Everybody is okay today, so I will not talk about this anymore with you." She turned and silently began sweeping the floor. He kissed John and put him down. He loved this precious one and spent more time with him than he had the others. Perhaps because he thought Sarah did not.

Silently and quickly, Lysander and John disappeared through the underbrush, Lysander back to his wife Rachel, and John back to Jenny and his children.

As John walked the old familiar trail, John recalled that day so many years ago in Scotland when he first saw little Jenny Dodds's soot- covered nose as she turned from Sir Walter Scott's fireplace she was cleaning and greeted his nephew. He loved her at that very moment, and he loved her more now. As he walked by the biggest white pine on the lake, he saw the wheel tracks. He knew those tracks. Uncle Wright, still running around the north country trapping and telling stories as an old man, was here; John liked nothing better than sitting on the porch, whittling, and listening to stories about the old days from Uncle Wright Rule, once known as the best horse thief of Jedburgh, Scotland. The noon sun shot through the green-leafed maple, splashing rays of light across the worn pine path leading to the little cabin perched on the shore of this magnificent lake. But what was uncle doing here away from a perfectly good workday on his farm?

# 2

## ROSSIE, NEW YORK

THERE WAS NO mistaking that sound above the wind whistling across the plowed field, picking up debris and rocks as large as baseballs. Thomas Dodds Jr. was plowing. Thomas was driving the horse team that pulled the stone boat while George Dodds jumped off to pick up rocks, throwing them onto the thick wooden sled then jumping back on. Usually, their cousin, Michael Wright, helped them, but Michael had rarely been off the farm and had begged his uncle to take him up north to the Adirondacks with him.

Michael came to live with his Aunt Catherine and Uncle Wright Rule as a young boy because a horse had thrown his father, causing a broken collar bone and broken leg. Even after healing, Michael's father was unable to do blacksmithing, the job he previously had done. The oldest son helped fill in, and Michael's mother took in laundry and did house cleaning, but things were still tight. Michael had loved his Uncle Wright from the moment he met him, and after the accident, Wright and Catherine offered to take Michael in. Since his mom and dad lived close, in the new town of Waddington, he did chores for them as well as his uncle and Thomas Dodds, but at thirteen years old, he was obsessed with hunting and trapping with his uncle.

"I wonder if Uncle Wright and Michael are at Jenny's yet," George yelled to his brother.

"Probably. They left yesterday."

"Don't know, Thomas. Uncle is a talker, so if there is anything to be told, it will be told." The men heard shouting, looked up, and saw Thomas's wife, Henrietta, and their daughter, carrying a big gallon jug. Thomas never could look at this woman without feeling his heart skip a beat. He remembered the first time he saw her in that store in Quebec, Canada. She still had long black hair, now streaked with a little gray. It bounced on her shoulders as she bobbed along.

"We have some lemonade for you," Henrietta shouted. She still had her French accent and was always confusing the past and present verbs; Thomas no longer corrected her. In fact, he liked the way she spoke. It reminded him of when they first met, and he liked looking into those large ebony eyes before he laid his head down after a hard day's work. "Well, you just amaze me, always come right when I don't think I can swallow another cloud of dust."

"Thought you'd be thirsty about now, dear." George eyed the bright yellow lemons floating inside the clear glass jug.

He smacked his lips, reached for the ladle and gulped it down before handing it to Thomas who did the same.

"Better take it easy," Henrietta cautioned. "You'll get sick."

"Not on your lemonade, Henrietta. Let's take a little break, George. Henrietta, walk with me. How is ma today?"

"She's not good, She's weaker. I'm worried."

"Me too. Uncle Wright and Michael left for the mountains. They are telling Jenny and Ann. I hope they get here in time."

"I know, I know," Henrietta, said shaking her head, "but, you know, Thomas, I worry about this stuff. They call it TB, and I wonder if you can catch it." "Doc says no."

"I know, but does he really know? I remember in Canada when my aunt came down with pneumonia and they didn't think that was contagious either, but it was, and my little cousin died of it. I think we need to at least keep the children away, and so does ma."

Little did they know that soon there would be more to worry about. It had been eight years since Henrietta and Thomas had tied the knot on the shore of the mighty St. Lawrence River. Now, they owned several acres of land that they plowed and logged. Young George worked for his brother and Thomas's oldest boy, seven-year-old Duncan, was eager to help. On this day, he ran out the screen door, his red curls bobbing on his head like corkscrews. He tore down the dirt path to the front of the barn where the two hired hands, Harold and Jacob, were hitching up the plow to the two gray dappled work horses. Thomas and George were in the barn finishing up the milking of their ten Holstein cows.

Just as Jacob finished feeding the steel pin through the hitch opening, Duncan came racing in, not wanting to be left behind. "Wait for me!" he shouted, as he ran toward the men.

"Whoa," shouted Jacob. As he was getting up to stop Duncan, the boy slipped in the mud, slid under the hitch, and hit it with his left foot. The unsecured hitch released, and the rock boat slammed down hard onto young Duncan's legs.

Everyone came running like ants out the doors of the house and the barn. Only Helen Dodds did not come because she was too sick. "Oh Lord," cried Jacob, "Duncan!" He turned, crouched down, and looked into the blue eyes of the frightened boy. "Duncan, it'll be okay. You just hold on."

"What is it? What's happened?" Thomas yelled, as he and George came running out of the weathered red barn. He knew as soon as he saw the brown boots on the ground. He knew it was Duncan and dreaded what he was going to see.

Frantically pulling up on the hitch lip, Jacob was able to lift it off Duncan's leg. By this time, Thomas was crouched down holding his son's head on his arm, his dark eyes scanning Duncan's body for injuries. Henrietta rushed out to the field through clods of dirt, rocks, and mud, to her small boy lying on the ground, stark white with his little legs bent in all the wrong directions. She kneeled in the mud and cradled his head while Thomas helped Jacob move the stone boat out of the way. Duncan screamed and then lay still in his mother's arms. Thomas took him from Henrietta. Tears welled up in his eyes as he looked at his young son and thought this boy would not become a man. "Duncan," he whispered as he proceeded to the house. "Duncan, it's daddy. Wake up." Duncan lay still and silent. He continued to breathe but did not regain consciousness.

Throughout the month, Old Doc Turner came and went, shaking his head as he quietly meandered down the worn path to his carriage. What a tragedy to lay upon this vibrant family so filled with hope. Thomas was just a young man when he came here, going on twenty years past, and now he was the proud owner of this farm. He worked hard just like his father; now he would need all the strength he had to get his family through the ultimate death of his mother and probable death of his son. Doc Turner stepped up into the carriage and looked out at the horizon. The sun was just setting on the newly plowed field. It was a ball of fire sinking slowly into the horizon leaving behind a red streaked sky. Well, thought Doc, I don't hold much with religion and don't even know if I believe in God, but if you are there and are making this blood- beauty sun right now, would you just take a moment and shine on this family?

Aunt Catherine and Uncle Wright visited Helen and Duncan several times in the next few weeks. Duncan had remained unresponsive for several days. They were grateful when he regained consciousness, but Doc told Henrietta that if the boy lived, he would never walk again. Henrietta never lost hope. She held him, talked to him, and begged God to heal her son's legs. One day Thomas came in to wash up for lunch. He thought he heard a sound coming from the boy's room. He hollered to Henrietta, and they rushed to the room. Opening the door, they saw Helen and Duncan lying on the floor. "Oh, my Lord," cried Henrietta as she rushed to them. She looked at Helen, felt for her pulse. Thank goodness, she was alive. Then she realized that Duncan was out of his bed. Thomas gathered him in his arms. Both Henrietta and Thomas stared at him.

"Gram, Gram. She fell. I tried.... I fell too."

"But how did you get this far away from the bed."

"I took steps. I took two steps, but I fell. Look what Gram gave me." He reached over on the floor and picked up the notebook Helen was so intent on bringing him. By this time Helen had opened her eyes and sat up. The three of them looked down on this little red-haired blue-eyed spit fire. And so, began the road back for little Duncan.

# 3

---

## The Journey Home

John Scott and Lysander Hall had parted ways at the fork in the trail after leaving the Keller house, Lysander heading north and John moving on south to his place. He traveled back on the same deer trail past the two red spruce and the white birch that now towered over the trail. John made a note that he needed to cut it down before it fell on one of the kids. All the children ran back and forth on this trail. Trees were one more danger the settlers faced in this wilderness. He rushed over the logs he had laid down across the swampy end of the brook that ran north to the Kellogg property.

John loved it when Uncle Wright came. There were raucous stories believable and unbelievable, and Uncle could hold your attention with his booming voice and thunderous laugh. Within thirty minutes the cabin loomed large in front of John. He hurried up the two steps, lifted the wood latch on the cabin door, and rushed in. Uncle Wright, Michael, Jenny, and their daughter, Julia, were sitting around the log table deep in conversation. Catherine was sitting at the wooden desk John had made for Ned several years ago. They had not heard him come in; one look at uncle's face told him them that the news was not good.

"Hi, Uncle," John said as he hurried over and shook his hand. "Michael, good to see you again."

"Morning," Michael said lowering his head.

"Well, sir, did you come down to hunt?" He scanned their faces again. "Oh, maybe not. What is it?"

"I wish hunting was the reason. Michael and I are here to watch the little ones while you, Jenny, and Julia go to see Helen. Patrick and your sister Ann, are on their way too."

"Are their kids going?"

"No, I understand Sam and Isabelle are staying with the Dornburghs."

Jenny looked at John. "We have to let Ned know."

"He knows," uncle interjected. "Patrick's sister was visiting when they got the news. She lives near Ned and was bringing the news to him yesterday."

John and Jenny's daughter, Julia Scott had grown up and married William Kellogg, son of Danny and Annie Kellogg; they had two girls, Mable, and Louise. The girls were nine and ten, and the Kelloggs lived on land between Lyman Mix and the north end outlet of the lake.

John asked, "Is Helen bad?"

"Yes, lad, it's her time. Doc says it won't be long now. Her breathing is shallow, and she is sometimes delirious, but she still knows everyone. You need to go now."

John rushed over to Jenny and put his arm on her shoulder. "Well, of course we will go, but you remember our neighbor. I don't trust him knowing we're gone."

"You mean Joel Plumley?" Wright asked. He remembered that Joel had first settled south of the Kellers on the outlet to South Pond. However, once he saw David Keller's farm sprouting lush green crops, he moved north near him. The Scotts had bought the lot they were on from David Keller, which put them close to Plumley.

"Yup, he just set fire to the Stanton's hay pile. I don't know what ails the man, but I'm worried about leaving the place."

"Well then, sounds like I'm just the fellow to handle an old curmudgeon like Plumley. Got it right here," he said, as he raised his rifle. He walked over and put his arm on John's shoulder. "You go and take as long as you like. I been cooking vittles for years, and Michael and I can hunt while were here. Don't you worry about anything. We'll take care of your place."

John and Jenny packed up that night, and when the sun rose over the great mountain to the east, the two hitched up the horses and headed for the Grasse River. They caught a riverboat to Ogdensburg where Robert Dodds picked them up. They arrived in time for Jenny to sit with her mother and tell her how grateful she was for her guidance, love, and understanding throughout the years. Jenny spent time with Thomas, Henrietta, and their children. The family spent the time reminiscing with their mother about their life in Scotland. The youngest, George, now grown and the ray of light in Helen's last days, loved hearing about the country where he was born but did not remember. He was a young boy when they boarded the ship to come to America. Ann and Robert talked about how they loved playing along the great river Tweed. They rehashed the time Robert climbed the silo and Ann got him down. Then, they laughed at the way old Sir Walter Scott, John's uncle, would plod along on his old horse visiting everyone in the countryside in Lessudden, Scotland. John reflected on his boyhood, visiting his uncle at the farm next to Laird Buccleuch's land where the Doddses lived and worked. "And you met me there."

"Oh, yes," John chuckled, "I met my sweet bonny Jenny in that place, but I couldn't keep her. I had to follow her all the way here to win her over."

"Uh huh," Jenny replied, smiling, "and if you hadn't been so boneheaded in the first place you wouldn't have had to come traipsing across Lake Champlain to find me."

"Oh yes, she's right, but it couldn't happen then. We were too young, and I was too lame brained." He hugged Jenny, and they all laughed.

Through the tears and the laughter, they all joined in saying their goodbyes to their beloved mother, wife, and friend. Soon she would be rid of the scourge of Tuberculosis. They buried Helen in the new Rossie cemetery under the row of cedar trees that Helen had planted thirty years ago when she and Thomas stepped out onto the land of the free where for the first time in their lives, they would own their land. Now she rests forever there.

Miraculously, no one else in the family contracted the disease. Jenny, Ann, and Henrietta sent notices to their relatives in Scotland. Helen's sister returned the notice. She wrote that she had said goodbye to her sister in 1819 before she sailed for America. They had conducted a funeral for the family at that time as many families did who knew they would never see their loved ones again. She wrote that she knew her sister was happy throughout the years she had lived in America.

Duncan continued to write every day in the notebook his gram had given him. Talking developed slowly, but soon he was able to tell the stories his grandma had shared with him about her childhood in Scotland.

While he was in his bed, his grandma had come to his room, and told him about the rivers and purple heather mountains of her homeland, and when he opened his eyes, he could see the purple heather through her eyes. She told him she loved him and that he was to never give up; she told him about his cousins living in the lush green forests and the mountains surrounded by clear blue waters. One day she told him that she had a gift for him. From the bottom drawer of her nightstand, Helen pulled out a book. It was titled *The Doddses*. She had fastened it with yarn fed through three holes she had made with her scissors. She said, "Duncan, this is the story of our life. One day you will continue our story." She handed him the book. "But, grandma, how?" He barely knew how to write.

"Shhh," she whispered, "You will, my sweet, you will. You will try hard." That was the last time his grandma spoke to him.

Days turned into weeks. Weeks into months. It was in the fall sometime that Duncan took his first steps with his crutches. Now, he frequently hobbled out to the cemetery to talk to his gram and write in his notebook. He remembered to try hard. He remembered her words about the green forests and blue waters, and he knew he was meant to one day tread upon that mysterious land called the Adirondacks.

# 4

## Two Old Thieves

In Long Lake, meanwhile, old Joel Plumley was in a feud with the Rutherfords, whom he had met in Chestertown. Jeff Rutherford believed that Joel had burned down his maple trees because he had confronted Joel for tapping them. Joel had claimed they were his, but Jeff had the plat showing that they were on Rutherford land. Now, Jeff and his family lived on Clear Lake several miles behind Joel Plumley, but even at that distance, he was not safe from the man. Nor was anyone else safe from that man.

Two nights after John and Jenny left for Rossie, Wright heard a ruckus in the hen house. He grabbed his gun and snuck out the back door. The moon was one night away from full, casting its light across the back woods and onto the barn. Wright silently crept through the pine path leading to the barn where he once again heard the chickens squawking loudly. He was within thirty feet of the barn when he saw the side door open. The shadow of a person quickly darted out the door and raced toward the woods. "Stop!" Wright shouted. He could see it was a man carrying something under his arm. Wright lifted his gun to his shoulder and shot into the trees above the person's head, hoping it would scare the fellow enough to stop him. Not so. The man never stopped and quickly disappeared into the darkness. Wright headed back to the chicken house to see what the man had taken. By this time, Michael, hearing the shot, had come out in his boots and long johns toting his gun. When he saw Wright, he ran toward the hen house. "What are you doing out here. We got a wolf?"

"No, we got a thief," Wright replied. "A thief?"

"Can't you hear, boy? Yes, a thief," Wright answered yanking the hen door open. Michael followed his uncle into the warm hen house.

Within moments, Wright noticed that the rooster was missing. "Well, looks like he wanted their best rooster."

"What? Are you sure it was a man?"

"For God's sake, Michael, I know the difference between the silhouette of a man and an animal. It was a man, and I know darned well what man!" Michael should know better than to question Uncle Wright about anything, especially anything in the woods. No one except Aunt Catherine knew how old Uncle Wright was, but Michael figured he was at least 80 and still scaring younger men off and sliding through the woods like a wild animal. Michael could barely keep up with him, and uncle kept telling him that he was slowing down.

"You think it was Plumley?"

"Oh yes, it was him. Dumb fella had that old torn-up hat he always wears. He either doesn't care if people know who it is, or he is just plain dumb. Don't know. Don't care. I'm going to his place and get that rooster back."

"Now?"

"Yes, now. You can stay or come; up to you." Wright turned and quickly disappeared into the black woods, leaving Michael standing there trying to wake up enough to understand what was happening. He couldn't let his uncle go over there alone. He still had nothing on and was freezing. He ran into the cabin, grabbed his jacket, thought of putting pants on, but changed his mind. He ran back out the door heading south, following his old fool uncle, and hoping to reach him before he shot Joel Plumley. Jenny had told him that Plumley had been sick, and Mrs. Stanton was taking care of him since his wives had all passed on; must be he wasn't all that sick. Michael ran through the trees and soon caught up with Wright.

"Oh, you decided to come. That Plumley fellow; I thought he was too old and sick to be still doing this stuff."

"That's what I thought," Michael replied.

"Not old and sick enough, I guess." Wright was fuming. There was not enough moonlight. Besides, no moon could penetrate the thick pines and dead decaying trunks piled up on top of each other like corpses in the woods. "God, uncle, why don't you ever take a path, even a deer path?" Michael gasped as he stepped up on another fallen giant maple.

"Element of surprise. Always, the element of surprise," Wright retorted, gingerly hopping over roots, rocks, and branches the size of logs. Michael was always in awe of how his uncle could navigate the Adirondacks in the black of night. All he could do was try to keep up with this white-haired man. The nights were already chilly, but the pace kept the cold away, and soon they were in sight of Plumley's cabin.

Michael grabbed his arm, "No one is up. Look!" The moon was straight overhead. The cabin was dark. "There ain't no lanterns on, uncle."

"Well, lad, do you really think the thief would leave us a light? He knows we saw him, for God's sake. I tried to shoot him."

"But...."

"Now, you just stay here out of sight. Don't want you getting hurt." "But...."

"No but. I said stay here. You hear me?" Reluctantly, Michael agreed to stay. Wright marched up the path onto the steps and began banging on the door, hollering, "Plumley, get out here, and bring me my rooster!" Michael followed quietly.

Wright opened the door. Most folks did not lock their doors. They had shotguns. "Hey, Plumley, where are you?" He could not see anything. "Plumley, I know you are here." His right leg hit the edge of the bed.

"What. Who ta hell is in here?" Joel Plumley hollered.

"I want my rooster!" shouted Wright pointing his gun within an inch of the voice he heard.

"What? Just a minute." Joel reached out, grabbed the lantern on the floor, lit it, and looked straight into a gun barrel.

"Where is my damn rooster?"

Joel squinted his eyes, pushed the barrel aside, and stared at Wright. His eyes drifted to the left to another man by his side. Too late to grab his gun and two men here, he thought. He looked again at the old man. "Wright? Is that you, Wright Rule? What to hell are you doing in my house at this hour?"

Wright looked at Joel in the lantern light. His eyes were heavy lidded, red streaks filling up the white. He had a shock of thick gray hair falling over his eyes. Joel brushed it away with his hand. "I don't have your rooster if that's what you're saying."

"You're lying. I followed you here. Now get up and go get me the rooster."

Joel looked long and hard at Wright. "Wright, I can't get up. I'm sick. Dying. You'll have to shoot me because I can't get you what you want. You know, my Sarah died last year so been fending for myself."

"Joel, I'm sorry about Sarah, but the thief had your old hat on. I recognized it."

"Nope, wasn't mine. Mine's right here." Joel reached under his bed to pull out his hat. It wasn't there.

"When was the last time you wore it?" Wright lowered the gun.

"Oh, I don't know. Been in this bed for mostly a week. Nobody been here except Lydia and Lavonia Stanton taking care of me. Blessing to that woman and her daughter. I'd be dead already without them. Now, who came in here and took my hat, and who is that young man with you?"

"This is my nephew, Michael. Okay, Joel, I believe you. We'll head on out, go home, and get some sleep."

"Yup, good idea," Joel said as he turned the lantern key to shut it off. Soon Wright and Michael were out the door and once again tramping through the woods.

"Stop," Wright said, as he pulled his nephew behind a large red spruce.

"What, why?"

"Shh. Just looking." He pointed toward Joel's cabin, which was now visible in the early morning light. "Just going to watch. You can go on home if you want."

"But it wasn't him," Michael whispered.

"Uh huh. Just watch." They were looking straight at the old barn Joel had built years before. Suddenly, the door to the cabin opened and there stood Joel Plumley.

"Hmm. Can't walk. I knew that bugger was lying," Wright whispered to Michael.

"Let's go," Michael whispered as he stepped out toward the cabin. "No, wait," Wright grabbed his arm.

Suddenly, out of the door to the barn stepped another man.

"You got it, right?" Joel hollered.

"Yup, it's in the pen."

"Ok, but you idiot, you stole my darn hat, and they recognized it. That devil Rule was there and tracked you straight here. I had to do some heavy talking to convince him I was innocent. Got to go back to bed but give me my daggone hat." The man came forward.

"Come on," Wright whispered to Michael. "Now." They walked out with their guns held high. "Stop right there, both of you, or I'll blow your heads off. Can't walk, Plumley? Who is this? One of your thieving relatives come to do you a favor?"

"Rule!" Joel spat out, his face getting red. "You didn't leave?"

"Of course not. I knew you were lying. I knew you were up to no good, and I knew you did it." Wright swung the gun at the young man still holding Joel's hat. His eyes were wild, and the hat was shaking in his hand. He didn't look to be over fifteen years old, but he was a tall one. Black hair, dark eyes, and ready to bolt. "You, son, will go to the barn and bring out that rooster. Michael, you stay with your gun on Joel. What's your name, boy?"

"Matthew. It's Matthew." "What are you doing here?"

"Joel's my uncle. I ran away from home in Vermont. Uncle Joel's letting me stay in the hayloft. Told me I could get work on that Carthage Road they were putting in, but when I got here, they had about finished it." "Oh, how good of him," Wright mumbled as he continued to follow Matthew into the barn. "And how well do you know your uncle?"

"Just met him two weeks ago. He told me he'd paid for the rooster but was too sick to get it and for me to go get it."

"Figures." They walked to the far-right corner of the barn, and there was the rooster along with several chickens.

"Okay, pick him up. You will be bringing him back to my place."

"Okay, mister."

When they were out in the open, Wright walked up to Joel who was now sitting on the steps looking at the barrel of Michael's gun. "Joel, that is darn low to get your nephew involved in your shenanigans. You know what, someday you really will be sick and dying, and if you don't straighten around you will die alone. Come on Michael." The three then disappeared into the woods to begin the trek back to their cabin.

Matthew listened to Wright's lecture all the way back to the house. The next day, Wright brought him to see Jeff Rutherford who needed a hand. After much trepidation about hiring a Plumley, Jeff agreed, figuring he would keep a close eye on Matthew and a closer eye on his uncle.

# 5

## STAGECOACH TO NEWCOMB

SAM FERGUS PARKER raced into town to wait for the large stagecoach from Crown Point. Today his relatives from Saratoga were coming. His dad was hunting. His ma was making bread, and his little sister was in the new school. Patrick, Sam's father, was an Abenaki Indian, and the Abenaki did not use surnames. Hence, Patrick's family went by Parker, his grandmother Evelyn's last name.

Sam's grandfather, Namito, had passed on, but his grandmother and Aunt Gizos were coming. Gizos had married Louis Joseph, another Abenaki born in the settlement just west of his grandparents' settlement. Sitting over many campfires, Sam's mom and dad had told the story of how his dad, Patrick, had saved their lives when his Aunt Jenny, Cousin Ned, and mom Ann, had made the trip down Lake Champlain to Whitehall and were ambushed by Canadian pirates. He always felt bad for his cousin Ned because Canadian pirates had killed Ned's stepfather on the horrendous journey down Lake Champlain when Ned was a young boy. Hence, the story of Sam's middle name.

Sam was proud of his mother, Ann, who was an expert hunter, trapper, and knife thrower. He loved the story about how she and his dad tracked Fergus's killers and made them pay for what they did: They tracked and abducted them and turned them over to Patrick's Abenaki tribe, delivering a just sentencing to these horrible men. Sam's Aunt Jenny told him that his mom was always running, climbing, or shooting something. She was the best shot with a bow in all of Newcomb. She was an amazing sight, running with the wind along the Hudson River, her long gray braids flying straight out behind her. She was as timeless as the mighty river that flowed continuously around the rocks and rotting logs, never stopping, never stalling, running true. Like his mom, Sam ran continuously, climbing the giant white pines as quickly as a bobcat, becoming an expert hunter, taught by a rugged Scottish lass and native-born Indian. He knew he had the best of both worlds. He knew he could do anything he wanted to, and he would.

Sam sat anxiously on a wood step at the stagecoach station next to the livery in this little Newcomb settlement. The sun was rising in the August heat. Dang, why didn't he bring water? He ran over to the well, pulled on the rope, took the ladle from the nail, dipped it in the old bucket he had pulled up, and gulped down some pure cold Adirondack spring water. He dipped the ladle again, and when he stood up, he heard the thunder of horse hooves.

He knew it would be four horses. He knew three would be chestnut brown and one would be black. He even knew their names. He knew because he had helped pa and ma raise them. He also knew Lucius Henderson, the driver, even though he was a new driver from the settlement to the east on a place called Long Lake. His pa had taken him hunting and fishing and visiting his cousins and friends, the Rutherfords, in that place.

Pa said the settlement was about fifteen miles away, and now instead of just a path, it was reached by a rocky rutted road that was best traveled by foot or horseback or by sleigh in the winter. His Uncle John and Aunt Jenny had settled on Long Lake. The Rutherfords settled on a pond just north of Long Lake. The oldest Rutherford, Jeff Jr., was married with several children, one being married to Danny Kellogg, a strange man from Scotland whom the Doddses met on the ship they chartered from Scotland to Newfoundland. Danny had saved Thomas Dodds's life during a vicious storm in the middle of the Atlantic on their way to America. Danny's wife's family, the Rutherfords, were neighbors of the Doddses in Scotland, and now they all lived within five miles of each other trying to eke out a living in this black-rooted forest land.

Danny Kellogg became a woodsman, husband, father, and local politician, attending all the town meetings and keeping company with another politician, lawyer, and man about town, Robert Shaw.

Sam set the ladle back on the nail and turned to the sound of his sister, Isabelle, running to the well. Soon, fourteen-year-old Melvin Blanchard appeared at the door of his father's store. "Who's coming?" Melvin asked, running up and screeching to a halt next to Sam.

"Our grandma," replied Isabelle. Isabelle had long red hair and freckles like her mom.

"Why ain't you in school?" Sam asked his sister.

"Why ain't you?"

"Because ma told me to meet the stage, but she didn't tell you."

"I don't care," Isabelle tossed her pigtails in the air. "I ain't sitting in that stuffy room while grandma is coming here. Besides, why should I have to go to school, and you don't?"

"Because I'm thirteen and you're eight; now get back in that classroom before pa catches you."

"No, and pa don't care anyway. He wants me to learn the Abenaki stuff."

"Well, I'm learning that too...."

"Shut up, you two," Malvern interrupted. "It's coming now." Sure enough, the dust was kicking up and covering everything like a sheet of snow. Old Elisha Bissel wandered out and stood by the door of the store with little Martha Bissell beside him. The stage roared up and parked in front of Elisha Bissell's store. "How was the trip?" he asked.

"Oh, nothing to note." Lucius Henderson, the driver, stepped down, and opened the door to the carriage. There stood a tall, thin man dressed in a skirt. This here is George

Robinson, a Scot from Jedburgh, Scotland. Says he knows Ann Dodds, but I'm told there ain't no Dodds in Newcomb."

"That's my mom," shouted Sam. "Really. Ann Parker is a Dodds?" "Yup."

"Only Doddses I ever run into was on a trip down to a place called Rossie," Lucius said as he pulled down the steps to the coach.

"Those are my aunts and uncles." Lucius scratched his head wondering how Ann had ended up married to an Indian, but in this business, he had learned to be okay with not knowing things about people.

"Well, I'll be," said the man as he stepped out of the carriage. Isabelle whispered, "But why's he got a skirt on? He ain't no girl." "Shh, Isabelle," her brother chided.

"Oh Lassie, I'm from Scotland, and this is what we wear in that country." Lucius just shook his head, looked at Elisha, and thought, God, another Scot, just what we need. He recalled the first Scot traipsing around town in a skirt and living at the new settlement. Nice enough fella who still came to town some but now wore pants, thank the good Lord. Lucius recalled delivering letters from Doddses in Scotland.

Soon a very tall thin woman stepped out of the coach. She had long gray hair in a long braid down her left shoulder. She wore deerskin boots that came to the hem of her skirt. A deerskin vest over a cotton blouse ended at her waist just a few inches over her skirt.

"Morning, grandma," Sam said as he reached out to take her hand. Lucius took her other, and together they guided her down the steep step onto the ground.

"Morning, Sam, my, how you have grown." He smiled.

"Grandma Evelyn!" Isabelle shouted and ran into her arms. Evelyn laughed and hugged her grandchildren. Isabelle was the spitting image of her daughter-in-law, Ann. She recalled the day her son, Patrick, had come home with Jenny, Ann, Ned, and Jenny's husband Fergus. Patrick had found them on the shore of Lake Champlain, tired, scared, and wounded. They had been attacked by river pirates and left for dead. Though they had tried to save Fergus, they could not. Patrick and Ann became friends when she moved to Chestertown; soon they fell in love and married.

"Isabelle, you have grown so much, and I think you have one less freckle than last time I saw you."

"Really! You think so? Ma says they will fade when I am older. I can't wait until they are gone."

"You a real Indian?" Malvern quipped.

"Of course, she is, you tadpole" Isabelle snapped back.

"Then how come she's got blue eyes? Indians ain't got blue eyes." "They do too, because she has blue eyes and she's an Indian," Isabelle sputtered. Malvern backed off muttering "Ain't no Indians with blue eyes."

Evelyn laughed and turned toward the man she had shared the coach with. "Well, Mr. Robinson, it was nice getting to know you; I see my son is here with my ride. Good luck in your new country."

"Thank you, and you too." Robinson picked up his box and moved toward the boarding house. Evelyn had enjoyed her talk with the Scot. She learned that in Scotland, he had worked for John and Agnes Rule in their store. Evelyn had recalled that her daughter-in-law's mother was a Helen Rule. She learned that John and Agnes were Helen's parents. She listened quietly while he continued. He told her that when the Rules received a letter from America, they would gather around the wood stove, and John would read it to everyone. One wintry day while John was filling his pipe with tobacco and opening another letter, George heard a loud thump. He looked over and saw John Rule motionless on the floor. George ran over and tried to revive him, but it was too late. The next day, Agnes asked George to mail a letter to their relatives in America. The letter was addressed to Wright and Catherine Rule. George recalled a man he knew by that name. He was a well-known horse thief who had fled to America. George Robinson memorized the address. He would go to this place. He would find Wright Rule, and he would get justice.

# 6

## TOWN MEETINGS, MEMORIES, AND SUGARING

IN THE MEANTIME, Long Lake town meetings went on with heated arguments about justice and roads. They finally began work on a road that followed the western side of the lake from Kellers' past Kelloggs' down to the foot of Buck Mountain. It was this road building that caused David Smith to storm out of the town meeting and leave Long Lake for good. He wanted this road to go to his place, which was between the Rutherfords' place on Clear Lake and the western north end of Long Lake. The town voted Smith's request down but built the road to go south to Zenas Parker's property. Since he was the road commissioner at the time, he persuaded the town to extend the road to his property on the southwest side of the lake about three miles south of the Keller property.

It was this road that Mary Ann Keller was riding one autumn day when the leaves were crisp and colored. Mary

Ann was troubled. She was a teenager and the prettiest of the Keller girls. However, she questioned too many things, like why couldn't she go to the town meeting, and why did women have to make the soap that stunk up their clothes and stayed in the skin for days no matter how many times they bathed?

She liked riding even though her choices were one of the two work horses and getting either of them into a trot was near impossible. She lived in the large house that her dad, David Keller, had built. Her father had built it straight up the ridge from the old cabin they had lived in when they first arrived many years ago.

She giggled as she recalled the men who had tried to court her: Barton Burlingame had come to Long Lake with Zenas Parker, and they had originally set up on Moose Island south of the Kellers across from Robert and Betsy Sargent. Later, Zenas bought the land southwest of the Kellers, and Barton moved in with him. Mary Ann thought back to Barton walking down the path or paddling down, hoping to get a glimpse of her sister, Sarah. He was in love with her first. Finally, he asked her on a picnic, and she went. Then, Sarah had to tell him she was marrying Abram Rice. He was heartbroken, went home, took his ax and his ale, and walked out into the woods to cut trees for firewood. Later that night, Zenas realized Barton was still not home and the ax was gone; he started to get worried.

It was on this dark starless night that Mary Ann Keller woke up to shouting coming from the lake. They all ran out to discover that Barton was missing. Everyone went looking including Mitchel Sabattis who found the man pinned by a tree in the woods. Christine Keller had some knowledge of medicine and used it on him, but he never really healed right. He could walk but he could not use his left arm and suffered with back pain. Mary Ann's mother sent her by horseback to check on Barton and tend his wounds. He began to fall in love with her; when she very kindly rejected him, and Zenas told him it was time to go home, he did. He moved in with his sister in Vermont, and Zenas finished building his place northwest of Moose Island.

Mary Ann rode Babe over the small bridge her dad and brother had built. She looked down the creek her family called Big Brook to the west side of the lake. It was there that she and her family had first stepped foot on the shores of Long Lake, at a bay called East Bay Landing by Joel Plumley. It was there that Zenas Parker and Barton Burlingame came with excitement and wonder for this new adventure in an untamed world. She always felt a heaviness in her heart when she thought of what happened to Barton, but at least he lived. Many men did not survive such injuries.

Her next suitor was Robert Sargent, Betsy Sargent's brother-in- law. Betsy and James Sargent had arrived before Barton. James was also injured in the woods, so his brother had come to help him. The Sargents lived just north of the first sawmill west of South Pond, about four miles south of the village. They made maple syrup, and Mary Ann recalled the first time Mr. Sargent came to sell it to her parents. She was playing in the yard when he paddled up with his daughter who was Mary Ann's age. Mary Ann greeted them.

"Hi, are you one of the Kellers?"

"Yes, I'm Mary Ann. I'll get my mom." She turned and ran up to the cabin, leaving James and Mary Sargent standing on the shore. Soon, Christine Keller came out the log door, stood on the porch and shouted, "James, come on in." She offered them tea that Mr. Bowen the hermit had left with her. "Mary Ann, please take Mary with you up to the barn to get your father."

She didn't understand why her parents sometimes bought syrup from the Sargents. Most everyone made maple syrup. She loved it because the people in the settlement gathered by the grist mill with the women stirring and boiling the sap in huge barrels. Usually Lydia Stanton, Harriet Plumley, and Jenny Scott headed up the boiling part of the process.

First in late February, Lydia's sons and the Plumley, Robinson, Austin, and Keller fathers and sons hitched their horses, loaded their sleighs up with wooden taps, buckets, and children, and slid off into the woods, stopping to drive the taps into the trees. The children hung the buckets from the taps. They would check them each day to see if the sap had started running. It was always a celebration when they came upon the first run. Then they loaded the filled buckets into large barrels they brought with them on the sleigh (or wagon, depending on the weather).

In the meantime, Isaac Robinson, Joel Plumley, and George Stanton built three fires outside. Lydia, Harriet, Jenny, and several other women and young girls placed their cooking pots on the fire; when the men came in from the woods, they poured the sap into the cooking pots. This was called "the sugaring." Most of the settlers came out for the sugaring. Some of the young men and women came home with their wooden molds filled with the soft sugar that they called candy. Some of the boiling took place in individual sugarhouses.

The Sargents owned the most maple groves, and they usually made their own and did not join in the sugaring. They boiled theirs in a large sugar shanty built directly across from the great falls. They always had enough to sell to people who had run out.

Sugaring was an exciting time because of the rise of spring, the sweet smell of syrup permeating the little town, and the children darting in to get the first taste of sugar on snow. They would pack wooden bowls with snow and cook some of the sap until it reached a certain thickness and a higher temperature than syrup. Then they poured the syrup onto the bowl of snow. It hardened and could be pulled off like taffy. Much of the maple syrup was boiled into sugar so they could have sweetener all winter. The syrup would mold, but the sugar would not. When they wanted syrup, they added water to the sugar. At the sugaring, old William Helms, Captain Doc Parker, and young Robert Shaw played music. The doc had arrived in a canoe and was staying at the Helms's place at the south end of the river. Sometimes at these gatherings Mitchel Sabattis would wear the traditional Abenaki headdress of his tribe; his sister and some of the Abenaki hunters would sing their songs and sell their handmade baskets and jewelry.

Mary Ann recalled the year the Sargents had promised to let Mary attend the sugaring party. "I can't wait until sugaring season," Mary said to Mary Ann as they ran out the door and down the steps to the barn.

"Oh, me too. You will love it, Mary. It is so much fun, and you know who will be there." "Him, right?"

"Right, and last year he played music."

"I'll finally get to say something to Robert. I never get to see anybody since I'm stuck way up there with the moose and the bear. Robert Shaw doesn't even know I exist."

"Maybe you can come and spend the night with me. We could row logs across the lake and go visit the Shaws." Most of the children who were old enough would straddle a log and paddle along the lake to get to their destination.

"Yes, that would be great, but they won't let me go because of chores. You know dad has never been the same since the tree fell on him. I must do a lot of the work, being the only child." Mary Ann had so many sisters and two brothers that she couldn't imagine being the only one.

"Well, Mary, I'm sure you will get your chance with Robert at the sugaring." Mary nodded, and they continued hiking up to the barn. Mary Ann liked Mary because she liked to shoot, fish, and climb trees like her. They reached the barn, walked in, and found her dad cleaning out horse stalls. Mary Ann told him the Sargents were there and then grabbed Mary and told her to shush while they scooted around the barn looking for Abram Rice. He was standing in the hayloft shoveling hay. Mary Ann looked at Mary, put her finger to her mouth, and said, "Shhh" as she creeped up behind Abram. When she was within a foot of him, she shouted, "Boo." He turned around with the pitchfork almost hitting her.

"Mary Ann! What do you think you're doing? I almost stabbed you." Abram shouted.

"But you didn't, and I scared you." She began to laugh

"That you did, but it's not funny, girl. Mary, did you think it was funny?" Mary put her head down. She did not want to betray her friend. "I don't know. Mary Ann, let's go climb that big maple."

"Yes, go climb something," Abram replied as he turned to finish spreading the hay for the cows. As the two girls were walking away, Abram turned and watched them thinking how young they were but how fast Mary Ann was growing up.

David Keller left the barn and soon was walking through the cabin door.

"Hi, James, you got some syrup for us?"

"Sure do, if you have some goat cheese to trade."

"We do. We do. You need any mutton?" "No, not today."

"How is the arm healing, James?"

"Well, it is better but still not good for paddling. Mary actually did most of the paddling up here."

"Heard your brother, Robert, has come to help."

"Yup, as much help as he can be. Wasn't much help in Vermont, though. He was always too busy courting the ladies."

David laughed, "Well, he is a young one, and they tend to be that way. Got one of my own would be that way if there were any girls near about."

James laughed, "Have to go to Newcomb for those." "Oh, yes, the Dornburgh girls."

Mary Ann rode along remembering the day so many years ago when her sister married Abram. Even as a young girl she had a sick feeling in her stomach when Abram and Sarah kissed. She wondered whether he would have chosen Sarah if she herself had been a few years older.

Mary Ann would never experience the sugaring party with her friend because in January of that year Mary Sargent came down with a fever and died within two weeks. The same year, Robert Sargent, who had begun to spend time with Mary Ann became lost in the woods during a blizzard. They found his body the next spring. He had gone hunting with his brother, and James came home without Robert. Amidst the tragedy, several people speculated that James killed his brother because he was jealous of any man who came near his wife. It was never proven, but there were whispers. Soon after Robert's death, James and Betsy Sargent suddenly packed up and moved out west and were never heard from again. Robert and Mary were buried on the bank of the entrance to their home beneath the sun's morning rays.

Mary Ann's thoughts snapped back as she approached the Plumley place and saw Jeremiah, Rachel, and Harriet Plumley sitting on the porch. Mary Ann pulled on the reins, turned her horse, and rode up to them.

"Morning." She looked at their faces and knew something was wrong. Jeremiah would never be sitting on the porch at this time. "Is something wrong?"

"It's dad," Harriet replied. "Is he sick?"

"Yes, I'm afraid so. Thank you for asking." John Plumley came to the door and shouted to them.

"I'll pray for him," Mary Ann said, as she pulled on the reins and guided Babe down the path to her house. Joel had done bad things to her family and friends. She prayed that God would give him whatever he deserved.

# 7

## WHEN HE WAS BAD, HE WAS HORRID, EPITAPH

WRIGHT RULE HAD warned Jenny and John to keep an eye on Joel Plumley, and though Mary Ann had said a prayer for him, within a few months of the rooster stealing ordeal, Joel had a heart attack. He survived, but it left him weak. Soon, Joel became bedridden. He had lived through two wives and fathered many children, but he was alone. His sons Jeremiah and John were guides supporting their families. His daughters were married, had moved away, or refused to tend to him.

Though he had done terrible things to his neighbors, including cutting the tail off their cow and setting fires, Lydia Stanton could not watch him die alone. When he became bedridden, she and Lavonia took care of the man, and he made his peace before passing on. She said that he was a changed man for real and left this world with the blessings of most of the ten settlers in the slow growing community of Long Lake.

Lavonia Stanton, whose family had arrived in '49 when she was nine, dreaded going to the Plumley home to help her mother care for him. She was now a young woman and had fallen in love and married Benjamin Emerson. They lived behind her parents' place next to Plumley's, and though she knew Joel had changed, she did not trust him. He had tried to burn them out, killed their animals, and withheld food from families in one of the coldest winters ever.

Lavonia recalled hearing stories from Mary Ann Keller about how Joel refused to give the starving Shaw family any potatoes when he was the only one who had any. The Shaws had come to Long Lake in December of 1847, carried in on a howling winter storm. There were no roads, and the post office was still fifty miles away in Chester. There were no doctors, and other than a small sawmill on the south end of the lake, the nearest one was a fourteen-mile ride or walk to Newcomb. Because of the horrendous winter of 1843, many cattle had died, so money and food were scarce.

In the middle of all of this poverty and cold, the Shaw family arrived believing they could move into an old farmhouse left by William Shaw, a cousin who had landed and left suddenly after the first winter.

George and Mary Shaw came with their daughter, Mariah, in a horse- drawn sleigh owned by Peter Van Valkenburg and driven by Amos Hough. Their two sons Robert and William followed with a wagon full of their supplies. The road was so narrow that Amos had to maneuver the sleigh from right to left to avoid some of the giant white pine branches. Amos listened to the murmur from inside the sleigh. He couldn't understand a word of it. William was from Ireland. Amos did not like this trip, but he did like the money. Little did he know that George Shaw had just given him the last of it. Amos imagined he wouldn't be making this run too much longer. He knew the state road from Lake Champlain was making some headway toward Long Lake, and when it did, it would bypass Newcomb. Amos deposited the Shaw family on the northeast side of the lake and watched as they began to carry their gear up a ridge that was too steep for the horses. He began to feel sorry for the children as he watched them hauling large packs on their backs. Instead of turning back for home, he jumped off the wagon and began helping them carry their equipment up the sharp bank to an old house that looked to Amos like it might fall in with a strong wind.

"You sure this is the place you want to be?"

"Why, yes, Amos it even has the big maple with the burial mark on the trunk. The native Americans notched the tree above where they buried a tribe member. Look, it is right here where John said it would be."

"Okay, then," Amos, said as they threw down the final load. "I thank you for your help, Mr. Hough."

"Amos, call me Amos, but I don't see...."

"We got it from here, Amos," George interrupted. "You better be headed back now. Look." They both saw that the peaks of the Seward Mountains were already white.

"Yup, another storm is brewing. You better get that wall plugged up and the old stove lit." They had hauled enough wood up the bank for a few days, but they would need to cut more right away and do some patching so they wouldn't lose all the heat out the sides where the moss had fallen out between the logs of the house. There was a six-foot gap in the west wall, and Amos could see the dirt floor in a few places beneath the snow.

He shook his head, turned, walked back down the new trail they had made with their feet in the snow, and headed north on the ice to East Bay Landing. It was past a bay just north of a little round island, and it was the end of the Newcomb/Long Lake trail. As he turned into the trail, he doubted he would see these people on his next trip. They would die or go back where they came from. Most people came here unprepared for what this settlement perched out in the bitter cold and wilderness had to offer. Mary Ann Keller told Lavonia that the only thing that saved the Shaws was the generosity of the old hermit, Bowen, who lived at the north end of the lake. He brought potatoes to most of the families living on the lake at that time.

One day, after arguing with her mother about bringing soup to her malicious neighbor, Lavonia stomped out the door and began the walk over to the Plumleys. She held her breath and hoped he was asleep so she could just leave the soup on the table next to his bed. She lifted the wood latch and slowly opened the door, willing it not to creak.

It did, and she heard, "Who is it? Who's there?" It was so dark in the cabin that she could not see anything.

"Mr. Plumley, it's me Lavonia. I've got soup." She stood in the doorway until he lit the lantern. Then she entered the room, walked to the bed table, and put the soup down. The cabin was much like the other cabins around the lake in that near the fireplace were pots hanging on nails. A gun was leaning in the corner to the right side of the door. Two pairs of snowshoes and many traps were hanging on the walls. The log table in the center of the room still held the embroidered table scarf Lydia had made for the Plumleys many Christmases ago.

She placed the soup on the table trying not to look at this man's face that was now a hollow mask. His skin was no longer burned by the snow sun. It was pale, and his brown eyes were rimmed in red. Lavonia wanted to leave. She turned and took a step toward the door.

"No Lavonia, sit down. Stay a spell. I got stuff to say." "But I...."

"But you ain't got time for dying man," Joel whispered.

Lavonia was trapped. How could she just zip out now? "Well, okay, for just a minute." She sat down and held her breath waiting for whatever blasted out of his foul mouth.

"Lavonia, I know I've lived a terrible life. I know I was a bad man to you and your family. I cut the tail on Keller's cow, shot your cows, and burned Boyden's hay, but I want to set the record straight; I did not set fire to John Boyden's house."

The Stantons had sold some of their property next to Joel to the Boydens. Joel was mad because he wanted the property. He didn't like neighbors. He had created so much havoc with the young couple that they finally moved across the lake. One night, soon after their move, their house burned to the ground, and they barely escaped out the window into the snow. Most people blamed Joel though they never could prove it. "I know I was a bad man but not bad enough to burn up people. Lavonia, I heard you're a writer of sorts."

"Well, no, not really."

"Your mom told me you write down everything that happens around here. Ain't that so? Well, I want you to write down what I said. I didn't start that fire. I did start the one that burned Rutherford's trees down in Chestertown, but I didn't torch Boyden's house."

Lavonia gulped. She had heard about the tree episode from Jeff and how there had been no proof that Joel did the burning. Here was proof, and now it did not matter. There would be no jail for Mr. Plumley. "Okay, Mr. Plumley."

"Then write about how I've found the Lord and I how I'm sorry for every bad thing I did here. I was wrong, and I want my children to know that I helped you once; remember how I came over when Benjamin was in that Civil War with Jeremiah and showed you how to plant?"

"Yes, I do, and that was very gracious of you."

"Gracious, yup, like that word. You can put that word in for me too. I was gracious." He sat up and stared out the window of the cabin he had built thirty some years ago.

"You know I was, well my whole family was, in trouble with the law when we came here. I suspect most folks that ended up in this wild country did not come on a winning streak. I know a few who came here to hide like me, and because I came here first, I claimed it for my own. I tried to run other people off, and some, I did, but the town, the blizzards, the freeze ups, and diseases came, and we fought them, and we won. Things like that can change a man."

He began trying to catch his breath. "Mr. Plumley, please, you need to rest." All Lavonia could think was, God don't let him die while I'm here.

"Yes, thank you," Joel whispered and closed his eyes. Lavonia breathed a sigh of relief. He was sleeping. She could sneak away. She got up and quietly left the Plumley cabin. She went out back to her cabin and wrote down what Joel had asked her to write, and when she finished, she prayed for his salvation.

Later, Joel was sitting up gazing out his window. He looked out at the black water of this giant river. He heard the waves splashing against the rocks on the shoreline. He marveled at the mountain's scenes, made clear when the Shaws moved on the eastern shore and timbered it. He prayed for his son, Jeremiah. It was a terrible war, and he did not know if his son would come home. Joel felt the warmth of the fire that his son, John, had started early that morning.

He smiled as he saw the lights of the Shaw house across the lake. He realized that should this town have been only his, it would be dying with him. Instead, the town would live. Long Lake would stay long after he was gone, and then his dark eyes crinkled, his mouth turned up in that crooked smirk, and he proclaimed, "But I will forever be known as the first white settler to step foot in this territory."

Some of his children came to the funeral. Some did not. All the town folks came to the burial, except one. Jeff Rutherford looked out at his beautiful, serene lake just a few miles west of the Plumley cabin. Today he would tap some maples.

# 8

## FIRESIDE CHAT

IT WAS DURING the freeze up on an October night that Lucius Henderson went out to the old worn barn on the western side of the lake to saddle up his team. It would be his fifth year of driving the stagecoach from Chestertown through Olmstedville, Minerva, Aiden Lair, and Newcomb to Long Lake. It would be a year of changes for the mail in the little settlement called Long Lake.

Rachel Helms, married to William who ran the small cabin hotel five miles from town on the southeast end of the lake, had been spouting off about how there needed to be a post office in Long Lake. She would walk to town to meet the stage and pick up the mail if it got there. Sometimes it was a month before it got through, and sometimes it never made it to the settlement. One day she received a month-old letter telling her that her friend Harriet Palmer's son, Ransom Palmer, had lost an arm in the Battle of the Wilderness fighting for the north in this raging Civil War.

She went into the small store Cyrus Kellogg ran in part of the new Long Lake Hotel on the corner of Carthage Road and the road to the lake. She remarked, "I declare, Cyrus, you would think in this age, one could hear about a loved one sooner than a month after the injury. Do you know about this?"

"No, Rachel. What is it?"

"Well, it is about your sister Harriet's son, Ransom Palmer."

"Oh, Lord, no," Cyrus cried, jumping over the counter, grabbing the letter, and reading it. "Oh no, he has lost his arm in the war."

"Yes, and that was over a month ago. I just got this letter from the hospital. I'm sure it was supposed to go to Harriet, but I got it."

Cyrus ran his fingers through his hair. "So, you think she doesn't know?" "Never said anything to me, nor you, I guess."

"No. Neither has Ezekiel. He must not know either." "Well, I guess we've got to tell them."

"Right. I guess." She held up the letter shaking it in the air. "For God's sake, he was shot and has lost his arm, and I couldn't even get a letter to him. He must think he has been abandoned." She plundered on about the incompetent mail system and how it was ridiculous that the town did not have a central post office. "We have to do something, Cyrus. We need to get our news faster than weeks after it happens, if we even get it."

"I agree." Later that night, he began to think: Why couldn't I have a post office at my hotel? He turned to his wife, Christine, "What do you think about having the mail delivered to the hotel and people coming here to pick it up?"

The next day, Rachel joined Christine and Cyrus in a discussion about the possibility of a post office. "Did you tell Ezekiel?" "Yes, he...."

"Had already heard. Harriet heard too. The state department sent a telegram. He is coming home soon, thank the Lord. You know, Cyrus, you can go to that town meeting and vote to turn a corner of this store into a post office. Darn shame I can't go. If I could go and vote, we'd already have a post office even if I had to put it in my place, but you have a central location and people come to the store anyway, so this would be perfect."

"I agree." Cyrus and Christine Kellogg said in unison. Just then, the door swung open, and Danny Kellogg strolled in. "I heard something about putting a post office in here. Uncle, you should do it."

"Uh huh." Just like that. He knew he would have to apply and be approved, and it was a process. "Danny, what are you up to this afternoon?"

"Oh, just came in to pick up some yarn for Fiona. She is making winter socks."

"She knits good stuff and makes her mittens and hats extra thick." Rachel replied. "She keeps you and the kids plenty warm."

"Yup, she does; you know she almost froze to death in Scotland when she was a little girl?"

"No, I didn't," Rachel replied. "How did that happen? Come sit by the stove and tell me." Cyrus had a pot belly wood stove with several cane chairs around it. People stopped by and chatted from time to time. Every morning, at six o'clock, he unlocked the door, built up the wood fire, and an hour later had the doors unlocked and the smell of coffee permeating the large wood room filled with fabrics, flours, grains, and tools for sale. Danny, Cyrus, Christine, and Rachel sat down, and Danny told the story.

"Well, there was a time in Scotland when Fiona's family was very wealthy, but most of their income was from the farm they ran. They sold produce, and her father was a prominent politician. He was what they called a Laird, and they lived in what sounds to me like a castle. Well, when the Industrial Revolution marched into Scotland, much of what the farm produced began to be produced by machines. This left the farmers who tended her father's land with no income. About the same time, the Highland Clearances began. During this time, many wealthy sheep owners moved in and took over the farms so people tending the farms were thrown out of their homes. Some went to work in the mines; others moved to Canada or America. In Fiona Rutherford's case, her father, the Laird Richard Rutherford, could no longer afford the huge expense of running the enormous mansion they lived in. They were a proud clan, not willing to reveal their secret to anyone. Without tenant farmers, the

Rutherfords could not keep the land, so they sold most of it and eventually the powerful Buccleuch Clan was anxious to take over their property. The Rutherfords were down to living on the few potatoes they could dig up and the deer Richard and his son Jeff could kill. The animals had long been eaten or sold. One day, Fiona, who was six years old, was so hungry that she left her home without her mother seeing her. She put her boots and thin sweater on and decided to walk to their neighbors the Doddses' house."

"Oh, my Lord, and was it winter?" Rachel asked. By this time Lysander Hall, his wife Harriet, Zenas Parker, Walter Jennings, and George Stanton had come in, heard part of the conversation, and joined the circle around the stove.

"Yes, Rachel. He said the child almost froze to death," Cyrus remarked. "Oh, hush, Cyrus," Christine snapped. "Let him finish the story."

"I believe it was February, which is winter, same as here, so Fiona began her trek to the neighbors. As I said, she had put on her red boots, but the snow became so deep that she lost one."

"Well how far away were the Doddses?" Zenas asked. "According to Fiona, about two miles."

"Two miles! My goodness!" Harriet Hall blurted out. "Quiet, woman," Lysander chided.

Harriet hit him with the end of her shawl. "No dinner for you tonight, mister." With that Lysander put his arm around her shoulders. She placed her head on his shoulder. "Go on then, Danny."

"Well, the wind was blowing so hard that at times she was blown backwards and fell down, pulling herself up and forcing her foot out of the snow. Finally, she saw the fence to the Doddses' place. She was so tired she just wanted to lie down in the soft snow, but she kept on. She reached the porch of the little house and looked through the window."

"Wait, wait, the Doddses, where have I heard that name?" Christine asked.

"Oh, your father-in-law's neighbor, Jenny Scott. She was a Dodds." Danny answered.

"That's right, and she married her neighbor in Scotland, John," George Shaw offered.

"Yes, well anyway back to Fiona...."

"Oh, so Jeff Rutherford up on Clear Lake was neighbor to Jenny Dodds in Scotland." "Yes."

"So, Fiona was his sister."

"Yes, now to get back to the story: It just so happened that on that very day Jenny Dodds was coming home from work and came upon the child peeking through the window. She stopped, realizing it was six-year- old Fiona Rutherford. 'My, my, little one, so what are you doing so far from home on this wintry day?' She squatted down to make herself eye level with this child whose blonde curls were poking out from the rim of her sheepskin hat.

'I'm hungry,' Fiona told her. Jenny invited her in and gave her food. Later, Jenny Dodds and her mother brought Fiona home. The Rutherfords were mortified and soon after set sail for America."

"Well, I guess that was the reason a lot of our ancestors came here; hunger, but how did you meet her?"

"I was working on the ship they came over on. I am a distant cousin of William Kellogg. I stayed with them when I first settled here." "Oh, my goodness, it is a small world," Rachel Helms remarked. "So that is why Fiona makes such thick winter coverings. She remembers almost freezing to death."

"Yes, I would say so," Danny replied, "and now I've got to get back to her with her yarn." He pushed his chair back and stood up as did Cyrus and the rest. They purchased their items and left the chairs empty until night rolled into morning, and once again, the men stomped in wearing their rubber boots and warm wool jackets to sit around the black potbellied stove smoking their pipes, discussing who left the settlement. Then they went on to work the day through. They mostly came in the winter, as spring, summer, and fall work started at dawn. Of course, there were always a few of the gray-haired men too old to work hard, and Robert Shaw who worked at talking and talked about working.

That next week was the town meeting, and both Danny and Cyrus Kellogg kidnapped the meeting and made it about the mail coming into Long Lake. Robert Shaw also voted for it, so it was not long after the meeting that Cyrus received word that he could open the post office.

A few months later, Jeremiah Plumley came back from the Civil War with a shot-off thumb. Benjamin Emerson came back without a leg, and young Ransom Palmer was missing an arm. A young man named Walter Jennings from Massachusetts who also fought in the war came to Long Lake looking for work. He found a job at a new hotel called The Centennial, which sprang up next to Zenas Parker's farm on the southwest shore of the lake. This place called Long Lake was growing and spreading its wings.

In the early morning mist as the dew lifted from new-fallen leaves, the clip clop of Lucius Henderson's horse team could still be heard by the waking townspeople, though the new post office shortened his route. However, now he would be paid, and he would be able to devote more time to his growing farm in the community folks were beginning to call Big Brook Village.

# 9

## REVENGE

AFTER GEORGE ROBINSON stepped off that coach in Newcomb several years ago, he vowed to find Wright Rule. George had worked for Wright's brother in Jedburgh, Scotland. He and Wright helped load and unload wagons with supplies for Rule's General Store.

Through the years, George had saved his money and bought two prize Clydesdale horses for the remnants of the estate he inherited from his ancestor, the Duke of Roxburgh. At the end of border fighting between Scotland and England, the Robinson clan was left with its magnificent manor home. George had married Isabelle Scott, and they lived in the Robinson home with his father the laird until he died. Five years later, the Industrial Revolution swept through Scotland and hit the Robinsons as it had the Rutherfords and the Doddses.

When George Robinson's father passed on, George, being the only remaining son, became the laird of the estate. Eventually, he had to go to work outside his estate to pay for its upkeep. Since the government taxed all male servants, George had to fire several of them. Many days, he resented being stuck with this monstrosity. He had not planned for it as he was not the oldest son until his older brother had died several years before and he inherited the property. He kept one tenant to plow the fields, plant in spring, and harvest in fall and two families to pay rent. However, it was not enough, so eventually, George and his young sons were tending the farm. Between working at the store and selling what he could from the estate, George was able to buy two draft horses. The horses increased production, and soon the estate was profitable again. George looked forward to the day he could quit working for the Rules and go back to only running the country house.

One spring morning George was awakened by his tenant, Patrick Walton, banging loudly at the door. He opened his eyes and looked out the window. It was still dark. "Hold on. I'm coming," he shouted as he stepped into the leg of his trousers, hopping to the door, and pulling them up. "Patrick. What is it? What is so important that you're waking me at this hour?"

"Mr. Robinson, oh, Mr. Robinson, the horses are gone!" "What?"

"The horses. Somebody took them. I went out to the barn. The door was wide open, and our two Clydes are gone."

George couldn't believe it. It was too horrible to absorb. Without those horses, he would lose the estate. "Okay, okay, Patrick. I'm going to the constable right now. Are you sure you didn't leave those doors open?"

"I'm sure. I remember dropping the latch like I do every night before leaving the barn."

"Well, this is a disaster. We've got to get them back." George rode into town and reported the theft. The constable assured him that his men would look for the horses, but since it happened hours ago, they might not catch the thieves. Once horse thieves were over the border into England, they were gone for good.

However, floating around in Constable Harrison's mind was one name: Wright Rule. Wright had been accused of horse thievery many times, but Harrison never could catch him. He was a slick one, and when Constable Harrison checked out the Rule house, it was abandoned. He checked the cottage, looked over the pens, and searched the barn. The Rule family was gone along with their animals.

Next, he went to Wright's sisters and brothers-in-law's store. He learned from John and Agnes Rule that Wright and Catherine Rule had sailed for America that morning. Harrison asked if he took any horses with him, but John didn't know. Constable Harrison went back to his office in Lessudden and erased the matter from his mind: The Rules were his friends, and if Wright were the thief, which had never been proven, he was out of reach and on his way to the colonies where he would not be found.

George Robinson returned to the store and told the Rules what happened. "Where is Wright, Mrs. Rule?" "He went to the colonies."

"What? He's gone to America. I didn't know he was planning to go there."

"We didn't either. It happened quite quickly, but that is how Wright does things. He makes up his mind to do something, and it is done. He and Catherine were to sail this morning."

"On the first ship?"

"The first ship out of Glencoe."

George walked away steaming mad. They could have caught him, but he knew the theft was planned. It would have taken them two days to get to Glencoe, so he knew they had left the night before, stayed in an inn, and sailed out on the first ship. Two days later, George traveled to Glencoe, walked into the ship's office, and looked up the manifest. Sure enough, there was Wright and Catherine Rules' names, and there were two horses with them. George threw his hat on the floor. "My horses. Blimey! He took my horses!" he shouted as the clerk stared as if hoping he would leave soon. He nervously eyed the gun that hung from George's belt. George saw the nervous twitch on the clerk's face. He put up his hands. "Okay, okay, I'll leave. You can take a breath. I'm not going to shoot you today." He turned and stomped out the door muttering, "If it is the last thing I do, I will get that thieving scoundrel, Wright Rule."

A few years later, his wife Isabelle and their children had to move in with her father and mother, Isaiah, and Mary Scott, who lived in Lessudden. George did not have the money to bring his family to America at that time, nor could he support them in Scotland. Though Isaiah Scott tried to talk George out of going to America, George was determined to go, buy a small piece of land, and send for his family. Isaiah gave him the address of his nephew, John Scott, who lived in a place called Long Lake.

He sold the estate, and with the little money he made, set sail for America by going through Canada.

He sailed the same route the Doddses had in 1819. He sailed into Newfoundland. Then, he came down the Richelieu River onto Lake Champlain where he overnighted in Crown Point and went on to Newcomb the next day. After arriving in Newcomb, George found out quite quickly where Wright Rule lived. Wright had made a name for himself as the best trapper in the territory. In addition, Wright's grandniece, Ann Dodds Parker was married to Patrick, an Abenaki Indian, and they lived on the outskirts of town. He befriended Ann by telling her of her grandparents in Scotland. Then he visited Jenny and John Scott, bringing news of his uncle Isaiah Scott and Jenny's grandparents, the Rules.

After learning that Wright Rule was living in Rossie, New York, George started the trek north with pure vengeance flowing through his veins. He would make that scoundrel pay and get his horses back. He arrived in Rossie the next day, found the Rule farm, and stood watch waiting for the right moment to confront him. He did not see his horses in the near pasture and assumed they were out in another field or had been sold; he bided his time and soon heard that Wright was in Long Lake and no one knew when he would return. George returned to Newcomb where he found some work on a farm. Revenge was his old friend soon to be joined by another Scotsman of the same mind. His name was James Dodds.

# 10

## FINDING WRIGHT RULE

It was autumn again on the Rossie farm. The leaves had fallen. The wood had been gathered, and the geese were flying south. Duncan Dodds was writing in his journal on the new front porch of their home when he saw two men riding up the driveway. One of them looked like a city dandy, dressed in a black coat, white shirt, tie, and big black top hat. The other wore a coonskin cap, gray wool shirt, suspenders, wool pants, and boots. What an unlikely pair, thought the young man standing up to his full height of six feet, tall by most standards for a fifteen-year-old boy.

"Hey!" he hollered as he walked over next to the maple tree where they had stopped.

"Morning, I'm James Dodds and this is George Robinson." "Dodds," Duncan said, looking up. "Hmm, you related to my pa?" "Is your pa Thomas Dodds?" Though James had never met Duncan, he certainly had the coloring with the red hair and blue eyes of some of the Dodds clan he knew back in Scotland.

"Yup, but who are you?" Duncan asked suspiciously. Few people came riding up to their farm unless they were from the area.

"I am your great uncle," replied James. "Oh, wow! You knew my dad in Scotland?" "That I did, Laddie. That I did."

"Well, come on in. My ma is in the house." James and George dismounted and tied the horses to the tree. "I'll get my dad and then give your horses a drink. Follow me down to the barn. My dad is milking." As they walked, James noticed the boy dragging one leg.

"Got you a bum leg there, I see."

"Ya, when I was six, they got squashed by a stone boat." "Oh, Lordy, so sorry to hear that, lad."

"Yes," George Robinson replied. "Tough break."

"Ya, they never thought I would walk, but I am, and I can even do chores, just not as long as pa."

They entered the barn, and the stench was more than James could stand. Several Holstein cows stood side by side in stations with a trough behind them. They walked down the cement floor. Duncan yelled for his dad.

"Down here, Duncan." Thomas was standing with a pitchfork feeding hay to the cows. He came forward and saw Duncan coming down the barn with two strange men.

"Pa, this is James Dodds and George Robinson."

Thomas squinted his eyes and looked again. "James, it's been a long time. I didn't recognize you." He reached out and shook James's hand.

"Hello, Thomas, meet George Robinson. His family...."

"Had the country house opposite Walter Scott's Abbotsford, almost into Jedburgh" Thomas cut in.

"Oh my, you remember?" James replied.

"Oh, yes, I was a young man when we came here. I remember the river and Cheviot Hills and the fair every year, and I remember that you were a schoolteacher."

"That's right."

"A schoolteacher that turned my uncle in to the police for horse thievery. Now, why would you be coming here, Cousin James? You know, Uncle Wright is old but not too old to knock you around if he catches you."

"I'm not the same man, Thomas. I want to see your uncle to apologize for what I did. I was a bitter man who spent too much time in the pubs. Someone bribed me to do what I did."

Thomas remembered his sister's husband, John Scott, telling him about running into James in Newcomb and how he was the same pompous chap he was in Scotland though he tried to pretend he was not. Thomas did not believe James and was not about to take him to his uncle without talking to him first. By this time Henrietta had come to the barn to see who had come to visit. Thomas made introductions and the pair were invited in for tea and biscuits.

"Have you gone to see John and Jenny yet?" Henrietta asked. "Oh, in Long Lake?"

"Yes, the older children have all grown, but John, Jenny, and their youngest are still there."

"Right," James replied, "and Ann and Patrick are still in Newcomb." "I heard you were working for the Whitneys," Thomas interjected. "Oh, yes, I was up until about two years ago. Since then, I have been back in Scotland. I'm here to help a friend and do some work on the side. I am now working for the local government in Edinburgh."

"Oh, what government job in Edinburgh?"

"Actually, right now I am running for political office in Scotland." "Wow! So, you are no longer living here?"

"No, but I keep a small home in Newcomb on the Hudson River." James replied.

"So, can we meet this uncle of yours? I hear he is the most famous trapper and guide between here and Newcomb." George chimed in. "Yes, that he is," Henrietta replied.

"He is the best," Duncan blurted out. "And is his farm close?"

"Oh, yes, it...." Duncan started to say. He stopped. He did not know this man, and he should not tell him where to find uncle. He began again, "He used to have a place in the area...."

Thomas broke in, getting out of his chair, "but it was too much for him, so he has moved on. Now, what I can do is tell him that you gentlemen are looking for him; where can he reach you?"

The two men realized that the conversation was over. They both stood up. James said, "We will be staying at the Parrish Hotel in Ogdensburg for a fortnight. Please have him contact us."

"Will do," Thomas said. "Now we need to get back to work. Come on, Duncan." He put his hat on, ushered the two men out, waved goodbye to them as they rode off, and turned to Duncan. "You don't ever give any bloke more information than you need to."

"Did our cousin really turn Uncle Wright in?" "Yes, son, yes he did."

"So, we don't trust him."

"That's right. Maybe he has changed, but we protect our family and we let uncle decide if that is the truth or not. Uncle will know." "That's right, Uncle Wright knows just about everything."

Thomas laughed and put his arm around his son's shoulders, "You've got that right. He's lived a long time, and that man knows things, son. He just knows things."

Uncle Wright was getting on in years, and when he heard about the visit, he listened and decided he would see James and George Robinson, but first he would be talking to his niece, Ann Dodds Parker, who had just returned from Scotland. Ann and her husband Patrick built and ran the new gristmill in Newcomb. They were also bounty hunters who killed coyote, bear, beaver, mink, and other animals for the fur trade, traveling up the St. Lawrence and the Richelieu Rivers into Canada to the trading posts. Now that their son Sam was grown and their daughter Isabelle was eighteen, they could run the mill while Ann and Patrick traveled into the woods and waters they loved. Ann remained the best archer in the area, and Patrick could throw a knife with such accuracy he could split an ear of corn. They both carried shotguns, and no one dared come up against either of them in a shooting match.

# 11

## The Ingenuity of Uncle Wright

O N A LATE autumn day in Newcomb, Ann Dodds Parker heard the clip clop of horses' hooves outside her home. She and Patrick still had the log home, though they had added a porch and a barn. She stepped out onto the porch and saw the shoulder-length white hair of Uncle Wright Rule jutting out from under his sagging brown hat. He was sitting on a beautiful chestnut stallion. Behind him was his sister's boy Michael Wright, Helen Rule Dodds's nephew. People sometimes confused Michael Wright with Wright Rule because they both had Wright in their name, a common name in Scotland but uncommon in America.

"Hey, uncle, to what do I owe this visit?" Ann asked as she stepped off the porch and hugged him.

"To me wanting some of your mincemeat pie."

"Aww, Aunt Catherine's pie is better than mine. You didn't ride all the way for a piece of my pie. Hey, Michael.

My, you are all grown up. I haven't seen you since Ma's funeral."

"I know. I been helping up at the farm."

"Well, come on in. Patrick will be home in a bit. How's the hunting been?"

"Good. We brought our supper." Michael lifted his saddlebag. "Venison?"

"Yup. Steaks."

"Oh, Patrick will love that."

That night, while the men sat around the old log table feeling the warmth of the fire, Ann and Isabelle cooked the meat and potatoes on their new wood stove. Isabelle set the table and Sam brought in more wood to fill the wood box. After dinner, Uncle Wright brought up the real reason he was in Newcomb. "Annie girl, tell us about Scotland. Patrick, what did you think?" Only Uncle got away with calling her Annie.

"I liked the green rolling hills they called mountains, but I could not understand most of what they said. Ann had to translate for me. I liked hunting for the red stag, though, and meeting her relatives. The best part was the Scotch whiskey from the distilleries."

"Patrick," Ann chided as she poked him in the arm.

"Well, I'm not much for whiskey but if I were, that would be my choice." "Yup," Uncle Wright remarked, "best whiskey in the world, and I must say I did taste a wee bit in my time."

"Uh huh, not what da told me, uncle," Ann said, smiling at him across the table.

"Well, your da was tasting it right along with me and sold it in the store." "I know; just pushing you, uncle. According to Ma, neither you nor da had a problem of that sort like some of the others."

"That's right. Now, Patrick, who did you meet over there besides Jenny's parents?

"I met some of her cousins on the Rule and Dodds sides. Then we visited Jeff Rutherford's old place." "Quite a place, huh?"

"Yes, it was a castle. In fact, all the buildings looked like castles, all stone and old, even the cabins." "Cottages," Ann corrected.

"Whatever they were, they've been there a long time: stark stone structures built against the rolling green pastures filled with those long-haired cows and horses and sheep scattered everywhere across the fields. Surrounding the stone buildings were tiny cement bungalows and small farms. The hills, or mountains they call them, were covered with purple heather. It was so beautiful, but the contrast of the houses showed a big difference between the rich and the poor. I saw where Ann grew up."

"Yes, much has probably changed since we lived there. Those small farms used to be estates owned by the wealthy who lived in the castles. Tenant farmers, like the Doddses, lived in those bungalows. We all worked for the wealthy and could not own our own land," Ann responded.

"Most of those mansions and bungalows were built hundreds of years ago," Wright added.

"Yes, uncle, like the Robinson manor outside of Jedburgh?"

"I worked for Laird Robinson for five years. He and the Rules were friends. He used to come into the store when I worked for Helen's dad. If I remember right, the Laird died and so did his oldest son, so the second son, George, inherited the place. He was struggling to keep it afloat while I worked with him before setting sail for here. Thomas tells me he was down in Rossie with your cousin James, looking for me. Did you hear anything about that?"

"Well, uncle, there was another rumor."

"God, always a blimey rumor. Give it to me girl."

"Well, while I was in Jedburgh, I visited our cousin Betsy McPherson."

"Oh, yes, she married my nephew, Fergus Rule."

"Yes, well the story goes that the Robinson manor was falling apart when Lord Robinson died." "Laird, girl, laird."

"Okay, uncle, Laird Robinson. Anyway, George did inherit it like you say, and he and his son ended up having to work outside the estate as well as on the estate to save it. With the money he earned at the store, he bought two Clydesdale horses."

"Yes; I think I remember that."

"Well, apparently, he woke up one morning and the horses were gone."

"Blimey, stolen?"

"Yes; they think so and by you."

"What? Are you daft? Me?"

"Apparently, the night they were taken was the night before you left for here, with two horses."

"Oh, Lordy, and all this time George was thinking it was me?"

"Yes, George and several others. I told them it wasn't you. I knew you never had any Clydesdales; the two horses you had were Highland horses, but George still thinks you ruined him because after that he had to sell the estate for pennies."

"So that is why he is looking for me, and that cousin of yours, James Dodds, is helping him find me. Such a waste, that one. Thought he was going to turn around for a while, but always been a pie-in-the-sky dobber, thinking he was better than anyone else."

"You say, they are in Rossie?" Patrick asked.

"Yes; they were up at Thomas and Henrietta's house looking for me." "What are you going to do? We'd better go back with you if you're going to meet with them," Ann picked up her rifle in the corner.

"Well, well, you are still the brave one, little Annie, and thank you, but I think we got this." Wright threw his arms around her and swung her in the air.

The next day, Wright and Michael saddled up and made their way back into St. Lawrence County. This time, they rode up to the Parish Hotel in Ogdensburg, left their horses across the street at the livery, walked through the wooden doors, and went up to the desk. "May I help you?" the clerk asked as she turned to face them and took a break from placing mail in the wood boxes behind the counter.

In the meantime, Wright pretended he was registering. In the register, he saw the two men's names he was looking for. "Yes; we are relatives of James Dodds and are here to visit him."

"Oh, Dodds. You are relatives of the Doddses?"

Wright and Michael looked at each other, and Wright said, "Yes, Lassie, that's right."

"Well, I'll be. I'm Eliza Martin. I know them."

"Eliza? Eliza?" Wright questioned. "Did you once live in Rossie?" "No, but my grandmother did. They moved south somewhere. A new settlement."

"Well, Lassie, it's a small world because the first place the Doddses lived when they moved to Rossie was in an abandoned cabin left by a schoolteacher named Elizabeth Scott."

"That was my grandmother. Like me, they called her Eliza. She has a brother south of here and went to live near him."

Michael and Wright looked at each other. They both asked in unison, "John Scott?"

"I think that was his name," she replied. Michael could not stop staring into her eyes. They were the most beautiful eyes he had ever seen: not just blue, but blue with tiny streaks of white like bursts of lightening. They reminded him of a sled dog husky's blue eyes in the snow.

"Well, thank you. Uh, sir, you wanted Mr. Dodds?" Michael was speechless.

Wright Rule didn't miss the moment. Hmm, he thought. I may not have my sidekick much longer. He looked at Michael and then at the girl, and stepped toward the counter, "Yes, Eliza, the room number please."

"He is in room 32."

"Okay, Lass. Thank you," Wright said as he headed up the stairs. Michael stood transfixed by the beautiful girl in front of him. Wright grabbed him by the arm. "Okay, son, time to go. Come on."

"Oh, uh. Yes." Michael stumbled along after his mentor, forgetting to even say goodbye to this blonde-haired beauty. Wright took the steps two at a time, and within a minute he was banging on room 32's door. There was no answer, so he banged again. Then, he heard a muffled, "Who is it?"

"It's the hotel. There's been a shooting," Wright quipped, knowing he would open the door. Within minutes, he heard the lock click. The door opened, and there stood a man dressed in a pair of gray trousers and white shirt with his shoes in his hand.

"What? Who got shot? Are we evacuating the place?"

"Well, well, well, George Robinson, don't tell me you don't recognize me," Wright said, as he and Michael barged into the room.

"No, and get out of my...well, if it isn't Wright Rule."

"Yup, that's right, and I hear you and that coward James have been looking for me. Well, look no more. Here I am, and what are you going to do about it?"

"Uh, I don't want you in my room. James, James!" he shouted into the hallway.

"You calling for James Dodds? He ain't going to help you, but let's get him in here, too. He put his double-barreled shotgun against the terrified man's nose and ordered him to call James again. "Michael, stay in the hallway, and as soon as you see his door open walk toward it. He doesn't know you. Then bring him here at gunpoint." Five minutes later James Dodds came through the door followed by Michael, who held a rifle at James's back.

"Ok, now we are here. We are going to have a little talk, or we're going to have a little shooting. Sit down." The two frightened men sat at the table looking into the barrels of the two guns. "So, why are you looking for me?"

James was petrified. He knew old Wright Rule was as crazy as they come, and there would be no talking him out of shooting if he didn't hear what he wanted, but James could talk. He had studied English and the law, so he had the words and the skill to deliver. "Wright, you know me. I would never say anything against you if it weren't true. I'm not really looking for you. George just asked me to show him the way to Rossie, so I did."

"Right, just out of the blue you travel all the way up here with a stranger. Here you are, an educated man, and you didn't ask why? I'm not educated, but I know that's a lie, and lies will get you shot, especially the big one you spread back home years ago about me being a horse thief; that lie right there ought to get you at least my fist in your nose a few times."

James backed away. "That wasn't me, Wright."

"Was too. You told the sheriff who just happened to be my brother's father-in-law. He had no reason to lie. What you did not tell him was that McPherson and I had a deal. He had traded me two horses for my dogs. He took the dogs and refused to give me the horses. Did you tell him that? Well, did you?" Wright moved the gun from George's face to James's nose.

"Uh, no. I didn't know."

"Right, you stuck this nose in where it didn't belong like you always do. Blimy, James, I don't know what to heck happened to you, coming from a good family like the Doddses, but they sure got a bad one when they got you." Wright turned his gun back on George. "Okay, now you. What are you accusing me of?" "You stole my horses."

"Uh huh, and did you see me steal your horses, George?"

"Well, uh, no, but we were working together at the store. I told you about the Clydesdales I had just bought, and the next day, they were gone, and you sailed for the colonies with two horses. So, where are they?"

"Okay, I haven't got time for much of this idiocy. Here, George, if you can read, read this; if you can't, give it to James to read." He pulled out the copy of the manifest of the ship he boarded in Scotland and threw it on the table. George read it and looked up at Wright. "Now, does it say anywhere on that paper that there were any Clydesdales on the ship?" "No, no it doesn't. Then you must have sold them."

"Right, George, I am going to steal your horses in the pitch-black night and sell them somewhere before dawn the next day. Think about it. Admit it, you idiot, it wasn't me, and I suppose you lost that place and came to America looking for me to blame. George, you never were the brightest cork in the rum barrel, and it is too bad your brother died because he would have saved your place, and you could have lived off him your whole life. I don't know what your beef with me or anybody is, James, but it is a shame you have that wonderful education, and you are throwing in with the likes of Robinson for a few dollars to spend the night at the nearest pub."

"But I don't...."

Wright put his hand up. "Don't even want to hear it, James. I won't believe it anyway. I've been to Newcomb and Long Lake, and I know Whitney fired you for dipping into his whiskey. If I remember correctly, and I usually do, it was the same thing that happened in Scotland."

He turned his focus back to Robinson. "George, I hope you find your thief, but after all these years, I would guess that isn't happening."

George shook his head. He believed the man. It made sense. He wasn't stupid. He could see that there was no way Wright could have taken the horses. "Okay, Wright, you can put the gun away. I apologize. God, I've been wrong all these years." Wright put the gun down by his side as did Michael. "Would you let me buy you a cup of coffee downstairs?"

They met in the coffeeshop half an hour later, and while they were talking, something occurred to Wright. "George, I just thought of something. You know, there is a family that moved to that settlement in the mountains by the name of Robinson. I know they were originally from the homeland. Any relation?"

"I'm not sure; my cousin moved somewhere around there." "Tall, skinny man like you."

"Yes, named Isaac."

"Yes, there is an Isaac Robinson in Long Lake. I met the bloke and his wife during sugaring last year. He told me he was building a sawmill and asked if I know anyone that needed work."

"It makes sense. My relatives ran a sawmill in Scotland," George replied. "His house is on the west bank about in the middle of Long Lake."

That day George and James headed back to the Adirondacks, George to Isaac Robinson's and James back to Newcomb and eventually to Scotland.

Lying in bed that night Michael Wright could not stop seeing those blue eyes staring up at him. He tossed and turned all night. The next morning, as he was loading up the hay wagon, instead of yellow hay, he saw her yellow hair. He saw her turned-up nose and pale skin in the snow while he was trapping and remembered the music of the voice of the girl at the Ogdensburg Hotel named Eliza when anyone spoke.

Finally, one day he confided in his mother. Michael had come to live with her after she had fallen from a stage-coach and broken her leg. Her place was in Waddington, a settlement only forty-five miles north of Rossie on the St. Lawrence River. For the past month, his mother had been getting around with a cane, so he began working in the local harness shop when he wasn't hunting, fishing, or trapping. He continued to stay with his mother at night.

He told his mother about his feelings. It was embarrassing to fall for a girl this fast, but he had to tell someone or explode. His mother advised, "Michael, go see her. How do you know she isn't going through the same craziness as you?" A few weeks later, after the spring thaw, Michael caught the stage to Ogdensburg that took him to the Parrish Hotel, a mammoth gray stone building with steps leading up to a thick wooden door. He opened the door and walked up to the counter expecting to see Eliza. Instead, a small man wearing round glasses greeted him, "May I help you?" he asked.

"Yes; I am looking for Eliza, the girl who works here."

"You mean the girl that used to work here," replied the man.

# 12

## The Last Panther, as told by Mitchel Sabattis

I T SEEMED THAT other things were disappearing besides girls named Eliza. For years, the black panther had roamed among the trees and rocks of the Adirondacks. Now, it was disappearing: shot by farmers who were trying to save their livestock, starved by brutal winters, and hunted by guides for tourists who wanted trophies on their walls.

On this chilly day, several men sat around discussing their trades. Mitchel Sabattis, Isaac and George Robinson, Henry Austin, William and Danny Kellogg, John Handy Plumley, Alba Cole, and Abram Rice were all gathered at Austin's. By now, tourists had begun trickling in from the cities looking for guides to take them hunting and fishing. These men, along with Wright Rule and Michael Wright, began working as guides. They would meet these "sports" at East Bay Landing or William Helms's log cabin hotel on the south end of the lake, take them out for one or two nights, and receive good pay for what they did every day.

Puffing away on his corncob pipe, Mitchel began talking about the last panther he shot. Mitchel was not a braggard or talker, but since the main talker, Lysander Hall, was not there telling his stories, newcomer George Robinson wanted to hear about Mitchel's last panther hunt.

"Well, it wasn't really a panther hunt," Mitchel began. "The sport that hired me wanted a moose, so I took him into Mud Pond out past Big Brook Village."

"Oh, right, out past me," Alba remarked. "Mud Pond's full of moose." "Uh, right," Mitchel said, clearly irritated by the interruption. "Now, as I was saying, so I take him out to Mud Pond, and we walk for miles heading back toward the lake where we leave the boat. We spend the night, and, in the morning, we sight deer but no moose. By now, my sport is hopping mad, but not mad enough to refuse my bacon, eggs, and biscuits or the venison we'd eaten for supper the night before. We are about halfway back to Long Lake when the snow comes blasting in; begins with a hard-fast snow, then lessens as we cross Sawmill Road and head down through that red spruce grove."

"Yup," William uttered, "know right where ya are, north of the Scotts's little place." All the men nodded their heads.

"Right," so we get onto a flat clearing. I look northwest to the sky, and I think I see movement up on the rocks. The late winter sun is breaking over the mountain splashing all over those rocks, so I figure it is playing tricks on me.

Meanwhile, my sport is mumbling about me being a stupid guide. I turn around, grab him by the throat, and shush him with the point of my knife because I see this movement again, and this time, I know it isn't the sun."

"'Why I....' the man sputters as I release his neck and tell him to shut up or I will shut him up my way. Then, I motion him to come with me. As we quietly start climbing up the ridge, I see the movement again. This time I see a flash of black. I know...."

"It ain't a bear." Alba interjects.

"No, too early. They're still hibernating, and it's too big to be a fisher, wolf, or badger," William Austin offers.

"Panther," Lysander says as he comes from around the cabin and sits on the steps. "It's that panther. I saw it there last week."

"Of course, you did," William Austin replies, "now just quiet you down. Mitchel's telling this story. Here, drink this cup of ale to keep your mouth busy for a spell." With little protest, Lysander accepted the tin cup. William Austin's ale was the best. No one would refuse his ale even though several people such as the Kellers did not approve of the drinking of spirits.

"So anyway," Mitchel continued, "we finally get situated behind a hanging rock, and I can see the panther standing there in a crevice between the two big boulders. Well, we wait, but that animal is not coming out. I climb a little higher until I am right in front of the opening to the hole. He is staring right back at me with those gleaming yellow eyes still pushed up against the rock wall almost knowing I got no shot. I tell my sport to get ready to shoot. The man is happy again because now he can take home a panther and brag about how brave he was to his sweetheart. Well, that animal isn't coming out, so I break off a branch from a low hanging pine and start to poke at the critter. He snaps, snarls, and backs further away, but I can see that from tail to head, that monster must be at least nine feet long. In the meantime, I glance over at my sport and he is kneeled down with the butt of his gun on the ground and the muzzle pointed straight up."

Lysander interrupts, "Oh my Lord. What's he thinking he's going to shoot, a bird?" He shakes his head. "Sports, I swear."

"I know, but we need them," John Plumley replies, getting another cup of ale from the barrel. "Anybody else want more ale? You know, I got a panther up Owls Head...."

"Sit down and shut up, you two," William and Danny Kellogg say in unison.

"Yes, let him finish his story," William Austin interjects.

Mitchel continues, "So, I see that my brave sport isn't going to be shooting anything. He's scared, and I'm glad because this may be the biggest panther I've ever killed. So, I poke it one more time, back off and shoulder my gun. Nothing, so I poke him again. This time that panther comes tearing out of that crevice heading straight for me. I barely have time to get my gun in position. By the time I pull the trigger, he is 10 feet in front of me. I shoot him right between the eyes and he drops. I step back almost tripping over the sport who is still frozen to the ground. The panther lands where I had been standing. I see it was a clean one shot."

By this time, the men are all sitting on the edge of their chairs. "Where is it now?" Lysander asked.

"Back at my place in Newcomb," Mitchel said, taking the cup of ale Lysander had given him.

"Skinned it yet?"

"Yup, it's drying."

"Well, hell," Abram piped up. "We want to see it."

"What? You don't believe me?" The men all murmured they did but wanted to see it since it was nine feet and maybe the last panther they would ever see. The next Sunday, they walked the trail to Newcomb along with Mary Ann Keller, James Rice, and two of the Kellogg kids. They reached the end of the trail on the west end of Rich Lake where Mitchel met them with his wagon. They rode in the wagon the half mile to his house. As soon as they approached the house, they saw the long black pelt hanging from the maple tree branch. It had to be hung from the second branch up on the tree, and it covered the entire tree trunk. "Lordy, Lordy," William Austin remarked, as he looked at Kellogg.

"Biggest one I ever seen," Lysander remarked as he jumped off the back of the wagon. Mitchel pulled the wagon up in front of the giant pelt, and they all tumbled out surrounding it and murmuring about how long it was and how they wished they had shot it.

"It would make me a nice coat," Mary Ann joked.

"That it would, girl. That it would," Mitchel said with a twinkle in his eye, "but the wife says it's going to make a warm rug in front of the fireplace so that's where it's going."

"You'll get plenty of meat from it," John Plumley said.

"Yup, got it smoking out there. They all looked out to the small shack with smoke billowing out of the chimney. "Come on in and have a cup of ale." William Austin remarked that it was too early for him, especially on Sunday.

"Ahh, never too early for a little nip," Mitchel replied. They followed him into the house where he dipped his cup into the ale barrel and handed out tin cups to the others. Austin, Kellogg, and Lysander took one to be polite, but they thought it was a mite early for ale. They just hoped Mitchel would be in good enough shape to get them back to the beginning of the Long Lake/ Newcomb trail. However, they stayed for a couple of hours: The women quilted, and the men smoked pipes, talked about the economy, the new hotel that Kellogg's son just started, and rumors about a man named Durant who wanted to put steamships on Long Lake.

"No way," Lysander and John said together. "No way that money- grubbing man is going to come up here and take our sports away from us."

"Except one," Mitchel replied. "He can have the one I had on the panther hunt with me." They all laughed "So, did your sport ever recover?" William Austin asked.

"Yes, but I don't think he'll be back anytime soon." They all chuckled, lifted their cups, and drank to Mitchel who was already well into the spirits on Sunday afternoon.

# 13

## SOBRIETY

ABRAM AND SARAH Rice could not move off her father's property. It was the largest farm in the area, and David Keller was getting older. David Jr. had his own place now, so James Keller and Abram had to shoulder the work along with seasonal helpers. Abram and Sarah had several children, and they all lived on the Keller farm. Hence, they continued to build additions onto the house. Most of the Keller women married local men, but although Christine Keller continually encouraged her daughter to find a suitor, Mary Ann refused to marry.

One day, Sarah went looking for Abram and found him in the hayloft drinking with Mitchel Sabattis instead of doing chores. "What do you think you are doing?" She shouted. "We need to get the cows milked and the sheep fed."

"Don't worry, hon; I'm doing it real soon. Mitchel and I are planning a business."

"A business. Is that right? You have a business. This farm!" She opened her arms.

"No, an ale business. We'll make ale and sell it to the sports, right Mitchel?"

"Yes, sir, uh ma'am."

"They're making a lot of money downstate doing just that."

Sarah put her hands on her hips, "Abram, you have enough to do on this farm; besides Barton Burlingame sells ale already."

"But he's leaving. That's why we want to start the business." "Are you sure?"

"Yes ma'am," Mitchel replied. "Barton can't keep up no more since the accident. That tree coming down on his leg messed him up, so we are all making the ale and whiskey."

"Well, I heard he is moving back to Vermont with his sister. That stuff is the devil's work. Look what happened to him. Besides, I don't like that David, James, and Abram Jr. are doing all the farm work while you are up at Palmer's Hotel trying to sell that stuff to the sports."

"But I'm making money. Besides, they are opening a new hotel up on the Carthage Road. It's where Bill Austin built his frame house. That'll bring in more sports to buy our ale."

"Well, it's all hogwash if you ask me," Sarah snapped. "Besides, I'm worried about Abram Jr. Have you even looked at him lately? He's skinny as a weasel; can't get food down him."

"Yup, he is a skinny one, but a little work doesn't hurt him. Besides, he only helps with the milking and haying. Probably help him." Abram Jr. had never been extraordinarily strong, and now that he was eleven, it didn't look like he was going to get much bigger.

"Won't hurt you either," Sarah snapped as she turned to go. Sarah was a formidable woman. She was tall like her mother and towered over Abram though Abram was tough as they come. A confrontation between them always resulted in Sarah eventually backing down.

By this time Mitchel was twitching and wanting to run out the barn door. "Abram, uh, I got to go anyway," Mitchel mumbled, as he straightened up, slid past Sarah, and exited the barn. Just then Mary Ann came around the corner of the barn with a cup of coffee. "Hi, Mitchel. Say hello to Elizabeth for me," Mary Ann said as she handed the cup to Abram.

"Yes, ma'am. Will do," Mitchel replied as he scooted down the path into the woods leading back to Newcomb.

"His wife isn't going to want to hear anything from him when he gets home. Just like this wife," Sarah spat as she turned and stormed out of the barn.

Mary Ann patted her sister on the arm, "Sarah, this coffee will sober him up enough so he can get the cows milked." Her heart went out to Sarah. She knew her sister had it tough with Abram. He was drinking more and more, and Mary Ann knew why. He was not a happy man, and Mary Ann knew the solution to that problem too. "Abram, drink this. You need to sober up so we can go milk the cows."

"Okay," Abram slurred as he took the coffee. Sarah stopped, turned, and glanced at the two of them sitting in the hay drinking coffee. Abram had always listened to Mary Ann even when she was a child. Now she seemed to be the only one that could do anything with him. Sarah shook her head and made her way back to the house. Today they were making soap from potash. A miserable, nasty-smelling job that took the Rice and Keller women all day to finish. "Mary Ann, I'll start the boiling within the hour."

"Okay, Sarah, I'll be there," she replied.

As Sarah glanced at them once more before exiting the door, she thanked God for Mary Ann. Sarah didn't know how she would manage when Mary Ann found a husband and moved away.

James Keller, David's youngest son, was praying too. He was praying for a preacher to come to this desolate community to stay. Since James Sargent had run that last preacher off in a jealous rage, they could not get anyone to come, and the few people who had come to Reverend Todd's makeshift church on the lakeshore had stopped coming. Though Mitchel Sabattis had periodically been playing his violin at the earlier services, he eventually traded the practice for drinking all night and sleeping in on Sunday morning, claiming it was the only day he could sleep in. Only his wife knew he was barely doing the milking anymore and wasn't getting up early enough to hunt. Lawlessness and havoc seemed to be winning out in this wild wilderness.

Havoc descended upon Mitchel and Elizabeth's marriage one Friday night in mid-May. After telling Elizabeth he would be working on his birch bark canoe with Caleb Chase all day, once again Mitchel came home drunk and penniless.

Elizabeth blamed herself for years. She had known he had an alcohol problem before she married him, but when she was fourteen years old and tried to break it off, she could not resist his boyish face, dark hair, and steel black eyes. Besides, he was amazingly skilled at hunting, fishing, and tracking, so he could provide for a family. When Mitchel and Elizabeth were courting, he would stop and pick her wildflowers and blueberries. Because Mitchel was Abenaki, Elizabeth's parents forbade her from seeing him. Undaunted, Mitchel left flowers and berries on her doorstep. This rejection of Mitchel continued until he left a deer on the doorstep. After he left game several weeks in a row, the Dornburghs began thinking Mitchel would be a good match and could take care of their daughter and grandchildren. One day, they met Mitchel at the door and invited him in.

"Mitchel," Mr. Dornburgh began, "what is it that you want from my daughter?"

Mitchel stared down at his feet. He had faced bears, panthers, and moose in these woods, but he had never been as scared as he was right now. His hands began to shake, and he couldn't get any words out. There was an awkward silence in the room until Mrs. Dornburgh asked, "Mitchel, you do understand English, right?"

"Uh, oh yes ma'am," Mitchel replied.

"Okay, good. Then answer this, are you in love with our daughter?" Mitchel stared at her and then looked down again. "Oh yes, ma'am." "Then, what do you want to do about it? Do you intend marriage?" "Marriage?" Mitchel answered completely dumbfounded that she brought up the subject.

"Well?" Mr. Dornburgh asked, "Look up at me, Mitchel; do you want to marry Elizabeth?"

Mitchel tried speaking, but no words came. Here was this vibrant tough woodsman cowed by the parents of his lady love. He prayed on his spirit to release the words. He saw his beautiful Elizabeth with her sky-blue eyes and strawberry hair. Finally, the word came out, "Unh-honh."

"What? What's he saying?" Mr. Dornburgh asked, looking at his wife.

"Mitchel. English," she said looking at him.

Oh no, he thought. It's Abenaki. English. What is the English word? Again, he envisioned the blue eyes. "Yes," he whispered.

A door opened, and Elizabeth stepped through. She looked from Mitchel to her parents and back again. "What's going on?" "Mitchel has asked for your hand in marriage." "What? My what? Mitchel?"

"Uh, hi Elizabeth." Mitchel moved from one foot to the other spinning the brim of his hat around with his fingers.

"You never talked about marriage?" Mrs. Dornburgh asked.

"No," Elizabeth answered. "You didn't even want me to see him, so we did not. Why am I the last one hearing about this?"

"Mitchel, take Elizabeth out to the porch. You two need to talk," Mrs. Dornburgh advised. So, Mitchel and Elizabeth sat on the bench on the front porch, and he officially proposed to her. After learning how Mitchel was blindsided by her parents, Elizabeth calmed down and accepted his proposal. She loved him and agreed to honor and obey him for the rest of her life. They took their vows a week later, and she had never regretted it. However, she could not face Mr. Bissell and make another excuse for missing the mortgage payment. She could not keep explaining to their three children why they were eating beans for supper again, and she could no longer look into the wizened contorted face of her once-handsome husband.

Elizabeth's brother was staying with them, and he had found Mitchel passed out in the woods leaning against a giant white pine. He got him up, slung him over his shoulder, and took him home. It was not the first time Mitchel had to be carried home, and Elizabeth was at her wit's end about what to do. Her husband had been the best guide in the north country until he wasn't. He was no longer working, and any money earned was spent on alcohol. Elizabeth took in washing and sold her jams and jellies to anyone who would buy them, though most settlers in Newcomb made their own. It just so happened that the night Elizabeth's brother brought Mitchel home, a friend of theirs named Lucius Chittenden had come to stay the night. He was a lawyer and politician from Vermont who had hired Mitchel on several occasions as a guide. Through the years, Lucius had come to admire this kind, gentle, generous man. He loved Elizabeth and the children, and he and Mitchel had become close friends. Lucius was around enough to know that Mitchel had a problem. He had tried to talk to him about it several times, but Mitchel always denied it, stopped the conversation, and pointed out how he never missed or was late for any of their hunting trips. He never was, until lately. The last two hunting trips Lucius planned with him never happened because Mitchel had not shown up. Lucius started having to hire Michael Wright or Jeremiah Plumley instead. They had some long campfire talks about Mitchel, and it took all of Lucius Chittenden's skill as a lawyer to get the two to say anything about Mitchel and alcohol, but eventually Lucius wore them down, and they divulged that they also thought he liked alcohol too much. Lucius swore he would never reveal that they had told him anything, and that night he decided he would pay Mitchel a visit.

By the time Lucius arrived at the Sabattis door, he had thought of a plan. Mitchel was not home when Lucius arrived. Elizabeth was delighted to see their friend but was embarrassed that she had little food to offer him. That evening they ate squirrels that her oldest son had shot, and Elizabeth cooked up some beans Lucius had brought with him. Lucius prompted her, and finally she began to cry and blurted it all out, "He hasn't paid the mortgage. They are selling the farm next week. What am I to do?" No sooner had Elizabeth got the words out than her brother, Henry Dornburgh, rolled through the door with Mitchel on his back.

"Where you want him?" Henry asked, looking at Elizabeth. Elizabeth pointed and Henry walked over and flung him down on the bed where Mitchel stayed until the next morning.

Elizabeth talked with Lucius into the night. The next morning, she arose before anyone, started the coffee, and began mixing the porridge for the children. She so wished she had something else to offer Chittenden for breakfast. When Lucius arose, she apologized for not having bacon or even eggs.

"Oh Elizabeth, not to worry. Look here." He bent over and pulled some salt pork out of his backpack.

"Morning. Hey, Lucius, what in the heck are you doing here?"

Mitchel asked as he slowly arose from the bed shaking his head and going toward the door. "Excuse me but I got to get a drink." He stumbled out to the well, pulled up the bucket, and gulped down the cold spring water. God, he felt like a darn cactus, and he would be needing a drink soon. He looked out into the woods; his eyes fixed on the old white pine where he knew he had a tin of ale. He looked back at the house and saw Lucius standing on the porch watching him. Lucius held out a cup of coffee and Mitchel stumbled over and took it. His hands were shaking so badly he could not hold it. Lucius took it back, dumped some of it out and gave it back, "Mitchel, you've got a problem."

"I do? I don't have a problem." He looked back at the tree. "Go get it."

"What?"

"You know. Come on." He motioned for Mitchel to follow him, and they began to walk toward the tree, coffee in their tin cups. When they reached the tree, Lucius told Mitchel to get his alcohol and pour some in the coffee. Without saying another word, Mitchel did just that. After a few gulps, the shaking lessened. Then they walked back to the little house, ate breakfast, and walked back under an old bent-over white birch to the white pine. Mitchel got another drink, and Lucius asked him to sit down. Once they were seated, Lucius began, "Okay, Mitchel, I want to talk with you about something."

"Oh, what?"

"Your mortgage."

"My mortgage. What is that to you?"

"You do know they are selling your farm next week?" "Uh, oh my Lord, Elizabeth told you."

"It doesn't matter who told me. Mitchel, you are good man. You have a beautiful family, and I am willing to help you if you will listen." "I don't see how anyone can help, but I'll listen."

"Ok, Mitchel. I'm going to ask you a question, and I want you to answer me honestly."

"I will."

"What would you give to one who would buy your mortgage and give you time to pay it off?"

"I would give my life, the day after I had paid the debt. I would give it now if I could leave this little place to Bessie and the children."

"Well, my friend, it won't cost so much. I will buy the mortgage if you promise to give up drinking and meet me at Bartlett's Lodge in August."

Mitchel promised instantly, solemnly. He rose from the ground, took the bottle leaning against the tree and dumped it out on the ground. Lucius saw the proud chief he had known. Mitchel stood up, turned, and faced the man who offered him help, "You may think you cannot trust me. I know I have let you down, but I will not let you down this time. When I am sober, I never lie, and I will tell you again when I see you and I am sober." When they returned to the house and told Bessie about the offer and the pledge, she was silent. He had never told her he would quit. He had never uttered a word about even having a problem with alcohol, and heaven help anyone else who brought it up. Humbleness engulfed the three of them as they stood face to face in trust. Mitchel put his arm lovingly around Bessie' neck. She began to sob, looked at Lucius, and whispered, "Lucius you can trust Mitchel. He will keep his promise. Thank you so much."

The moment passed, and Lucius replied, "We will hope for the best. Now, I must go, but Mitchel, remember the second of August at Bartlett's Lodge, and in the meantime, no whiskey." And he left. On his way through Elizabethtown, Chittenden stopped and bought the mortgage to the Sabattis home.

# 14

## THE FIRST CHURCH

SEASONS PASSED, AND the people in the young community began to hear rumblings of new schools, new roads, and new businesses. Abram Rice was a carpenter, and he and his sons helped build many of the new buildings. By now there were several frame houses but no minister or church. The makeshift church Reverend Todd had set up was long gone. The only remnant of that church was the bible the reverend had put in David Keller Sr.'s hand before he left the settlement for good. The Keller family read that bible every night and prayed for someone to come to help build a church. David had passed the bible on to his youngest son, James.

One night, soon after dinner, there was a knock-on James's door. James opened the door, and there stood a man with a shock of white hair jutting out from his chin. James noticed right away that this man's eyes were different.

 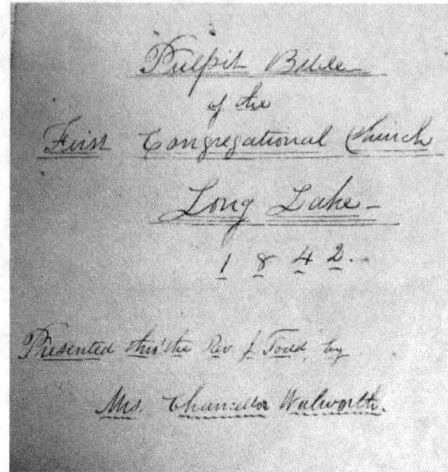

One of them was partly closed and the other wide open. He had a musket hanging from his shoulder, and David thought the man was not well. He picked up his own musket, walked out on the porch, and greeted the man.

"What can I do for you, mister?"

"I understand you have been praying for a preacher," the man said. James was taken aback by the soft voice coming from such a rugged- looking man.

"Uh, yes, yes we have."

"Well, I have come to bring you a minister, James." "Wait, uh, who are you? How do you know my name?"

"Sorry. My name is John LaPelle, and I have come from Crown Point to answer your prayers. I know your name because I heard you." Just then James heard rustling in the leaves and was doubly surprised to see Mitchel Sabattis coming up the hill.

"Mitchel, what's going on. Who is this man?"

"He is a good man. I met him in Newcomb. He is friend of the Van Valkenburghs."

"Okay, but what is this about a minister? Are you a minister?"

"Oh no. I am a surveyor and farmer, but I want to bring a minister here."

"Where is your horse?"

"I didn't bring one. I walked."

"From Crown Point? That is almost sixty miles from here."

"Yes, and a beautiful walk, I might say." James was amazed by this man and a little afraid; however, because Mitchel knew him, James invited him in to meet his family. From that day forward, a friendship blossomed, and great events would come to pass because of this friendship.

John LaPelle soon moved to Long Lake and married Moriah Shaw, but Moriah died young in childbirth. John was devastated. He turned to a church friend, Lavina Van Valkenburgh, and a short time later married her. They built a house off the new road coming in from Essex County where they befriended the native Abenaki and Mohawk men, letting them stay with them while hunting. John saw the Long Lakers (Long Lake was then called Goughville) as "ungodly hellraisers" that needed taming. Taming would come with a church. James Keller, Mitchel Sabattis, and John LaPelle began discussing plans to build a church, but they had one big problem. None of them was rich, and none of them had land close enough to town to build a church.

The next year, Mitchel decided to move from Newcomb to Long Lake. John LaPelle and Robert Shaw helped Mitchel build his house on the water south of the village on Carthage Road, and many a morning Mitchel and John would meet on the shore below his house to catch some fish for their families.

All was well until one night after a bitter fight with Elizabeth, Mitchel slammed out the door, walked across the road deep into the woods, and pulled out a tin of ale he had put there when they first moved to Long Lake. He knew it was foolish. He figured he would never drink it, but he liked knowing it was there. He sat down with his back against the large red spruce listening to the woodpeckers hacking away at the cedar tree a few yards away. He picked up the tin: I can't do this. I just can't. My life is good. My children are healthy, and I have a new home, but I just need a little nip to take the edge off.

"Hey Mitchel," a soft voice came from behind him. Mitchel jumped up, putting the gun to his shoulder, and shouting, "Who's there?"

Big John LaPelle came out from behind the tree with his hands in the air. "Hey, don't shoot me, my friend."

"For Jesus's sake, John. What are you doing out here?"

"You don't want to do that, Mitchel, for everyone's sake including Jesus." "But how did you know?"

"I know. I know things." He took the tin from Mitchell. They talked for some time and many times after that, and so in August Lucius Chittenden and Mitchel Sabattis sat on the bench in front of Bartlett's Lodge on Upper Saranac Lake surrounded by the mountains they loved, cementing the promise that Mitchel had made. Mitchel gave Lucius a payment toward the loan and told him all that he was doing in Long Lake and about the new canoes he was selling. They hunted the next day and parted, two men with great admiration for each other and a deal for Mitchel to pay $100.00 per month until the loan was paid off.

On one of the coldest, stormiest February nights in Vermont, a man bundled from head to toe came to Chittenden's door in a handmade sleigh drawn by two horses borrowed from his guide partner, Michael Wright. Mitchel had traveled to Lucius Chittenden's home through Newcomb and then the corduroy Carthage Road over the mountains to Crown Point with a sled heavily loaded with food, game, and valuable skins to offer as gifts.

The fire was warming Lucius Chittenden and his wife when they heard the knock on their door. "Lucius, was that somebody knocking on the door or the wind beating at the shutters?"

"Must be the wind. No one would be coming to our door in this storm."

But Mitchel Sabattis was not bothered by the weather. As a boy hunting with his father, Peter Sabattis, he had slept under trees, on pebble beaches, and under his canoe. The early spring rains lulled him to sleep when they spattered through the leaves and pelted the forest floor. When the rains gave way to late spring, he basked in the damp smell of the earth as they lay talking of the day's hunt. When winter storms reigned, he donned his fur-lined outer garments and welcomed the warmth of the heavy snow. He knocked again, harder this time.

"Lucius, someone is at the door."

Lucius rose from his chair, walked to the door, picked up his gun, and shouted, "Who is it?" "It's me, Mitchel."

Lucius quickly opened the door and there stood Mitchel covered in snow. "Come in, come in. Honey, it's Mitchel Sabattis."

"Oh, my goodness," Mrs. Chittenden said as she stood up and came to her husband. "Come in. I just fixed a pot of tea." Mitchel hung his coat up on the hook beside the door, removed his boots, and followed Lucius to the fireplace. The first thing Lucius noticed was the color of his eyes. It had been some time since he had seen Mitchel's eyes without red lines scattered through the whites.

That night he told Lucius how his wife now filled their house with boarders and that his oldest son was now also a guide. "Lucius, I'm here to give you back part of the loan. He reached in his pocket and pulled out an envelope and handed it to Lucius. "I thank you for your trust in me." He told Lucius about John LaPelle and how they were trying to start a church but could not find the land. Lucius listened intently. The next morning, he watched as Mitchel began the long trip back to the Adirondacks.

Lucius sat down at his desk and wrote a letter to two of his close friends, James and Mary Mulholland, who owned land in Long Lake, asking if they could deed a small plot of their land to build a church. The Mulhollands immediately contacted John LaPelle and Mitchel. John did the surveying on Lot 82, the piece of land the Mulhollands donated, land that fronted Carthage Road and bordered Robert Shaw's and Ann Houghton's property.

Mitchel, this once drunken man who could not stumble out of a hayloft by himself, left his home in the woods and asked for money of wealthy men and religious groups. He traveled from Boston to New York to Philadelphia and returned with $2,000. The Mullhollands had deeded one-fourth of an acre of that land to Mitchel for $25.

In 1865, the Wesleyan Methodist church was born. Robert Shaw became its first pastor. David Keller Sr., who had remained the sole member of Reverend Todd's church and had prayed for a real church, would not live to see it built. He died in 1860, but his wife, Christina, was among the first to attend the new church.

Five years would pass before her children would place Christina Keller in her grave beside her husband at the bottom of the hill near the Keller house.

They had brought their children to the new land never knowing what would take place. They watched many torn and beaten settlers pack up and move out west to milder climates and more fertile ground. They left a legacy of land for their children and permanent ties with the little community that continued to grow slowly but surely with sons and daughters tilling the dark soil and building a life.

# 15

---

## DOWN THE RABBIT HOLE

WHEN THESE FIRST rugged settlers passed on, they left bibles, buildings, and brave children behind, children like Mary Ann Keller who one day in a fit of anger, walked in on the men in the town meeting and announced that she was staying. She was sick of the men not letting women vote or learn anything about what was going on in their town just because they were women. Although their first response was to escort her out of the meeting, after the urging of John LaPelle and Abram Rice, they voted to let her stay if she kept quiet, and, of course, she could not vote.

That night Abram Rice walked her home. When they entered the house, Sarah approached her sister. She had already heard about the ruckus at the meeting and confronted Mary Ann about overstepping her bounds. "And I heard how you stuck up for her, Abram." Sarah stood in front of him with her hands on her hips. "Abram, you shouldn't be encouraging her to step into a man's world. It is going to get her hurt.

Mary Ann, no man will ever marry you if you don't stop this nonsense. You barely know how to spin or bake bread." "Ahh, Sarah, I think it's fine that she rides, shoots better than any man, and wants a say in the town her family started."

"We have a say. Both James and David Keller have positions on the board, and you vote."

"But Sarah, they don't know what us women want," Mary Ann replied. "Yes, they do if you are married," Sarah said putting her face within inches of her sister's.

"Well, maybe I don't want to get married."

"No, maybe no man will marry you. That is the truth of the matter." "Now, Sarah, that just isn't true. Why, I would marry her if I were a young man," Abram said smiling at Mary Ann.

"You would!" Sarah snapped. "Of course, you would because you are you, Abram. You never grew up. Always out laying around never getting any work done!"

Abram shouted back, "Sarah, enough! If I didn't work, this farm would not be doing as well as it is; besides, it is never enough for you. If I worked night and day, it would not be enough!"

"I'm going up to my room. Good night, Sarah," Mary Ann said, throwing her arms up and climbing the steps to her room.

"Good night, Mary Ann."

Two hours later after the house was quiet, Mary Ann heard tapping at her window. Clinging to the cedar tree, Abram smiled in at Mary Ann. She opened the window.

"Abram, what?" She watched as he put one leg over the windowsill and climbed in.

"I needed to talk to you."

"Okay, but here in my bedroom? This is not appropriate, Abram."

"I know," he whispered, "but I have to tell you. I can't keep holding this back. Mary Ann, when you look at me, what do you feel?"

"Huh, well you are family, so I guess I have good feelings toward you." Her eyes darted from the door to his face. She was imagining Sarah walking through the door at any minute. He was staring at her when she looked back. Their eyes met, and she could not tear away. She began to shake, and tears sprang to her eyes. "I...I."

"I know, Mary Ann; I feel the same way," Abram whispered, as he pulled her into his arms. "Oh, God, Mary Ann, I have loved you forever."

Mary Ann had never felt such warmth. It permeated through every fiber of her being, a warmth she could not pull away from, could not fight. This feeling was more powerful than the mountain lion, the bear she faced two years ago, and the moose she killed last winter. She did not know what it was, but she melted into Abram's arms and held her breath. Abram pulled back and looked at her. His face was inches from her, and he said, "I don't know what to do, but I can't stay away from you."

The break stopped the warmth, and she was able to find her voice. "Abram, we can't do this. You must go. Please go."

"Okay, Mary Ann, but I know you feel the same way. I will go and try not to see you." He turned and put his leg over the sill, onto the tree branch, and quickly climbed down the tree.

In the weeks that followed, Mary Ann and Abram avoided each other as much as possible. There were furtive looks at the dinner table and glances at her riding off down the pasture, glances that stopped his heart. She spent most of her time away from the house except for chores. Shelling peas with her sister one afternoon, she looked up to see pigs running loose through the field past the gate that was supposed to be holding them in. "Oh, darn, those pigs are running amok again," Sarah saw it too. "Mary Ann, run and get the boys to help you round them up." Mary Ann ran off the porch and up into the field where she saw David Keller and James Rice working in the field. Running straight toward the two men, hollering that the pigs were loose, she failed to see Abram running toward her from the other field.

"What's the matter?"

Mary Ann turned at the sound of his voice, stared, and then came to her senses. She pointed toward the east end of the barn. "The pigs are out and running away."

"Come on."

"Okay, we need to get them before they get to the bank," Mary Ann shouted as she ran. The two of them ran like wildfire, catching up to the animals and herding them back to their pens before they reached the bank. When the last one was in the barn, they leaned against the whitewashed walls and gasped for breath. With their backs against the wall, their hands accidentally touched. Mary Ann put her fingers around Abram's fingers. He turned his face toward her. Their faces were inches apart and then ever so slowly, ever so lightly, the kiss happened. Like a feather, a whisper, but a kiss. With that kiss, the siege was over, the siege to attack and defeat this powerful force that had taken over their lives. "Meet me tonight," Mary Ann whispered. "The window." She let go of his finger and ran out of the barn not waiting for an answer, running, running from that force within her that was taking control and driving her to disaster.

That night, Mary Ann once again heard the tapping at her window. This time she rushed over to the window, opened it, watched him step in, and fell into his arms. "There is no going back now, Abram," Mary Ann whispered as she pulled away and stood there staring up into his face.

"No, sweetheart, there is no going back."

"But, my God, Abram. I have thought about this for so long, since the last time you came to my room and I just keep thinking, what about Sarah? What if she finds out? She will be heartbroken."

"No, she won't. Mary Ann, she never loved me. She will be mad, I am sure, but not heartbroken. I thought she loved me, but she did not. She married me because her father wanted to keep me on the farm working for him."

"But you loved her."

"Yes, I did, or I thought I did. I was a young boy infatuated with an older woman. I suppose she was kind at first, but she did not want all the children, and we kept having them. She is right that she works hard, but she is wrong that I don't work."

"I know. I see you doing the haying, the milking, and tending the sheep. I too have always cared for you, but I tried to pretend I didn't."

He looked her straight in the eyes, "Mary Ann, I love you. I always have."

"I love you too. What are we going to do?"

"We are going to kiss," and they did, a passionate deep soul- wrenching kiss that they had been holding back for years. Mary Ann's mind was churning. Doubts and shame rolled in. She pulled away.

"Abram, we have to stop. I should move away. I could go live with James or go to uncle's house in Chestertown. I could get a job there." "No, no. I will leave."

"But you have the children. You can't leave the children."

"I know. I know." He hung his head, letting reality seep in until he looked up into those beautiful eyes. Those eyes. What were they going to do? "I will be leaving for a few weeks anyway. I have to go to Crary Mills and help Michael Wright and Eliza with the farm they are starting."

"Does Sarah know this?"

"Yes, it is a good time of year to go. The boys can manage, and Simeon Cole is coming over to help while I am gone."

"I will miss you, but maybe I can get used to not being near you."

"Yes, yes, maybe." He hugged her one last time, turned, and stepped out the window.

It was painful for Abram to climb down the cedar tree. It was painful to leave her. It was painful to crawl into bed beside his wife with thoughts of another woman swirling around his head. There would be no sleep for Abram Rice on this night.

# 16

## MICHAEL WRIGHT AND ELIZA MARTIN

THE DAY MICHAEL Wright left the Parrish Hotel in Ogdensburg was one of the saddest days of his life. Eliza was gone. Why didn't I come sooner? he thought as he stumbled down the steps of the hotel. Then he remembered that his Uncle Wright said the Scotts settled in a little town outside of Ogdensburg. The new owners of the hotel were strangers, but somebody must know her. He went to the general store and approached a young man who was sweeping the floor.

After introducing himself, he described Eliza to the young man. "Yes, I remember her, but I ain't seen her in a while." He remembered her because she was the prettiest girl in town. All the boys remembered her. "You might try over at the blacksmith shop." He pointed to the building across the street. "The Parrish family runs that, and they know everybody who comes in and out of town. Those people own most things around here including the hotel."

"Okay. Thank you." Michael walked across the street and ambled into the shop. A man wearing a mask was bent over a forge heating a long black instrument. Michael stood in the doorway for a few minutes. "Mister. Hello." The man could not hear him. Michael took a few steps closer. He did not want to touch the man for fear he would startle him and one of them would get burned. He continued standing, waiting for the man to finish the piece he was working on.

"What you need, mister?" Startled, Michael jumped to the side, turned around, and saw a large red-faced man.

After Michael caught his breath, he said, "Morning, I'm Michael Wright, and I am looking for someone. The people at the store said you might be able to help me."

"Okay. I'm Frank Parrish. Who are you looking for?" By this time, the man at the forge had finished, put down the poker he was making, and joined Michael and Frank.

"I'm looking for the woman who used to work at the hotel." "You mean Eliza?" Frank asked.

"Yes, that is her name. So, you do know her?"

"Yup, and just what would you be wanting with Eliza?" He stepped a little closer to Michael.

Michael saw the man's eyes change from friendly to guarded. "I'm a friend."

"Oh, you're a friend. Strange I ain't never heard of you." By now Michael knew he could be in trouble. A third man had entered the shop and was standing on the other side of Michael.

"So, I hear you're looking for my fiancé." He had blonde hair and looked younger than the other two. The man stood tall and puffed out his chest.

"Your fiancé?" Michael repeated.

"Yup, we are betrothed and set to marry next month. Now I think you best be moving along." All three men were closing in on him. Michael knew when to retreat. "Well, thanks. Good morning to you." He removed his hat, turned, and hurried out the door. Michael was tough but not stupid.

He jumped on his horse and rode to his cousin Thomas Dodds's farm. After he told Thomas and Henrietta about Eliza and what had just happened at the blacksmith shop, Henrietta said, "Michael, they are not engaged. I know it. Eliza is a close friend. Why didn't you come here first and ask us? She's living down in her grandmother's old cabin. Joe Parrish keeps trying to court her even though she keeps turning him down. In his head, she is his, but she is not engaged. I heard she has been hired on as a housekeeper someplace a few miles from here." After getting directions, Michael left and rode straight to the cabin. He knocked on the door. No one came. Just as he was about to knock again, he heard the latch click. The door swung open, and there she stood. He was struck silent at the sight of her.

She opened the door wider. Her jaw dropped and she said, "Oh my Lord, Michael Wright, what are you doing here?"

"You remembered my name." He stepped from one foot to the other now that reality was returning. "Uh, I was in the neighborhood visiting my cousins," he lied. "They told me you were here so I just thought I would drop by. I hope it is okay."

Eliza smiled, "Come on in. Yes, it is okay." After they discussed the fake engagement, they began dating. Young Joe Parrish gave Michael some trouble in the beginning, but when Eliza threatened to spread the rumor around town that he had lied about being engaged and agreed to say he broke it off instead, all went well.

Three months later the young couple married and moved to the small town of Waddington set on the edge of the St. Lawrence River. Eliza worked in the general store, and Michael worked for his cousin on the farm. Within two years, they had their own farm in a town thirty miles from Tom Dodds's place.

His longtime friend, Abram Rice, arrived the day after they moved in to help him start up the farm. For two weeks, Abram worked alongside Michael, Uncle Wright, Tom Dodds, and his sons. At the end of the time, Michael was sad to see Abram go, but he knew he had responsibilities in Long Lake, and Abram had Mary Ann Keller in Long Lake.

# 17

## MIDNIGHT MADNESS

FOR MARY ANN and Abram, the torture continued: The two weeks he was gone were very lonely followed by the joy of seeing Abram ride up to the porch and then Sarah meeting him with a hug. Mary Ann stood behind staring into Abram's eyes wanting to be Sarah right now.

They were trying to stay away from each other, trying to function as if nothing had happened, trying to talk themselves out of this wild painful journey. Each time they vowed to stay away; each time Mary Ann talked and cried to her friend, the hermit, Ebenezer Bowen and vowed to stay away from this man. She failed. She failed behind trees on Sawmill Road, in her room in the dark of night, behind the barn with a stolen kiss; she failed, and she grew thin and quiet no longer wanting to hunt, and during the quiet endless nights, she cried, imprisoned in the room above where her love and her sister slept.

Abram Rice and Mary Ann Keller lived in agony until one early morning, when the mist was rising off the lake and they met at the big rock by the river's edge, Abram said the words that would change their lives forever, words that could not be taken back once said. As the sun rose east over Kempshall Mountain, Abram uttered the words, "Mary Ann, run away with me."

Those six words fueled a plan that culminated two weeks later on a cold October night in the dark after the bright harvest moon. Mary Ann never changed her mind once she agreed to go. She loved him like she did anything else, completely, and full steam ahead. That was who she was; she hunted harder than anyone else, rode and pushed for what she knew was right, and was a formidable adversary in anything she competed in. Her heart was in full throttle, though her head attacked her at times like when she watched Sarah and the children fixing dinner and when her best friend talked to her about boys and how they shared everything. She wanted so much to tell Lydia Stanton and her brother John. She wanted to lift the guilt embedded in her heart by calling the whole thing off, but in the end, love won. She told no one. She stopped at nothing. Instead, on that night, at midnight, she climbed out her window, climbed down the cedar tree, and raced to the barn with only her small pack basket. For an instant, she stopped and looked back at her home. What would her father think of her now? She was grateful he had passed so he would not see her betrayal. She was choosing sin. She stared into the darkness. Where was Abram? She heard a voice in her head, "You can't go." Mary Ann turned and took a step back toward the house.

"Mary Ann," Abram whispered. She turned toward the barn and saw Abram. "Mary Ann, we must go; you can't stand there. Someone could look out and see you. Come on." He motioned her over to him.

"Oh Abram, I don't know." Now she was sobbing.

He put his arms around her. "Mary Ann, please." He looked at her face and wiped away the tears. "I know this is hard. I can't imagine leaving the children, but I can't stay. I just can't stay in this marriage. I love you, but if you can't go, I understand. I am going with or without you."

"You would go without me?"

"Yes, this is it for me. If I don't leave, I fear I will go another way." He lifted his gun and looked intensely at Mary Ann.

"Oh no, Abram, no, please."

"I'm sorry sweetheart, I didn't mean that; I just, well, I am going now. I think you need to stay here. I don't think you can leave." He put his lips on hers and kissed her hard, pulled back and said, "I will always love you. There will never be anyone in my heart but Mary Ann Keller. You take care of yourself. Watch over your sister and the children." He turned and walked away. Mary Ann watched until the dark forest swallowed him up. She stood there in the emptiness, feeling it all around her, feeling life without Abram. She looked back one more time, and this time she saw a shadow in the upstairs window. She was staring into the eyes of Abram's nine-year-old daughter, Lucinda. She gasped and covered her mouth. The tears burst forth in an avalanche. She looked away and slipped into the woods after Abram.

Sarah Keller woke at dawn and was surprised that Abram was already up and out. When he had not returned by 10:00, she sent the children out looking for him. They did not find him. She sent her oldest daughter up to wake Mary Ann. Her daughter returned with the news that her aunt was not in her room and her bed had not been slept in. Sarah and the children scanned the farm again; then Sarah discreetly inquired around town as to whether anyone had seen her husband or her sister. She knew in her heart what had happened, but Sarah could not entertain the humiliating reality of such a betrayal by two people she loved.

The whole town was abuzz. Most figured they had run off, but there were stories about robbers and ghosts. The strangest thing was that the horses, carriages, and wagons were not taken. If they fled, they fled on foot. Sarah could not believe her sister would take her husband. Abram was thirty-four and Mary Ann only twenty-three. After a few weeks it became clear that she could not run the farm by herself and raise these children. She needed help. Her brother, James, and his wife, Ester Seaman, came several days during the week to help, but he had his job and commitments with the town. Her sister, Gitty and husband, Robert Shaw, took in James Rice. Isaac and Margaret Keller took David. George Houghton took Malvina. Almond Hough raised John, and the Perrys raised Lucinda. Abram Jr. went to stay with his uncle and aunt, David and Tina Keller.

Sarah eventually accepted her fate and focused her energy on the farm. More work was piled on her and her children's shoulders. Even though they were living with others, Abram, David, and James Rice helped Sarah do the daily farm work. During haying, harvesting, and plowing, most of the town pitched in to help her. Steven Lamos, who kept his cows on an island south of East Bay Landing, had moved in and settled where the Shaws had first landed.

It was now called Tarbell Hill due to the Tarbell family setting roots down the road from Steven. The makeshift road now began from the ridge above the lake and ran to the new trail coming in from Newcomb.

Steven Lamos gave a hand when needed. He and John LaPelle became good friends, and the two maintained the little church and school on the hill above the Long Lake Hotel. Steven and John also helped Sarah with the planting and harvesting, and Lysander Hall showed up several times with an "extra" deer, rabbit, or turkey. At times, Sarah felt guilty about others raising her children, but sometimes when she looked at them, she would tremble and go off to her silent place.

# 18

## SEASONS COME AND SEASONS GO

WINTER BLEW IN, covering the fields with white, finally giving way to spring flowers and plowed fields. Many seasons had come and gone since Abram and Mary Ann had run away. They had run to the Wright farm where Abram worked with Michael and Mary Ann found a job in the local general store.

On this morning, Mary Ann sat out in the field next to the small pond beneath the maples that peppered the rocky pasture, recalling the night she had left her home in Long Lake. Now, she was throwing stones in the pond they swam in, watching the ripples form from the center. The leaves were sporting their colors in the gentle breeze of a clear autumn day. She thought, this is so different than Long Lake. I can see for miles. She could see the large gray barn looming like a giant elephant below the moving clouds. To the right the woods lined up like soldiers above the pasture and were filled with the blackberries she had picked for pie throughout their seasons. She liked it here, but she could not deny that she missed the blue waters of the lake and the green Christmas trees that surrounded the waters. On a day like this she would have seen the reflections of the maples, beeches, and elms in the clear open water. She recalled riding bareback in the early morning dew, listening to the cry of the loon, a sound so distinct when it echoed across the lake that even the children knew it. Here, perched on this rock, she heard the twitter of the squirrels as they gathered for winter, the chick-a-dee-dee alerting her of the coming winter. The musical song of summer had been replaced by a more rapid warning of the need to gather, organize, and prepare for surviving the onslaught of wind and snow. She thought about being young and laughing with her sisters and friend, Mary Sargent. She recalled the face of little Lucinda in the window on the night she left. What would she look like now after all of these seasons? She thought of David, her brother who always antagonized her when Mary came over. How she would give anything for him to antagonize her again. She would give anything, but not Abram. No, she had made her choice, and she knew there was no going back. Sarah and the children would never forgive her. She loved little Melvina Rice and thought about young Abram Jr. growing up without his dad. Guilt filled her sometimes, flooding her like a suffocating avalanche.

A sound in the breeze pulled her from the place she was going. She looked toward the house and saw Leafie, Michael and Eliza's oldest daughter. She had her hands cupped around her mouth and was yelling something. Mary Ann listened and heard her name. She got up and began walking, "What is it?"

"Dad has some news. Come to the house." Mary Ann followed Leafie as she opened the torn screen door and walked into the hall leading to the kitchen. She wondered if she would ever see Long Lake again. It was early fall of 1864, and she would not wonder long.

In June of that year, Abram Jr. had begun to cough and sneeze. By the end of July, the cough had intensified, and by August, he had developed a fever. Tina Keller gave him broth and put camphor poultices on his chest, but the cough became severe, and the fever would not go down. She notified his mother who came and tried an old remedy her mother had used. She mixed turpentine and lard and rubbed it on his chest and then gave him hot elderberry tea. Still the fever raged. "We need Doc Parker," Tina whispered one morning.

"But they say he isn't a real doctor," Sarah replied.

"I know, but we aren't either. Besides, he was a doctor at one time, and he helped me through the grippe last year."

"Well, okay. I'll send John for him." John Rice harnessed up Babe and headed out to the captain's place well past the South Pond mill. Captain Parker, the only semblance of a doctor they had in town, had been a doctor in southern New York. One day he showed up on the beach of William and Rachel Helms's log cabin hotel south of the great falls and the South Pond sawmill. Rumor was that he had lost a patient because of a surgical mistake and was so guilt ridden that he could no longer practice medicine. The only peace he could get from this guilt was living frugally in the great forests of the Adirondacks. He had stayed with the Helmses for a few months and was soon moving closer to the village. He did not want to practice medicine but at times helped when there was a need. There was a need at the Keller home today.

When Captain Parker arrived, his six-foot-two frame filled the doorway, and his long white beard hung down to his belt. Tina led him upstairs to the little attic bedroom where Abram Jr. had slept for the years following the disappearance of his father. Doc Parker heard the cough before entering the room. He knew that cough. He knew Abram Jr. had the dreaded consumption. He went in, and there was the young man, blonde hair stuck to the sweat on his forehead. This boy had experienced so much pain and loss, and now this. Oh, Lord, no, thought the doc.

"Hello, Abram. How long have you had this cough?"

"Don't know, doc, think it started last winter, but the cough keeps getting worse."

"Have you taken anything for it?"

"Just what Aunt Tina gave me. It isn't helping though. It's the bad stuff, isn't it doc?" "Well…."

"It's okay. I know. My friend had it." "Who was that?"

"Henry, Henry Parker." "Your cousin, right?" "Yes."

Where is Henry now?"

"Newcomb. They moved to Newcomb." "You been around your cousins?"

"Ya, we go hunting and fishing together."

"I've got some medicine here you need to take. You need to rest. I'll check on you tomorrow." Oh my, we need to check on the Parkers too, thought the captain.

"Ok, doc. Thanks." The captain nodded. Tina, Sarah, and David Keller were outside his door when doc came out.

"So, Doc, what can you give him to get his fever down?"

"I am so sorry, but I don't think he is going to get over this. All we can do is keep him comfortable. I'll check on him tomorrow."

"Oh no," Sarah cried, tears welling up in her eyes. "It isn't a cold?" She knew what it was. Sarah and Tina had suspected it for the last month. They knew it was the deadly consumption, and there was no cure for it. Eventually, his lungs would fill, and he would not be able to draw a breath. Sarah did not know how long he had been fighting this disease. Abram would have hidden any signs, and she did not know about Henry Parker's passing.

On October 10, 1864, young Abram Rice, just sixteen years old, took his last breath. In his deliriums at the end, he thought that David Keller was his father, Abram Sr., and David let him think that, but Abram was nowhere near him when he died.

Michael Wright was hunting near Long Lake with Albert and Charles Hanmer, Isaac Sabattis, and Lyman Russell. They came in from three days in the woods and heard the news about the Rice boy. He jumped on his horse and rode hard back to the farm. He arrived late in the afternoon, dismounted his horse, put her in the barn, and began the dreaded trek up to the house to tell Abram and Mary Ann. He hated having to do this. He knew this couple had risked everything for love. He saw both in their moments of regret. He watched Abram staring off into the fields at nothing and Mary Ann writing letters that were never sent. He did not necessarily approve of what they did, but they were here now, and they were his friends, so he would stand by them. At first Eliza was against helping these people who had left their families. Michael convinced her to at least talk with them. Eventually she agreed to let them stay because of Michael's persuasion and because they were desperate for farm help. Michael was increasing the Holstein cows, and now they were expecting another child. Eliza demanded that Mary Ann write and tell their families where they were so they would not worry, but each time Michael went into the Adirondack forests, the notes and letters Mary Ann had written remained behind. However, he carried with him the money Abram and Mary Ann gave Sarah Rice for the children. It was anonymously left under Helmses' door and then Doc's door after he moved. The first payment said simply, 'For Sarah Rice.' Eliza kept asking and was always told that the letter would go the next week. Fear came instead, and Mary Ann was never able to post the letter. Michael never said another word about it. He was gone much of the time. He was not a farmer. He was a woodsman, and Eliza knew that when she married him. She was grateful to have Abram on the farm. He was a farmer and was now running the farm better than it had ever been run.

Michael stepped up on the porch, opened the screen door and shouted, "Mary Ann, Abram!" It was late afternoon, and Eliza was punctual, so he knew she and maybe Mary Ann would be preparing supper. He hugged Eliza and told Leafie to go tell Mary Ann and Abram to come in. Soon, they were all gathered in the large kitchen Michael and Abram had built on the farmhouse.

"You're back," Abram remarked. "How was the hunt?" "Oh, good. Got us plenty of meat for winter."

"We got the corn all in," Abram remarked. "I see that. Saw the field as I came down."

"Michael, why are we all here?" Mary Ann asked as she rushed in behind Leafie.

"Uh, Abram, I don't know any other way of putting this, but I got some bad news."

Eliza looked at Michael's face, put her hand up to stop him, glanced down at Leafie and said, "Leafie, I didn't finish gathering the eggs. Please go get the rest of them."

"But, what's the news. I want to hear too."

"You heard your mom," Michael said sternly as he pointed to the back door. Leafie turned and stomped out the door.

Mary Ann put her arm through Abram's and leaned into him. "What is it, Michael. Is it the family?"

"Yes, I am afraid so. Abram, it's your youngest boy."
"Abram Jr.?"

"Yes, Oh Lord, Abram, I hate saying this, but he became very sick and everyone did everything they could."

Mary Ann's hand went to her mouth and she gasped, "You mean, you mean...."

"He didn't make it. Michael, for God's sake, tell me he isn't...." Abram whispered.

"Yes, Abram. I am so sorry, but your boy died yesterday."

Eliza gasped and put her arm around Abram who was sinking slowly to the kitchen floor. Mary Ann and Eliza took his arms and sat him in the rocking chair.

"I'm so sorry, Abram, so sorry," Mary Ann whispered.

"Please, everyone, please, just leave me alone for a moment." Abram sobbed into his hands, bent over as if to pull in the pain of the guilt that was washing over him.

Later, Abram and Mary Ann decided that despite the chilly greeting they would receive in Long Lake, they would go to Abram's funeral. Abram suggested he go alone, but Mary Ann refused to send him by himself. "Abram, we will go together. We will pack now and leave at dawn." She turned to go up the stairs to pack.

"Wait," Abram said, grabbing her arm. "We need to plan this. We can't just walk in after being gone all these years, and you do not need to do this, Mary Ann."

"I don't care. I need to see my nephew and my sister. I need to be there." Abram knew that you didn't try to persuade Mary Ann Keller of anything. "I'll go by myself, Abram." She put her hand on his arm, "It's okay. You know I can get there by myself."

"No; we will both go. Pack my bag." The next day, they were on the stage to the Adirondacks, terrified of what awaited them when they faced the townspeople.

Figure *1*. The Huntley Farm (1835) originally built by Joseph Martin, Eliza Martin Wright's brother.

# 19

## The "Homecoming"

Abram and Mary Ann arrived at Robert Shaw's Long Lake Hotel in late afternoon in the middle of a terrible rainstorm. They hurried out of the carriage and ran up the steps into the building. Robert greeted them stiffly and declared that they had to rent two rooms. He stated, "I am deeply sorry and know you are in tremendous grief over your son, but you will not be sinning in my hotel."

Mary Ann started to protest.

Abram put his hand on her shoulder, looked the reverend in the eye, and said, "That's fine, Robert; we'll take two rooms."

They were shown to their rooms; later, Mary Ann chided Abram, "Why did you let him talk to us like that? I don't feel like a sinner." "Mary Ann, you know Robert as well as I do. He was always judging everybody even when we were kids, and I think most of the town is going to have the same opinion. We are here for Abram. We just need to get through this horrible time, be a little humble, and leave as soon as we can."

"I'll be on my best behavior."

"Umm. I don't think that will work. Your best behavior is most people's worst behavior."

She walked over and put her arms around him, "You are right, Abram, and I am so sorry. I will be silent no matter what happens. I am really scared to see Sarah and your children."

"Me too." That night while Mary Ann slept, Abram sat up most of the night staring out the window that faced the hill leading up to the little white church. The silence was over-whelming. No birds sang. No wolves howled. Abram thought about his boy. He remembered how excited he was to have this son and how happy it made him that Sarah agreed to give him his first name. He wished he could go back and do things differently, but his son would still be as silent as the animals lying among the great Adirondack trees. It was as if they were joining his boy in his silent sleep. He was not alone. Abram fell to his knees and asked God to forgive him. When he raised his head, dawn's light was slowly cov-ering the little church on the hill.

That morning, Gitty and Robert Shaw were up at five o'clock. They had eaten breakfast, and Robert was leaving. Gitty brushed a kiss on his cheek before he opened the door and went out. At the same time, young Amanda Kellogg, the daughter of Danny Kellogg, old William Kellogg's rela-tive, was mounting the steps to enter the store. They had hired Amanda after Robert Shaw and James Keller opened the hotel and store.

Gitty put a few more chunks of wood in the large black stove, filled the tin pot with water and coffee and waited for her guests to come down. She was a petite woman who was recently married. When Mary Ann disappeared and they were all searching for her, Gitty was frantic. She was five years younger than Mary Ann and adored her older sister. She was not the outdoors type like Mary Ann and spent many hours inside sewing, knitting, and playing games with her sisters. Mary Ann was an excellent seamstress, and she taught Gitty how to sew. When they realized that Abram and Mary Ann had disappeared, some neighbors thought they had drowned. It was a frequent tragedy on this lake. The waters could change from placid as a mirror to a raging river with fierce white caps and strong winds.

Gitty recalled that first day that Mary Ann was missing. There were questions. She had no idea where Mary Ann would go in the blackness of night. They even talked of someone kidnapping her. David and James saddled the horses and rode down Sawmill Road, her usual ride. They stopped at the hermit's place and talked with him. Ebenezer asked, "Have you checked with any of the Rice family? Perhaps one of them saw something."

They had not, but of course they did not know that Abram was also missing. They thought he was working out in the field. Ebenezer shook his head and rubbed his whiskered chin, "Uh huh, of course." He knew. He had seen things, but he wasn't the one to say more. He also knew that Sarah knew. David and James rode away puzzled, searching for their sister. When they reached the house, they gathered all the Keller and Rice children and asked if they had seen anything. Young Lucinda Rice stared at the floor in silence.

It was not until mid-morning that the Kellers knew Abram was also missing. Then they thought Abram had kidnapped their sister. However, Sarah, like Lucinda, was speechless because she knew. Ebenezer was right. She had known for a while. She had seen the looks between them. Sarah had felt Abram drawing away from her. She had even confronted him about not wanting to be intimate anymore, and he had blamed his inattention on being tired or preoccupied with work. Yes, she knew but never dreamed they would run away together and leave her and the children.

Gitty and Robert Shaw spent hours trying to comfort her and eventually brought James home with them to live. Now, here was James's delinquent father back, and Gitty had to serve him coffee. She realized she had to tell James before he came down for breakfast. "Amanda, I'm going to get James. Watch the coffee."

"Okay, Mrs. Shaw." Gitty climbed the wooden stairs, turned right, and slowly walked into his room. He was awake. "James," she whispered. "Aunt Gitty. What time is it? Am I late?"

"No, son; Robert went off by himself this morning. I have something I need to tell you."

"Oh, okay." He sat up and looked at his aunt's face, seeing the pain etched around her eyes. "What is it, Aunt Gitty?" He was thinking that it was the pain from Abram Jr.'s death, but everybody knew about that, so why would she be telling him? No, it was someone else. "Oh my gosh, did someone else die?"

Gitty reached out and touched James's shoulder. "Oh no, James, nothing like that. I don't know how to say this other than to just blurt it out to you; your father and aunt have returned." "What?" His head snapped up, "What?"

"Yes, they came for the funeral. They checked in last night. They will be at breakfast this morning."

"Oh, my gosh. Aunt Gitty, they are here? You and Uncle Robert let them stay here?"

"Yes. We have a business, and they arrived last night in the pouring rain with nowhere to stay. If you don't want to see them yet, you can go out the side door. Uncle Robert is up at the mill cutting trees. You will have to see them at the funeral, but maybe it would be easier to face them with Uncle Robert or Pauline." Pauline Houghton was engaged to James.

"I think I'll go over to Pauline's, but what about you. Are you okay?" "Of course. I will be fine. Now, you go be with Pauline."

James had recently asked Pauline Houghton to marry him. Gitty was happy with that news. They were both twenty-one, and Pauline was the oldest Houghton girl, a family that was moving in to be near their relatives, the Hendersons and Houghtons. Pauline was Josiah Houghton's cousin. James worked with Josiah one summer and they soon became close friends, one summer before the Houghton family moved to the town. From the first time James saw Pauline, he was smitten, and now his heart was beating faster than a windmill and he wanted to be with his girl. He grabbed a tin cup of coffee and walked up the road to Josiah's house where Pauline was staying until the wedding.

Gitty returned to the kitchen where Amanda was removing the freshly baked bread from the oven.

"Oh, I love the smell of fresh bread," Mary Ann remarked as she came into the kitchen. Gitty did not acknowledge her. Amanda offered a hesitant good morning not knowing if she should speak to her but being too young to know for sure what had happened before between the two sisters.

When Gitty walked into the store without a word, Amanda offered Mary Ann a table and asked if she would like coffee and bread with jam. By this time Abram had arrived, sat down, and Amanda served them. Gitty stayed in the store section of the building. When they were through with their breakfast, Mary Ann pushed her chair back, turned and walked into the store. Gitty was behind the counter.

"Gitty, can't you say something to me?"

"I've got nothing to say except I can't believe you came back here. I can't believe you two would ever show your face in this town again." "We came for Abram."

"For Abram! You came for Abram! Where were you and his father all the years he needed you? You come now, now when he doesn't need a father anymore."

"I know. I am so sorry. I had to. I love him, Gitty."

"Of course, you had to. You always had to do whatever Mary Ann wanted to do. You certainly better be in love with that man out there if you gave up your whole family for him." Mary Ann put out her hand and placed it on Gitty's shoulder. Gitty pushed it away, "Don't touch me, Mary Ann. You betrayed us all. I looked up to you. Now you disgust me. Just go; go to the funeral. I will be there and so will James, his son that he abandoned, and I will be by his side."

"Oh, Gitty, please...."

"Just go. Go," Gitty sobbed.

Mary Ann walked outside where Abram was waiting for her. Tears ran in torrents down her face. She buried her face in his shoulder as he circled his arms around her and held her tight. She felt his warmth and the safety of his arms. She took a breath. She was safe.

"You know they are all going to be like that." "I know," she whispered. "I know."

"Are you going to be okay?"

She nodded. "Abram, I'm okay. I will be by your side."

"I love you, my girl."

"I love you too." Abram snapped the reins, and the couple turned the buckboard he had rented from Ai Shaw westward down the path toward the Keller house where Abram was laid out for viewing. Gitty watched out the window. She felt no relief from the stabbing wound in her heart, as she remembered the excitement she felt when she would see her sister ride up on Babe, with whatever game she had shot for dinner that day. She could hear the high pitch of Mary Ann's laughter as they ran through the wheat fields and out on the frozen lake in the winter. Her heart lay still. It no longer beat for Mary Ann Keller.

The buckboard bumped along on the crude road. They came up on the new three-story building across from the water's edge of the swamplike pond. "I heard from Michael that the Hanmers opened a store there," Abram pointed.

"Somebody is out there washing windows," Mary Ann said. As they approached the building, they both could see that it was a woman in a gray dress. She was quite a large woman with her hair tucked neatly beneath a white bonnet. Suddenly, the woman turned and waved as if she wanted them to stop. "Abram, she is waving us down. Oh, my Lord, I think it's your daughter. I think its Melvina."

Abram squinted his eyes and looked again. "Maybe, but…."

"Dad, stop. Please stop!" the woman shouted. Abram pulled the horses over and looked at the woman before him.

"Mel? Is that you?"

"Yes, it is. Oh, my Lord. I heard you were in town." She reached up and took his hand. He stepped down, and a shocked Mary Ann watched Melvina put her arms around him and hug him. She did the same to Mary Ann when she stepped out of the rig. "Dad, I married Josiah Houghton. Josiah and I work for Bill Hanmer here at the store. I am expecting your grandchild." She patted her stomach.

Mary Ann did not speak but nodded and smiled. Abram fumbled around for words to cut through the awkward shock of seeing his little girl pregnant.

Finally, Mary Ann spoke. "Congratulations. Melvina." "Thank you. Are you here for Abram's funeral?"

"Yes."

"Dad, he was so sick. At least he is in peace now. I wish you could have been there for him." "I didn't know."

"I know, and everyone is mad at you but me, I think. I was so sad when you left. I cried for days, weeks, and then I finally accepted that I would never see you again. I want to hate you, but I can't."

Abram once again wrapped his arms around his precious Melvina. "I am so sorry, Mel. I know I hurt everyone. I can't explain to you why I had to go, but love is powerful, making you do all kinds of crazy things.

"Dad, I get it. I love Josiah, but I would never leave my little one. Mary Ann, I hated you for a long time, but I will not shun you. You saved my life many years ago, and I will never forget it." Mary Ann nodded her head and smiled.

Just then a tall thin man came out of the house. His face was darker than most and his black hair was combed straight back and hung to his shoulders. Mary Ann suspected he was all or part Abenaki or Mohawk. He was dressed in black wool pants and a black jacket. "Melvina, who are you talking to?" he asked as he came down the steps and stood beside Melvina.

"Josiah, you never met my father. This is Abram Rice."

"Oh, hello; well, Melvina, we have to go. By the time it's over, it'll be time to open the store, and Bill is going to the funeral too. Better get your coat." He moved from foot to foot, visibly uncomfortable.

"And Josiah, this is Mary Ann Keller. She saved me from a panther when I was a young girl."

"Well, thank you for that." He nodded his head. "Come on Mel. We've got to go now."

"We understand your hurry," Mary Ann quipped, "but he is Melvina's father." Abram nudged her arm and shushed her.

"Oh, yes, and you are not her mother. Mel we've got to get ready now!" He put his arm around her shoulders and started to turn her back toward the house.

"Okay, Josiah, okay," she turned back around and said, "dad, it was good to see you. See you at the…" she put her head down and began to weep. Josiah led her up the steps to the house.

"Yes, dear, good to see you too," Abram managed to spit out before they disappeared into the house. Abram and Mary Ann climbed back into the rig. Abram took the reins and they started up the hill. "I told you not to say anything, Mary Ann."

"I know, but the man looked like he wanted to be any-where but standing there before us sinners."

"I know, and here we go into the rest of them who will be looking at us the same way. At least Melvina could forgive me."

"Yes, I know. Melvina is being who she is. She sees the good in the world, and I have always liked that about her."

"Yes, always has. She will be a great mother. I am surprised by Josiah's reaction, because I'm sure Sarah was not happy about Melvina marrying a half-breed."

"Well, it's not so uncommon anymore, and Michael told us Sarah didn't keep the children after you left, remember?"

"I know, I just hate to remember that." They rode on past the mill, past Robinsons' house on the ridge, and right down the new Sawmill Road that would lead to the Keller house. Mary Ann thought of all the times she had ridden Babe on this dirt path, all the times she had cleared the path in spring when new shoots jutted out in the middle of the dusty road, all the times she had used this road to meet Abram in the woods. She held her breath as they crested the knoll, turned their heads to the left and saw the long porch filled with the people of the town they had abandoned.

Figure 2 The Keller House

# 20

## THE GATHERING

ABRAM PULLED HARD on the reins, guiding the horse up the dirt path past the house to the front of the barn. Abram jumped off the buckboard and tied the horse to the hitching post, and helped Mary Ann down. Then they took a deep breath, turned and began walking toward the house. They were all standing around staring at the couple as they walked toward them. Mary Ann took in a another deep breath, held her head up, and ran into her brothers, David Jr. and Charles, halfway to the house.

"I wondered if you would come," David said. "I wondered if you even knew about Abram since you didn't tell anyone anything."

"Yes, we found out the day before yesterday and came straight here." "Who told you?"

They knew David was fishing for where they were living.

"We heard through a passing peddler."

"Well, at least you are alive, Mary Ann. What a terrible thing you did to your family."

Mary Ann looked down, "I know. I know." David stared at her waiting for an apology that did not come.

"Well, good luck. There are a lot of hard feelings up on that porch and also right here," he made a fist and touched his chest.

Instead of joining all of those on the porch, Mary Ann and Abram stood to the right of the steps and said their greetings. No one responded and instead stood glaring at the two. The couple was not invited inside or onto the porch. Finally, Lucinda Rice, who was now a teenager, walked up and grabbed Abram's hand and pulled him toward the house. Tina Keller stepped forward, "Lucinda," but David Jr. stopped his wife. Abram looked quizzically at David who stood closest to them on the porch.

"Lucinda hasn't spoken since you two left!" Sarah Rice shouted angrily. "Not one word. See what you did! You not only betrayed me but also your children," she began to sob. David Keller put his arm around her shoulders. Tina put her arms through Sarah's and rushed her inside. Another silence followed while Lucinda led her father and Mary Ann inside to where Abram lay in state. Sarah had been taken upstairs.

The viewing had begun two nights before, and this was the last viewing for the family. Mary Ann and Abram kneeled on the wood floor beside the casket. Lucinda stood behind them. Abram looked down at his son; so young. Too young to be gone from this world. A deep saddness stabbed his heart, and he knew it would never go away. Tears rolled down his cheeks as he turned to Mary Ann, "Maybe I could have saved him. Maybe if I had been here...."

"No, Abram, we promised we would not do this. You could not have saved him. The doctor could not save him or all the others who are dying from this disease."

"I know. I know. You are right." They prayed silently. Then, they stood and slowly turned to walk away. Abram, glanced back one last time at the son he had left behind and then he looked down at his daughter who stood beside him and could not talk. There was no depth to the sorrow he felt. There was no way back. He had made his choice years ago, and he would either live by it or die by it; right now, he just wanted to lie down and die.

When Mary Ann and Abram stepped out onto the porch, Reverend Shaw and Gitty had arrived. Most of the towns-people including the Kelloggs, Mixes, Dornburghs, Parkers, Austins, and Halls were there. Abram Jr.'s best friend, Farrand Austin, looked up at Abram Rice. Tears filled his eyes. He could not believe that his friend who had climbed the apple tree outside the barn with him, stayed at his house, and swum in the lake was no longer here. Even old Isaac Robinson, his wife Christina, and their children attended. There was something special about young Abram Rice, something special that would bring Isaac out to his funeral. He never attended funerals. He thought they were unnecessary. "They're dead. Don't need us rallying around 'um anymore. They got the good Lord to rally round 'um," was his philosophy.

They gathered inside while the reverend prayed over Abram. Then, they headed toward the bottom of the side hill, the family burial ground. Charles Keller and John, James, and David Rice carried the casket in front of the procession. Abram was buried beside David Sr. and Christina Keller. When the service was completed, they walked back up the hill, and the townspeople left. The Kellers, Rices, and relatives stayed for the food that was set out by caring neighbors. Abram and Mary Ann were not invited, and no one spoke to them, no one except Lucinda. When Abram turned to step up onto the buckboard, he leaned over and gave his daughter a hug. Lucinda hugged him back. She whispered in his ear, "Goodbye, Dad."

Abram pulled back and looked at Lucinda directly and said, "My God, child, you can talk." Mary Ann heard what Abram said and turned around.

"I can now, Dad. I saw you that night." Abram was still in shock, "Saw me when?"

"I saw you and Mary Ann run away in the night. I was watching out my bedroom window."

"Oh, Lord, I am so sorry. I wish I could have told you." "Me too. Why didn't you? Why didn't you tell me?"

"I guess I didn't think you were old enough, and I didn't want anyone to stop us."

"Dad, I never would have told. You knew me."

"I know, but I thought it would be a lot for a young girl to carry." "You thought I would tell."

"Yes, I guess I did, and that would have been okay. If I had it to do over again, I would have told you."

"Okay. Will you tell me where you live so I can write you?" Abram looked at Mary Ann and then back at Lucinda and then he told her about the farm he lived on and how he would love for her to write and come for a visit.

Lucinda stood in the middle of the gaping opening of the barn door as she watched her father pull out onto the rocky muddy road and disappear over the knoll. She vowed that she would never tell where her father was living. She would show her father that she could be trusted. Lucinda turned and walked back up to the house, came through the screen door, walked up to Sarah and asked her what there was to eat. Sarah fainted.

# 21

## THE ABENAKI, THE POLITICIAN, AND THE CONGRESSMAN

BOTH ROADS LEADING into Long Lake were rock filled, sometimes impassable, wagon trails in the spring mud season. Although an act was passed years before authorizing the construction of a road from Lake Champlain (Crown Point) on the east, westward across the mountains through Newcomb and Long Lake to Carthage, it was an arduous task, much of it being a corduroy road (logs placed across the muddy swamp trails). The roads in some places were not traveled from one year to the next, especially west of Long Lake where trees grew up in the wagon roads such as those leading to Zenas Parker's place and north to the Kelloggs' place on Big Brook.

In the middle of the 1800s, the main link with the outside world was still the Carthage Road. The Town Board, Cyrus and Asa Kellogg, Josiah Wood, William Helms, Ezekiel Palmer, George Shaw, and David Keller, passed a resolution that the Carthage Road between the Essex Hamilton County line and the Herkimer Hamilton County line to the west should be divided with mileposts into sections of one mile each. The town issued work contracts to the lowest bidder in each section. The Board also voted to develop the agriculture of the county by improving several wagon roads. The main problem with this vote was that there was no money for these projects.

Cyrus Kellogg agreed to write to the New York lawmakers about the condition of the roads into Long Lake, the difficulties of getting to the remote settlement, and the economic need of having tourists visit the region. The lawmakers did not answer, in part because the Civil War broke out and in part because the Adirondack wilderness was easy to ignore. Hence, travel to Long Lake was confined to two well-traveled, plank, root-infested roads.

At the next town meeting, Mitchel Sabattis suggested they invite one of the politicians to Long Lake, which would take him through the arduous journey from Albany. This was a three-day journey by horse and buggy. One of the New York politicians, Robert Van Valkenburgh, took the bait because he was born in Plattsburgh, New York, and had relatives in the area. However, he had never been in the Adirondacks. When mud season ended in late May, Mitchel Sabattis and Robert Shaw, now also an attorney, met Mr. Van Valkenburgh at the train station in Whitehall. Mr. Van Valkenburgh was dressed in his fancy long black coat, white shirt, and black top hat. Robert whispered to

Mitchel, "Oh Lord, he's a dandy." Mitchel just shook his head. Shaw walked straight up to the representative and put out his hand, Congressman Van Valkenburgh, I presume?"

"Yes, yes, I am. Please call me Bob."

"Okay, I am Robert Shaw, and this is my friend and your guide, Mitchel Sabattis. Do you have all of your bags?" He looked down at the small bag the congressman was carrying.

"Yes, yes. I believe I do," Bob replied.

"Okay then, we will proceed to the ship." They walked to the Whitehall boat livery on Lake Champlain and boarded a large steamboat, which took them to the opposite shore of Burlington, Vermont, and on to the New York side of Port Kent. Here, they boarded a horse-drawn coach and, after six miles, arrived at Keeseville for lodging at the well-known Ausable House. Then came a fifty-six-mile trip into the mountains mostly over plank roads to Martins Hotel on lower Saranac Lake. The next morning, they placed the congressmen in the middle seat of Mitchel's new birchbark canoe and paddled him through lower, middle, and part of upper Saranac Lake. Next came a mile walk across the old Indian Carry to Stoney Creek Ponds, where Mitchel launched the boat into the Raquette River. The winding section of the river from Axton Landing to the foot of Long Lake was difficult because they were rowing against the current with a heavy load. By this time, the congressman was stiff and dirty. His bones ached, and he had long since lost his hat and used his fancy coat as a seat cushion.

Mitchel and Robert were amazed that the man never complained, but when they rounded a bend in the river, and he heard Raquette Falls and saw the bottom waters rushing and swirling over the visible rocks straight ahead of them, the congressman's mouth dropped open, and he asked, "We are not going through there, are we?"

"Oh, yes, if you want to get to Long Lake." "But...."

"Just hold on," Mitchel yelled above the roaring of the falls. He began to paddle quickly in unison with Robert Shaw. The congressman went white and silent. He held on tightly to the sides of the boat, prayed, and became violently sick over the side of the boat.

After six miles of water and what seemed like three miles of rapids, the visibly shaken man was glad to walk the one-mile carry around the two falls. He was exhausted, but he had to carry his baggage since his guides were carrying the boat, oars, and supplies. By now, Bob's once white shirt was tattered, gray, and sweat stained.

"Didn't you bring a change of clothes?" Shaw asked when they were sitting by their last campfire eating the fish that Mitchel had caught for dinner.

"Well, yes, but I don't want to change until I get to the hotel where I can shower and put my other shirt on. I had no idea it would take this long."

"Hotel." Mitchel said looking at Shaw.

"Shower? What's a shower?" Robert whispered back. Mitchel shrugged his shoulders, and before Mitchel could say another word, Robert Shaw said, "Good idea, Bob. You can get a nice hot bath at the hotel." Little did the congress-man know that there were no luxury hotels in Long Lake. There was old William Helms's log cabin on the south end of the lake, the Long Lake Hotel, which was full, and Palmers' new place, originally built by William Austin now owned by Ezekiel Palmer. However, none of those had hot showers. They booked the congressman at Palmers.' Palmers' did have baths, but Robert had heard they were lukewarm at best. Later he told Mitchel it was better to let the congress-man find that out for himself, as well as that Ezekiel Palmer was barely on the cure side of Smallpox, claiming the veg-etable pills he bought from newcomer Benjamin Brandreth had cured him: No sense in raising any alarms right now, even though there was talk that the pills were quackery. [Quackery or not, Benjamin was a master marketing busi-nessman, and soon his grandfather's pills had become nationally known. Benjamin, a wealthy man, bought a lake and a tract of land southwest of the Rutherfords' on Clear Lake.]

Another six miles upriver brought them to the foot of Long Lake. Ten more miles took them to the settlement where Congressman Van Valkenburgh spent the night at Uncle Palmer's. Feeling sorry for the young congressman, Harriet Kellogg Palmer took his tattered clothes, washed, and mended them, and gave him supper. He would stay three nights at Ezekiel and Harriet Palmer's. Returning to the city after another rough ride, the congressman imme-diately filed a measure to fund new roads.

With this money, the two road commissioners, Cyrus Kellogg and George Shaw, granted Ezekiel Palmer's request to construct a road beginning at the end of the bridge over the outlet of South Pond, traveling south to the line of Palmer's lot near James Sargent's vacated property, eventually connecting with the Carthage Road that ran east to the Long Lake Hotel.

By 1867, William Kellogg was running the new Lake House, and John Rice was working for him. Long Lake was welcoming home their men from the Civil War, including John's brother, James, and they were planning for a new bridge that would connect the east and west sides of Long Lake.

In the meantime, the west side of the lake continued to attract and hold men such as Scotsman George Robinson who now hunted and traveled the route from the Adirondacks to the Wright farm in Crary Mills, New York, alongside Michael Wright and Abram Rice.

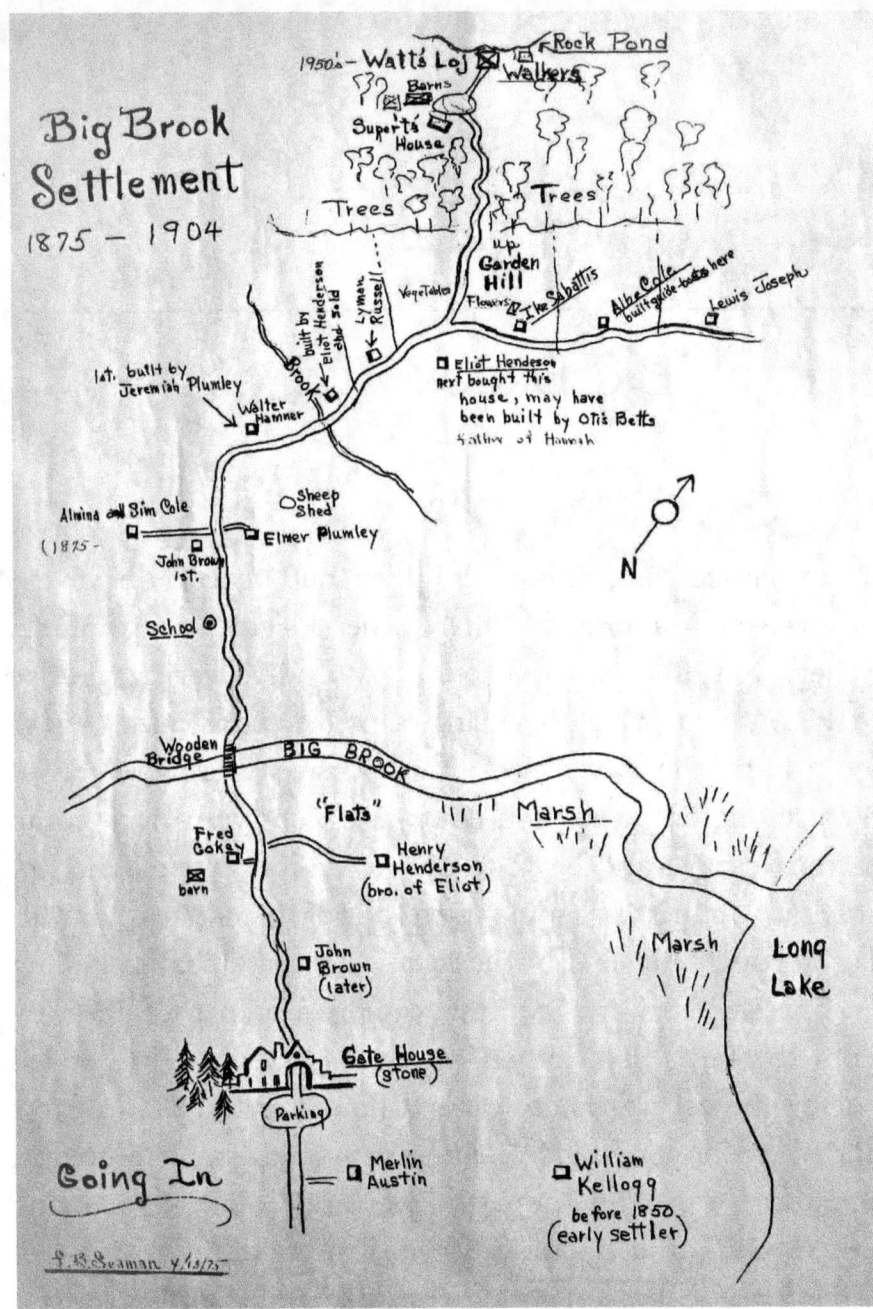

Figure *3* Big Brook Village

# 22

---

## BIG BROOK VILLAGE

BY MID-CENTURY, SEVERAL families had moved above the western shoreline where the Plumleys, Stantons, Kellers, and Kelloggs had settled. After discovering the rise of the waters during the spring rains, several families chose to move off the water, even though travel was more convenient living on shore: You could walk out your door, jump in your canoe, and be gone. However, convenience did not stack up against sweeping water out of the house and wading in mud after one of the spring torrents came blasting in. The Kellers were the first to move up on the hill away from the lake. Soon others followed, having been flooded out by the severe rising waters some springs. The narrow outlet at the north end of the lake would begin to hold in the waters from the Raquette River and Cold River causing the swelling and flooding of the settlers' land and sometimes their cabins. Though the men built several wagon roads, the main method of travel was still by water.

One of the families who built north of the lake was Lucius Henderson's family. They built near the large brook that flowed into the lake. Lucius Henderson had married Joel Plumley's daughter, Harriet, and they had one of the largest farms on the southeast side of Big Brook Creek next to what folks started calling "The Flats." At times, this brook sped along churning up rocks and debris, like a tidal wave into the lake. However, during the late summer it was as mild as a millpond.

Soon Ike Sabattis, son of Mitchel, built a cabin near the deep blue water of Rock Pond. Joining the Henderson family were Alba and Sophia Cole and later Simeon and Almina Keller Cole. Almina was David Keller Jr's daughter, and their property bordered the brook.

After Henry Russell put down roots next to Ike, the community became known as Big Brook Village. Soon, there were close to a dozen families living in this community, including Jeremiah Plumley. Every family had at least one cow, an ox, horses, pigs, sheep, and poultry. The thick forests of spruce, balsam, pine, and hemlock continued to dominate the territory. Maples, beech, cherry, and oak meandered through the forest floor sharing the space with the green pastures cleared by those who continued to be lured by cheap land and visions of lush grasses and crops.

One such family was John and Ruby Brown and their six children, who came from Canada and settled in Vermont. John heard stories about the lush farmland in the Adirondacks, so he brought his family to Long Lake.

Instead of rich land he discovered a thin layer of sand atop infertile layers of leaves, needles, twigs, and rotted roots.

John had read about Jeremiah Plumley through the advertisements of a man called Adirondack Murray. Murray was the Reverend William Henry Harrison Murray, and in the fall and winter of 1867 he wrote about his visits to Long Lake for the *Meriden Literary Recorder* and then authored a book, *Adventures in the Wilderness*. He wrote, "Long Lake is a good starting point for a party, as it is situated midway of the forest, the center of magnificent scenery, and the home of many guides. All it needs to make this route one of the best is that roads should be improved, and a good line of coaches established." Along with Murray were the land merchants and the peddlers touting their wares, encouraging more buyers to move to this desolate though beautiful area. However, reverends, merchants, and peddlers were not farmers.

John Brown believed the hype about Long Lake and its rich black soil just waiting to receive crops and give a farmer a good living. He moved his family to Long Lake to look at the plot of land just to the south of Jeremiah Plumley's land. John and Jeremiah were among the men who cleared the land and settled in Big Brook. They were followed by several others including sixteen-year-old Canadian-born Alex Duane. He met Esther Henderson, adopted daughter of Lucius Henderson. Alex and Esther had a whirlwind romance, married, bought land from the Mix family, and settled in Big Brook near her parents' farm.

The Browns arrived by sleigh in March with all their belongings including lumber for the barn, seed, an ox, cow, pig, and goat. It took only a shovelful of dirt for John to realize that this was not fertile soil. He bought land that bordered William Kellogg on the east. William, his nephew Danny, and his two sons had built the bridge that spanned the waters. His closest neighbors were Alba Cole to the west and Elmer Plumley to the east.

One morning in early June after trying to plow all morning and getting only one corner done, John heard a voice in the distance. "Tough ground we got up here, huh?"

John turned around and followed a black hat skimming past two white birch trees that lined the path leading into the woods. He knew that hat. "Mitchel, good to see you," John remarked, walking over, and shaking his hand. "Yup, digging is terrible, and so is the dirt if you can even call it dirt."

"I know. I tried to warn you."

"I know, Mitch, I know, and I wish I'd listened to you, but I was turned by the price, and those people swore this soil was black and fertile." Mitchel had picked him up at East Bay Landing on his first trip up the lake, but it would be a few more years before John and Ruby made the decision to leave their home.

"Well, it's black all right, but not fertile. You might better get to trapping and shooting the local game for meat and fur."

"Hmm, yup, guess I could. Trying to get the land set up, though. I never done much trapping. I've got a few traps but...."

"Then put them in along the brook. Your boy could do that."

"Right, pa, I can do it," John piped up. "Mitchel, would you teach me?" "Well, it would be up to your dad." John Jr. looked at his father.

John looked at Mitchel, squinted his eyes and said, "Uh huh. Well, that's all good, but I need you for harvesting the vegetables right now, John. Mitchel, Ruby's got a rabbit for dinner. Want to stay?"

"No, maybe some other time, when I can bring Ruby a big trout or some deer meat."

"Well, don't know as you need to do that, but suit yourself, Mitch. Good seeing you."

"Yup, John; winter comes early up here. I better leave you so you can get to it."

With that, Mitchel turned and walked silently back under the white bent birch trees and down to the rocky shore where he stepped into his canoe and began the trip to the south where he now lived with his wife and children. John Brown was a proud man; sometimes that was a good thing, and sometimes it killed you.

In early September, William Kellogg and his son, Cyrus, paddled down the lake and brought the Browns MacIntosh and pear apples they had harvested. Mrs. Kellogg had sent some jelly along with a dinner invitation. They knew the Browns planted fruit trees, but it would be three years before they produced any apples. Ruby Brown thanked them, and before she could put them away, two of the boys were chomping on apples. It had been a long time since they had eaten a fresh apple. Cyrus Kellogg and Alba Cole had told John to hunt and smoke as much meat and fish as he could to prepare for winter. "Well, I plan to as soon as I finish the barn and pen," John replied, becoming quite irritated that everyone was telling him what to do. He had survived plenty of winters in Vermont.

"We'll help you with the barn, John." William replied.

"Naw, don't need no help. Got my kids here." John had three boys and three girls. The oldest boys were John Jr, fourteen; Richard, twelve; and Alex, ten years old. The girls were younger.

William Kellogg knew not to argue with someone like John Brown. He was a loner and not about to listen to anyone, and he did not want him as an enemy. One enemy in these parts was bad enough. Because the Kelloggs and the Rutherfords were related, Joel Plumley had automatically become an enemy, and the Kelloggs had certainly been through enough with him.

Ruby Brown stood on the porch churning cream into butter. She heard the conversation and later confronted John, "Maybe we should let up on the barn for a couple of weeks and get some meat in the shed."

"No, the most important thing we have to get up before winter is the barn."

"But we only have one cow, a pig, and chickens."

"That's right, and they will need cover this winter." He wasn't about to explain to her again how they could butcher the animals if need be, and they would have eggs all winter if the animals had shelter.

"Okay, then I will go hunting."

"No, no you can't go out there. It isn't like Vermont where you can see from one tree to another. Sure, as anything you'd get lost."

"But Harriet Henderson, Mary Ann Keller, and Mary and Livonia Stanton go hunting, and they say the winters are bad."

"Uh huh, same as Vermont. Besides, Harriet Henderson is a Plumley, and she was raised like a wolf in the woods having Joel for a father, and how do you even know these women go hunting?"

"Well, they all live just down the way, and our son and John and Elizabeth Henderson have become friends."

"Uh huh. I don't see any good coming out of that, and you'll see, we got enough to get us through the winter. I'll do some more hunting next month. I'll stock us up then, just like we do every year." The next morning, Ruby walked back through the rows of green beans they had planted. She knew there was no convincing John of anything he had his mind set on. She looked out over the rolling hills that led down to the lake. She could see the mountains in the distance, and though it was a warm September day, she thought she saw white on the top of the highest mountain. Ruby knew John was not going to ask the Hendersons for anything. He and Angie Henderson were half brother and sister, and there was a story, but John was never willing to tell it.

By late September, they had harvested the garden. Ruby and the girls had finished the canning and then helped Mrs. Kellogg with her canning. John and the boys completed the barn and pens by mid-October. There was some meat in the larder, and John planned to go hunting with John Jr. the next day.

On October 26, they woke up to large white snowflakes falling softly on the grass and trees. "Pa, it's snowing. It's snowing already." "Okay, that's good, son, good for tracking. We'll just eat breakfast and go." He could smell Ruby's coffee perking. She was frying bacon, and the sweet aroma filled the cabin and made John's stomach growl. This bacon was from the pig that John had to shoot because a wolf had attacked it in the dead of night. John shot the wolf before it dragged the pig into the woods but not before the poor animal was damaged beyond help. To make matters worse, it was a sow and pregnant. They were counting on adding to their pig stock, but it was now down to one.

"John, it's been snowing since last night, and I don't know if you can hunt."

"Sure, we can with the snowshoes I made. I like hunting in the snow."

"Okay, John, you just make sure you keep an eye on Junior." "Ma, I can snowshoe, and I can hunt. You don't need to worry about me." The younger children were all up now and peeking out the little window excited about this early snow.

"Well, I guess that is it for the corn, then," John sighed. The last two nights had been below freezing, and the corn was not ready to pick.

It would die. John wondered how anyone could grow corn here: Plant too early and the spring frost killed it; plant too late and the September freeze killed it. They finished eating, put their winter gear on, and lifted the latch to the heavy log door. The door flew open. Strong winds mixed with snow blew in, forcing John Jr. into his father and John to let go of the door. It blew completely open, blowing the lantern out and the tin breakfast plates off the table. John pushed Junior away, stepped toward the door, grabbed it, and managed to shut the door.

"My Lord, it's a blizzard out there!" Ruby said as she began sweeping the snow off the table.

"I guess we aren't hunting today. Can't believe we got snow and wind like this in October." Ruby looked at her husband. People had been telling him all summer. She looked at the two little ones sitting in highchairs. Ruby grabbed a towel, ran over, and wiped Hazel's hair.

"Winter or no winter, we need to get the rope tied to the barn," John said. Even in Vermont, they had to have a rope guide leading them from the house to the barn in case of a blizzard. They had to get to the barn to milk and feed the livestock.

"Were you going to milk her before hunting?" Ruby asked.

"No, thought I'd have the boys do it while Junior and I were hunting. She'll be okay, though. I'll go out and milk her as soon as this snow calms down. We'll hunt tomorrow. I am going to need the rope, though. It's in the darn tool shed, so I'll need to get down there first to get that."

"No, you don't," Ruby replied. "I brought it onto the porch a couple of weeks ago."

"Really," John said, "good thinking, dear, so all we need to do is get it to the barn. It doesn't look like it's stopping anytime soon, so I best go now." He peeked out the window again and saw a world of white. A pinecone hit the window with a bang. John jumped back. "Lord, I wonder how long it's been snowing like this?"

"It was snowing the first time I looked out about five, but I don't know when it started," Ruby replied as she wrapped her scarf around her neck.

"There's got to be at least a foot of snow out there. Must have started hours ago," John said as he pulled his boots up over his wool trousers. Soon John, Ruby, and Junior had bundled up with sheepskin hats, wool scarves, and Ruby's mittens. John and Junior pulled on the door until it opened, letting the snow in once again. Ruby told her eight-year-old to watch the little ones as she stepped out into the snow accumulating on the porch. The wind knocked Junior against the side of the cabin. He grabbed the rail and held on until he had planted his feet securely on the porch. John tied the rope to the porch railing while Ruby and John Jr.

watched him go toward the barn. They would watch each other and wait for John to signal that he was at the barn. He would give the rope a yank and swing the large lantern. They should be able to see the light even through the snow. Then they would wait for him to return. Then, he and Junior would go down to milk and return later to prepare the animals for the night.

Blizzards were dangerous because they blinded you so you could think you were going straight but since there were no visible landmarks, you could easily veer off course. Along with that, today the snow was knee deep so keeping your footsteps straight was almost impossible. Ruby could barely see the octagon barn through the thick veil of snow. By now, Ruby and Junior had their mittens around the rope waiting for a pull from John indicating he was at the barn. Suddenly, the rope went limp in their hands. "Are you there, John?" she yelled, her words sinking into the howling wind. They heard nothing and saw nothing but the swirling snow. John Jr. shouted, but still nothing. Ruby worried that he had fallen when she felt the rope loosen. She pulled the rope a little, and it gave way easily. She didn't dare pull on it for fear that if he had fallen, it would be torn out of his hands. "John, John, are you there? Junior, I have to go find him."

"No, ma. Maybe he tied it and it came loose. We need to wait for the light."

"Okay, we'll wait for ten minutes, Junior." Ruby squinted and covered her eyes with her mittened hand, willing John's lamp to shine, but no light shined. After what Ruby thought was ten minutes, she told Junior to stay with that end of the rope. She would follow it to the barn and find John. It had now been about twenty minutes since John left. It was a five-minute walk to the barn.

"No, ma, I should go."

"John, stay with your brothers and sisters. If anything happens, you take care of your sisters and brothers until you can get help at the Coles's. She looked over toward the Coles's house, but it was not visible. Ruby stepped off the porch into snow past her knees. God, she couldn't believe it had fallen that much in a few hours. What was this God-forsaken place? She prayed as she took another step, tightly grabbing the rope and her boot filling up with snow.

It was not tight, but it had to be secured to something because it was not coming completely loose in her hands. With each step, she craned her neck and yelled for John, but still no answer. A sudden burst of wind smashed against her face. She fell back, sitting on top of the snow because she could not get her boot out of the snow fast enough to catch herself. Luckily, she still had the loose rope. She stood back up and realized that now the rope was taut again. She grabbed the rope with both hands, willing herself to stay upright and shouting again for John.

"I'm right here, Ruby." Suddenly, appearing directly in front of her stood John looking like a giant ghost.

"Oh my God!" Ruby screamed, "John, where were you?"

"Ruby, what are you doing out here?"

"Looking for you. What on earth do you think? What happened?"

John looked confused, his eyes squinting as he tried to figure out what was happening and why Ruby would be out in the middle of this mess.

"Nothing. I got to the barn, tied the rope, went in and fed the chickens, and milked Sally."

"What?" Ruby screamed. "You were supposed to swing the lantern and yank on the rope."

"I know. I did hold the lantern up. Didn't you see it?"

"No, no, John, I didn't. Why didn't you come right back?"
"Oh, I did some things in the barn."

"But John, Junior and I were waiting on the porch for you to come back or signal or something. We thought you were lost or dead, God forbid, and the rope was tied and then it was loose."

"Oh, ya, I dropped it at one point and had to run to catch it. Come on Ruby, let's get back." With that Ruby stamped back toward the porch muttering under her breath. Young faithful John was still standing on the porch shivering.

"Dad, you're okay!" he shouted wrapping his arms around him. "Sure am, John. Let's go in and thaw out. They all went in, took their snow-covered wet clothes off, and sat by the hearth getting warm. This was winter, and there were six months to go. Ruby felt that they would not make it. She just prayed that there would be some hunting days. But these days would be few because the wild animals bedded down in the winter, and some days it was too windy to hunt. The animals could smell the hunters when they were within two hundred feet or more of them.

By late December, the jars of canned vegetables were gone. The pork was finished for Christmas dinner along with potatoes that they still had. They waited for the January thaw that folks talked about, but it never came. When they prayed, Ruby asked that they be thankful that they had plenty of wood for heat and the children were not stricken with disease like some of their neighbors. They tried fishing by cutting a hole in the ice, but the fish were not biting. Ruby watched out the window as her husband came through the yard, fishpole in hand and once again, no fish. Fear and sorrow were etched deep in the folds of his face.

# 23

## THOSE IN NEED

ONE EARLY MORNING in February Sophia Cole stepped out on her porch to hang out the clothes she had just washed. The morning light peeked through the late-night darkness. She heard a tapping sound. Thinking it was the woodpecker attacking the large cedar tree between her porch and the neighbor's barn, she continued hanging clothes. Sophia loved this time of day when Alba was down at the barn and the children were still asleep. Sharp winter silence surrounded her save for the woodpecker. The sound continued; she looked into the distance and saw someone digging a hole in the snow. She moved over to the other side of the porch and watched a woman in a black wool shawl shoveling. It was Ruby Brown. She recognized the shawl; she had made it as a housewarming gift. She wondered what on earth Ruby was doing. She watched as the young woman continued to dig and then pull up the brown sticks and vines of rotting plants. She put them in a wooden pail and after looking in both directions, began walking back to the cabin. At this moment, Almina Keller, came out the door to help. "Sophia, let...."

"Shh." Sophia whispered; she put her finger up to her mouth and pointed toward the Brown place. Almina looked over and gave Sophia a quizzical look. Almina was newly married to Alba Cole's cousin, Simeon Cole. They rented this property from Alba and Sophia because Alba had bought another piece of land up the road closer to the lake. Alba was good with his hands and loved boats. His dream was to build, evaluate, and sell guide boats, which were beginning to be in greater demand as more people from the city were finding their way to the Adirondacks and needed guides.

Sophia and Almina ducked behind the porch corner as they watched Ruby until she opened the door to her house. Sophia went inside, fixed them a cup of hermit Bowen's tea, and sat down at her new log table with Almina.

"Well, obviously they have nothing to eat. That poor woman is digging up weeds," Sophia said. "I'm going over there."

By now Alba and Simeon had returned from the barn. "Going where?" Sophia told him what she had seen. He thought for a moment, "Sophia, stay out of it. I'm sure John would not want you bringing food over there."

"No, not food. I'm just going over and at least be neighborly. I haven't visited Ruby since fall so it would not be unnatural for me to visit."

"Well, I still don't think so. Me and Simeon are going out back to chop down a few more trees; wood pile is getting down."

"Ok, dear. Here, here are some new gloves I made you." She handed him the thick gray gloves.

"Thank you, dear. He gave her kiss on the cheek." The two young ones hugged, and they were out the door.

As soon as the woods swallowed them, Sophia grabbed Almina, "Come on. We're going over there. We'll wait about an hour and make sure John is gone, and then we'll go visit and see what's what."

"But Alba…."

"But nothing. We're going." They waited about an hour. Then they put on their coats, hats, boots, and mittens, grabbed the snowshoes from the porch, and began snow-shoeing to the Brown house. In front of the porch step, they unhooked their snowshoes, stepped up onto the landing and knocked on the door. In a few minutes five-year-old Henry Brown answered the door.

"Hi, Mrs. Cole."

"Hi, Henry, is your ma around?"

"Yup, she's right here." The cabin was one room like most of the cabins. To the left was the great fireplace where a cook-ing kettle hung. To the right of that was a curtain enclosing a box bed, and beside the curtain was another bed. The rough log table was in the center. It was three hewed logs resting on two stumps on each end. Each side had a log bench. A large black stove was to the right of the door.

"Why, hello, Almina. My goodness. Sophia too. Come in. Come in. I'm sorry I have no tea right now. but please sit." Almina smelled a strange medicinal odor coming from the pot hanging in the hearth.

"How is John?"

"Oh, he is fine. Out trying to find our cow."

"Ya," Henry piped up, "so we can eat it. Dang cow ran away because she knew we were fixing to eat her."

"Henry," chided Ruby, "now that is just not true." "Pa said."

"Henry, go out and help your brother with the woodcutting." "Don't know why. Ain't nothin' out there he'd let me help with." "Go!" Henry dressed and went outside to join his brother, John Jr.

"Ruby, what is going on? I know this is your first winter. How are you getting on?" Sophia asked.

"Oh, we're doing fine. So wonderful that you came by, though."

"Are Vermont winters like the ones up here? Is it what you expected?"

Ruby's eyes began to water. Pride tried to hold back the tears, but pride lost. "Oh, Sophia, no, no, we did not know it would be this cold for this long. We were not prepared, and now there is nothing left to eat. I fear that we will starve before spring. Please, don't say anything to the men. If John knew I was telling you this, he would never forgive me."

"Ruby, I wasn't spying, but I saw you this morning digging up the bracken."

"You saw me?" "Yes."

"I was trying to find anything. I have already found all the rotten potatoes. Now I am boiling the stems of milkweed, bracken, and witch hobble for broth."

"Really? I've used witch hobble for headaches and colds but never to eat. You know, you can't eat bracken. It will make you sick." "Oh no; I didn't know."

"Yes, it is poisonous."

"Oh Lord, I almost poisoned my family." She jumped up, took the pot from the hook, walked to the door, opened it, and threw the liquid out."

Almina and Sophia watched. Finally, Sophia spoke up, "My goodness, Ruby, we still have some potatoes. Let me bring you some." "Well, we would have to do that without John knowing."

"Maybe we could say you found some while digging. Let me think about this awhile, and we will see what we can do. The two women rose from the table, said their goodbyes, and snowshoed back to the cabin. Almina loaded some potatoes in her backpack and took them to Ruby.

That afternoon Sophia sat in her rocker and finished her darning. Sewing always made her mind work better. She knew one thing, pride or not, those children needed food, and she was not going to let them starve. Almina was sweeping out the house with a hemlock broom. Suddenly she stopped, "Sophia, I have it. I have an idea how to help the Browns. I'll get Almira to help me." Almira Keller was

Almina's twin sister. Like her Aunt Mary Ann, Almira could ride, shoot, and trap.

"Oh, wait a minute, Almina, remember, no one can know we are helping," Sophia cautioned.

"No one will except Almira, and she is the most secretive person in town." Her parents did not know about Almira and Farrand Austin, barely teenagers, who were beginning to court behind their parents' back. Almina's parents were already not happy about Simeon and Almina. They only consented to the courtship because they knew that Simeon would support their daughter, and she moved in with Alba and Sophia to help with the housework. "She will not tell."

Then, Almina told Sophia that her idea was to ask Ebenezer Bowen for help. He was smart and could figure out things other people could not. Sophia agreed that it was worth a try. Almina stood up, went out to the porch, secured her snowshoes, and began the half mile trek to her father David Keller's house. She arrived, burst through the door, and told the sad tale of the Browns to her sister. That afternoon, Almina and Almira harnessed up old Babe and made the journey to the north end of the lake to hermit Bowen's place on the pine ridge at the foot of Buck Mountain. He lived next to an old military road that he had used when he first arrived from Elizabethtown. He always had a fire going, smoking meat, fish, and anything else he could. hermit Bowen was an intellectual man who had turned his back on society years ago, come to the end of

Long Lake, built a shack, and sold charcoal, eggs, and tea. No one knew a lot about his past, but Robert Shaw regularly visited him, always trying to bring him into religion. The hermit was not religious, but he liked to help people. He had come to know Robert Shaw when Robert was a boy. They too were starving when they first came, and no one could or would help them. Ebenezer Bowen brought the family food in the night until George and his son Robert secured work at the mines near Newcomb.

Mary Ann Keller knew this because she managed to find out things about most of the people in the community. She seemed always to be behind a tree or in a barn stall or somewhere within reach of information. She slipped out at night when the family was asleep. She saw and heard things before sneaking back in, sometimes just before dawn's light. At times, Mary Ann rode with Almira, and soon Almira knew much of what Mary Ann knew.

The twins rode their horse off the ice right up to hermit Bowen's door. He came to the door fully dressed in wool pants, white shirt, vest, and fob. Ebenezer opened the door a crack. A gust of wind snapped his long white beard out, where it shuffled in the wind. "By gum, it's the Keller girls. What can I do for you, young ladies? He pushed the door open wider and stepped out. His blue eyes sparkled in the afternoon sun reflecting off the snow.

"Mr. Bowen, we wondered if you could help someone." Mary Ann had said that this old hermit could see right through you into your soul. He knew things, things Almira did not wish him to know. Almira explained the situation, and he assured her he would help if he could. Soon, they were on their way back home, knowing this kind but mysterious man would manage it from here.

When the new day arose, everyone in Big Brook Village discovered a bag of potatoes on their doorsteps. The following week everyone woke up to eggs, and this continued until spring. Zenas Parker thought it was the Kellers. Old Henry Olin Russell and Henry Austin joked about the Big Brook Fairies who delivered food, and old hermit Bowen continued to sell his charcoal and keep his potatoes cold and chickens warm.

These were the early families in the village. By the late 1800s, several more made their way into Big Brook Village, building a school and a guide boat shop where paddling down the lake on a hot summer day you could hear the tap, tap, tap of Alba Cole building his boats.

# 24

## A LIFE FOR A LIFE

DURING THIS TIME, the nearest general store was still fourteen miles away from the Long Lake settlement. There were no roads going north or south. During the summer months, Alex Duane helped on the Henderson farm, but in winter, he ran a logging camp where his wife and daughter, Jane, helped in the kitchen.

One winter, a young, half-starved man wandered into the lumber camp. His name was Isaac Clement. He had been born in Michigan, where he had grown up extremely poor. While still a boy he was sent to live and work for a farmer all winter. The farmer paid his family a bushel of wheat for Isaac's labor. One day before his sixteenth year, Isaac met another man who came to work for the farmer. The man was from the northern mountains of New York. He told Isaac about the log camps popping up: You could live in the camp, get fed, and have a place to sleep at night. He also told him about a newly discovered titanium mine called Tahawus where he could find work. One week later, Isaac began the journey into the Adirondack Mountains. The train ride to Port Henry, New York, took all his meager savings.

All Isaac knew was that the camp was on the east side of what was called the Hudson River, near a place called Calamity Pond, where a monument was erected in memory of a Mr. Henderson who accidentally shot himself at that place.

After leaving the train station in Port Henry, he began walking toward the mine. It was winter, and the snow was up to his knees. He muddled through the snow for miles. He thought he would die before he could even live. Determined to live, he dragged himself another few miles until he was so exhausted that he had to rest. He saw the top of a stone sticking out of the snow and decided to rest on that. As he got closer, he realized it was strangely shaped. He approached and wiped the snow off the top and sides and saw writing. Though he could not read, he knew he had found Henderson's monument. He looked around and knew he must be close. With renewed energy, he kept walking. Growing up in Michigan winters, he knew the last thing you do when out in a winter storm is close your eyes. He knew if he did that, he would never open them again. He also knew he could not last much longer. He began to look for whatever form of shelter he could find. Night was falling, and soon it would be too dark to see anything. He had to rest. He found a large white pine, sat down under it, and covered himself with snow hoping that at least it would give him enough warmth not to freeze to death. He pulled his hood tight and started to lie down so he could completely cover himself with snow. As he turned his head, he caught a flicker of light. He thought he was hallucinating. He blinked his eyes several times, sat up, and looked again. It was still there! Isaac stood up and began walking toward the light. After he managed to pull each frozen foot out of the snow for about thirty feet, he suddenly realized that the light was gone. He blinked several times and looked all around. Nothing. Nothing but blackness. He must have imagined it. Isaac's knees buckled, and he fell. He closed his eyes and thought he was going to die here… never fall in love or marry or….

"Hey, fella, what are you doing out here?" Isaac thought he was hearing things, too. He opened his eyes; standing in front of him was a man holding a lantern. "Well looks like you ain't dead. Come on son. Let's get you to camp." This man, or ghost, grabbed Isaac's arm, pulled him up, and helped him walk. Isaac could not feel his feet. Soon he saw the outline of a building and the man hollered, "Hey, somebody get out here!" Soon, Isaac had another man on his right, dragging him up onto a porch and into a large room. The first thing Isaac could see out of his snow-laden eyelashes was the roaring fire. They carried him to the large chair in front of the fireplace and began to unlace his boots.

"Looks like you got some good frostbite going on there, son. You're at my logging camp."

"I am? I'm not dead?"

"No, son. You ain't dead. Old man winter didn't get you this time. I'm Alex Duane." Someone handed Isaac a hot cup of tea. They helped him off with his wet clothes and wrapped him in blankets. The pain in his fingers and toes came about ten minutes later. For that, there was whiskey. Later, after Isaac introduced himself, he found out that Alex was visiting the outhouse, and it was his lantern he saw. It disappeared when Alex went inside the outhouse. "What are you doing way out here?"

"Looking for work." "What kind of work?" "I'll do anything." "Ever cook?"

"Uh, yes, some."

"Good; old Pete just took off on one of his drunks. Don't know when he'll be back," Alex said shaking his head. "So, tomorrow morning you'll get up at three o'clock. The men that run the sprinkler wagon go out to water down the ice road early. We eat bacon, eggs, pancakes, and potatoes. You pack sandwiches and we'll be back before dark for supper. The rest of the men will be down at four."

"Uh, okay," Alex mumbled, terrified of the prospect of cooking all these things. He had never cooked for others and had trouble understanding Alex's Canadian accent. He had never heard, if he heard correctly, of a sprinkler wagon, but he did hear the time he had to be up and cooking. One of the men showed him to his bunk. He fell onto it and slept five hours until he heard a knock on his door.

"Yes?"

A woman said, "Time to rise."

"Okay." He was confused. Where was he? That was a woman's voice. He had seen no women last night. He stepped out onto the rough wood floor and sank to his knees. Pain shot up his leg like hot lava. He groaned, pulled himself up on the bed, sat, and began to rub his legs. The right one hurt the most, but after a few minutes, the pain subsided some; he tried to stand again. This time it worked. He dressed and slowly wobbled out into the kitchen where he saw two women busy at work, one with a coffee pot in her hand and the other stocking the stove with wood.

"Morning," he said.

They both turned around. Isaac saw that both women had sandy brown hair and big brown eyes. There was no doubt that they were mother and daughter.

"Hi, I'm Esther, Alex's wife, and this is our daughter, Jane. I understand you met my husband, Alex, and you will be taking over the cooking from now on."

"Hi, uh, yes. I guess." "You guess?"

"Uh, I mean yes."

"Okay, I understand you almost died and have some frozen toes and hands, so this morning why don't you watch us? We will show you where to find things and what to cook."

"Ok." His body began to sway. Jane grabbed the stool and put it under him.

"You sit and watch," Esther said.

After biscuits and coffee, Jane began to show Isaac around the large building with Esther following behind. "Okay, this is where we keep the flour and sugar." Jane went to a large wood cabinet, opened the doors, and showed him where several items were kept for cooking. Isaac's eyes widened in fear as he looked at the gigantic black stove. Esther glanced at the boy several times. "Isaac," she whispered, "Isaac, have you ever cooked on a stove?" He started to lie, but instead he looked into her eyes and the lie vanished. He shook his head.

"Ok, have you ever cooked?" "Uh, not really." "

I thought so. Listen, you meet me down here at 3:00 am tomorrow. I will help you."

"Why? Why would you help me?"

"Because you need help; Jane, this will be our secret." Jane nodded. She liked secrets, and she liked having someone closer to her age around. Her brother, Henry, was only four years older, but he was always with his dad and his friends or gawking at Annie Scott when she came up to Long Lake. She was a beautiful blonde-haired blue-eyed girl who stayed with her grandparents quite often. They lived down the road from Big Brook Village where Henry lived on the Henderson farm with his grandparents and parents except during logging season when he worked in camp. The Scotts had never moved up off the lake like several others, so Henry could follow the path through the woods straight down to their house. Esther knew about this infatuation and was glad the Scott girls weren't there very often, because to find Henry for farm work during that time was impossible.

Isaac looked into Esther's face. He heard what she said. This helping concept was so foreign to Isaac that he did not believe her, but he did not say so. No one helped. He remembered being four years old after his father died, being left alone, begging on the streets, and people passing him by. People took care of themselves.

That morning Isaac woke up at 2:30. He came out and saw Esther in her long gray skirt and white bib apron coming toward him. "Good, you are up. Well, come on. We have a lot to do before they'll be in here needing to eat so they can get out there."

For the next hour, Esther and Jane taught him how to cook pancakes, eggs, potatoes, and bacon. Esther made bread for Isaac to put in the oven. When the men came in, Esther disappeared into her room but before she left, she told Isaac, "Don't tell them you had help."

"But no. You did most of...."

"I know, but if these men or worse yet, Alex, knows you did not cook this, you could lose your job, and you need this job. You will not tell. Is that understood? If you do, I will not help you with dinner."

Isaac agreed, and at the breakfast when they were all sitting down eating and complimenting Isaac, he did not utter a word. Soon Esther and Jane came out of their room, sat down, ate, and remarked how well the new cook did and how old Pete better watch himself when he decided to come back because the new man could outcook him. Alex looked at his wife and looked at Isaac. "Humm," he said, as he piled a large spoonful of jelly onto his toast.

It was exactly four days later that old Pete returned just before supper on a cold rainy night. "I'm back," he shouted as he shut the door against the sharp wind. Everybody groaned. The men had begun to like the young boy. He certainly had come up with some different versions of food, but they felt sorry for the skinny kid and ate whatever he put out. The day before Pete came back, Henry shot a pheasant just outside of camp on his way to work. He rushed back in, dropped it on the table, and asked Isaac to have it ready for supper. Henry rushed back out the door leaving Isaac standing there looking at the bird. He knew from talk that he had to put it in a boiling pot and steam it to pull the feathers out. He did that, plucked all the feathers and about an hour before dinner, put it in a big kettle to boil. At the supper table, he put it on a big tin plate in the middle of the table and gave everyone knives. They began cutting into the bird and as they got down to the breastbone, the last logger who was cutting saw all the innards suddenly fall out of the pheasant onto the table. They all stopped and stared at the mess, put their knives down and kept on eating everything but the bird. Later, Alex said, "Boy, did you ever cook a chicken?" Isaac shook his head.

"I could tell. Next time, take the innards out first." That was all he said. He turned and walked away, mumbling to himself, "Sure, that boy knows how to cook. Sure, he does." Thank the Lord old drunk Pete had returned. The next day, Alex gave Isaac a job in the woods with the rest of the men, and he became an exceptional logger. One day Alex joined Isaac on the walk home. "Well, I'll say this. You make a much better logger than you do a cook." Isaac nodded his head. "And the wife wants to know if you would come to dinner on our next leave." Through the years, he came to several dinners and through the years, he and Jane grew fond of each other.

When Jane was fourteen years old, Isaac asked her to meet him in the place under the red pine tree where they had met and talked before. She met him as she had done the previous week. This time as she stood against the old tree, Isaac bent his tall frame down and kissed her gently on the lips. She stood there frozen, not knowing what to do. Isaac broke the silence by saying, "Jane, I am in love with you." She wanted to say she loved him too, but she was speechless. Isaac started to say something else, stopped, turned, and hurried off into the forest. Jane felt stupid. She loved him, but what would her father say? She was terrified of her parents finding out he had kissed her. So, she avoided him all week and cried all night. One night after she and mother had returned to the farm in Big Brook, Esther heard her daughter crying. She entered her bedroom and sat on the bed. "Jane, what is the matter?"

"Nothing."

"It is not nothing, dear; you are sad, and I want to know why." "You would not understand, ma. You would not understand."

"Oh, wouldn't I? It doesn't have anything to do with that young man you've been meeting in the woods, does it?"

Jane's head snapped around. She looked at her mother. "You know?"

Esther nodded.

"But...."

"Mothers know," Esther replied. Mothers with spies because Jane's brother Henry told Esther about their meeting. Esther had followed them out the next day and saw them. They were only talking. She decided to leave it alone.

"Mother, he kissed me." "Really."

"Yes, and I didn't do anything. I acted like a tree, just stood there. He even told me he loved me, and I still said nothing."

"Well, do you love him?"

"Yes, I think so. Are you mad?"

"No, I'm not. I like Isaac. Better someone court you I know well than someone I don't know."

"But now I've ruined everything. I bet dad will be mad he kissed me." "Maybe. We'll see."

"Are you going to tell him?"

"No, not yet. If Isaac is the fine man I think he is, he will make it right. We'll see. Don't you worry."

"Okay, I'll try. After her mother left, she sat up in bed and thought about her life. She felt so much better. Her mother always had a plan, and things always worked out when she told her the truth.

That night, Esther had the talk with Alex. She told him she thought Isaac was sweet on Jane.

"I know."

"You know. What do you mean, you know?"

"He told me; pulled me off into the woods yesterday and asked me for Jane's hand."

"She doesn't know."

"I know, and you are not to tell her." "Okay, but what did you say?"

"I gave him my blessing and told him if he ever treated her bad, he would have this in his face." He balled up his fist and shook it in the air.

They both laughed. Esther grabbed his wrist, pulled it down and kissed her husband. He was a tough burly lumberjack, and she was sure he had scared Isaac enough to give him nightmares for a few nights. The following week, Isaac asked Jane to meet him at the red oak, where he proposed. They were married on her family farm and lived with Alex and Esther until they built a small house down the road.

Then they bought land from Christina Kellogg who lived on Sawmill Road and built across the field from them. Isaac painted the house white even though few houses were painted. He had an artist's eye and began to build rock walls, sometimes having to live away from the family through the week.

When their first child, Elizabeth, was two years old, they bought land across from the Robinson sawmill on what became known as Clement Road. Isaac cut the timbers for his house and sent them down the sawmill chute that ran from the top of the hill to the Robinson's mill on the creek below.

During that time, Jane had her own work to do, spinning, planting wheat, and vegetables, gathering to dry for winter use. Since Isaac acquired two sheep, there was shearing and cleaning to send away to a carding mill in Warrensburg, New York, to be made into rolls for spinning. When Isaac was away, the Keller or Plumley boys took Jane's wool to the mill. Along with spinning the wool into yarn, Jane made most of the clothing for winter for her family, which soon included four more children.

# 25

---

## Last Days at the Logging Camp

IT HAPPENED WHEN Isaac was no longer working at the logging camp and Alex should not have been working at his age. It happened after Cyrus Kellogg built the Lake House Hotel; it happened in March, two months after his granddaughter Esther Clement, was born.

It was a burly March morning. The wind blew down from the north like an angry ogre. Richard Parker (Zenas's son), Melvin Cole (Alba's son), and Henry Duane had left to harness the horses and hook them to the log sled. Alex hung back to stoke the stove with wood to last the day. He was taking his jacket off the hook next to the door when Richard came running in. "Alex, we can't get that darn sprinkler to work."

Alex shook his head, "Not again. We had some trouble with it yesterday, but it was working fine by the end of the day. All right, I'll look at it." Alex finished putting his coat on and walked out the door into the pre-dawn chilly air.

He grabbed the kerosene lantern off the porch nail, lit it, and walked out to join two men who were looking at the machine. "Trouble with it again, huh?" Alex said shaking his head. He figured it was the sprinkler wagon valves. He thought he had fixed it just unplugging the valve on the right side of the machine. "Did you look at the valves and see if they are plugged?" The men all nodded.

"We checked. The valves are clear," Richard said, as he joined Alex inspecting the side valves of the sprinkler.

"Okay, I'll look. Henry, you stay here. Richard and Mel, go with the logging wagon. We're running late."

"Okay, boss," Mel said, as he and Richard stepped up on the logging wagon seat to drive the horse-drawn machine back into the woods where they had cut yesterday. Alex had Henry hold the lantern while he worked on the sprinkler wagon. They walked over to the back of the machine. Alex handed the lantern to Henry, bent down, and checked the valves on both sides. They were clear but no water came out. Then he knew it was plugged further up the tubing from the tank. "Dang," he muttered as he stood up scratching his head. "I'm going to have to crawl under this thing and let the water out. I need you to go get the big wrench in the toolbox on the porch." "Okay, dad," Henry said as he turned to go.

"Hey, leave the lantern there on the wheel. It's light enough for you to see but not for me under this machine." Henry put the lantern on the large wheel and started back to the house. Just as Alex began to crawl under the wagon, the wind gusted. It caught the lantern, lifted it up, and brought it slamming down onto Alex's back. Alex screamed and tried to wiggle out from under the wagon while trying to knock the lantern off his back. Henry heard the scream, turned, saw fire under the wagon, and ran back. He grabbed Alex's boots and pulled him out. The lantern rolled off his back, but his jacket was on fire.

Henry rolled his dad over on his back into the snow. The flames went out. Luckily, Alex had his jacket, winter underwear, and a thick wool shirt on. He was able to stand, and Henry helped him into camp. When they got the layers of clothing off, they found a deep burn about twelve inches long and five inches wide. "My God, the burn is actually the size of the lantern. It burned straight through."

"Henry, go get some snow. Take the bucket over there and fill it with snow and put it on the burn," Alex grunted.

Henry stared at the red welted skin and wanted to run. He paced back and forth looking for the bucket. "Ah, where is the bucket? I can't find it."

"Oh, for Lord's sake, get something; anything; and get out there and get some snow!" Alex yelled.

"Uh, ok, ok." He scanned the walls and the floor looking for something. His mind raced. He couldn't focus. He looked down at his feet, pulled his boot off and went outside. He filled the boot with snow and came back in." Alex was bent over the chair with his face buried in the crook of his arm.

"I've got it, dad. I've got the snow."

"Okay. He got up and lay down on his stomach on his cot. "Now, put the snow all over the burn." Henry did as he was told. Ten minutes later, Alex instructed Henry to get the willow bark off the beam above the stove. Henry retrieved the container of bark, mixed it with water and smeared it on the burn. His mom had used this when the cooking pot had fallen on his hand and burned him. Everyone had some in their homes. "There is torn sheet cloth under this bed. Use that to wrap around me to cover the burn," Alex instructed. After covering the burn, Alex got up, groaning and wincing with pain; Henry watched. "Well, son, you going to stand their gaping all day or you going with me to get some work done?"

"But dad, you can't...."

"Ahh, a little burn ain't going to make me lose a day's work. Come on.

You are fixing that darn wagon." By now, the morning sun was shining off the glittering snow. With Alex's instructions, Henry got under the wagon and found the problem in the upper part of the tube coming from the tank. They fixed it and made it out into the woods, only losing an hour's time.

The problem did not come that day or the next day. The problem came when Alex woke on the third day in terrible pain. Richard Parker had tried to get Alex to let him look at the wound and put a new bandage on it, but Alex would not. The next day, the pain was so intense Alex let Richard remove the dressing and look at the wound. Richard silently gasped when he saw the large red blisters bubbled up on his back. "This is not good, Alex, you need to go see a doctor."

"What doctor? We ain't got no doctor in Long Lake." "We got Robert Shaw and Doc Parker."

"They ain't doctors."

"I know, but Robert has a new salve he made, and he can treat wounds with it." Richard knew Alex was the most stubborn man around, but he also saw Alex's bloodshot eyes and could feel the heat coming off his body. He knew something was not right and that Alex needed help. Finally convinced, Alex left camp and went home. After looking at the wound, Esther chided him for waiting so long and then sent Henry to fetch Doc Parker and Robert Shaw. Both men came within the hour. Both men shook their heads. "How long you had this, Alex?" the old doc asked.

"Oh, a few days."

"A few days! You should have come in immediately." "I couldn't; had too much work."

"Well, you won't be working now," Robert interjected. "You won't be working at all."

"What do you mean, he won't be working?" Esther asked, her face scrunched up in worry.

"Esther, he's got Pyemia. There is no coming back from that." "What? Py what?

"His blood is tainted now. It got infected and there is nothing we can do." "What?" Esther just could not understand what they were saying.

"For Lord's sake, woman, I'm dying. They're saying I'm done. How long?" "Not sure, but you better get your affairs in order. Now get some rest."

They turned and walked out onto the porch with Jane, Esther, and Henry. By now Richard and Melvin were back home and came over to see how he was. They all stood out on the porch. "So, Doc, what will happen? Will it be painful?" Jane asked as she clung to her mother.

Doc Parker spoke up, "Well, I've only seen two of these cases before. He already has the fever. He'll eventually lose consciousness and go quietly. Just give him this. I gave him a dose. It will let him sleep and help with the pain."

"I am so sorry," Robert Shaw said as he touched Jane's arm. "We will pray for him." That Sunday prayers were said for Alex Duane and his family. The next Sunday at 7:00 am, Alex took his last breath. The whole town came to the burial.

Within the group of mourners stood John and Jenny Scott. Gray tendrils pushed out from Jenny's scarf, and John's beard was now full gray. They still lived in the cabin on the west side, never feeling the need to move, never wanting more than each other and their freedom. They had many talks in front of the fireplace with their granddaughters who came to stay, talks of their love surviving across an ocean onto two countries. Jenny was thinking about her friend, Esther Duane, and John was thinking about his friend, Mitchel Sabattis and the hunt tomorrow.

# 26

## THE LAST HUNT

IT WAS THE winter of 1881, and the Adirondacks were once again blanketed with snow. Big Brook Village was abuzz with activity as the Browns prepared for winter. This time, they had plenty of meat and vegetables. The children went to school down the hill while Elmer Plumley raised sheep and sold mutton and milk to the new hotels that were sprouting up.

This year, this season, this dark dawn, John and Jenny Scott sat at the old wooden table with their coffee and reminisced about the hills and valleys of their lives. "Well, Jen, time to go. Got to get us some meat for the winter."

"John, must you go this morning? I think it is going to storm." "Never stopped me before."

"You were never this old before. Besides, you know, Ned, Patrick, and Ann have offered to fill our larder for the winter. It is time, John. Let them do it."

"Jenny, I'm still standing, and I'm meeting Mitchel anyway," he remarked as he stood up.

"Okay, I see. One old man leading another," she chided.

"Aw, Jen, my bonny lass. No more worry. We will be fine." He grabbed his winter gear off the hooks, shouldered his rifle and opened the thick log door. Jenny hugged him and watched as he ambled down the worn path they had begun so many years ago. Jenny saw the bend in his back, the curve in his leg, bowed from years of work. The wind blew across the lake, and she felt the bitter snap of winter wind. She shut the door and began picking up the breakfast dishes. There were no more children home. They were all grown and married. She dressed and went outside to feed and milk their two cows. By the time she reached the barn, the snow had begun, and by the time she finished, there were several inches added to the layers on the ground. She loved the snow if everyone was safe inside. John had hunted in all kinds of weather, and he preferred snow hunting, but if it kept snowing at this rate, she knew he would have to cut it short. When he wasn't back by early afternoon, she began to worry, and when he wasn't back by 4:00 pm, she began to fret and imagine the worst scenarios: Did he leave Mitchel and then lose his way in the snow? No, she knew that was unlikely. John knew how to get home blindfolded, and though it was snowing hard, she could still see the barn. Is he sick and Mitchel is trying to get him home? Did they go out on the lake and break through the ice?

Dark rolled in early, and the cows needed to be milked; she would have to do it. She began the trek out to the barn, fighting the bitter wind pulling at her scarf and made it into the barn, yanking the door closed behind her. She leaned against the door gasping for breath. Oh Lord, she thought, I'm not going to be able to do this much longer. She pulled off her gloves and looked at her hands, now covered in brown spots. The winds ripped at the door as Jenny caught her breath. She picked up the pail, milked the cows and made sure the animals had enough hay to keep warm through this winter night. She slid the door open and was greeted by a stinging wet snow slapping her in the face. She could barely make out the cabin though it was only thirty feet away. She pulled her scarf up over her face and began trudging through the snow. For God's sake, where was John? He wouldn't be home because if he were, he would have come to the barn to milk. She was halfway home when she saw him. He was covered in snow, loaded down with meat, and walking so slowly that Jenny thought he had stopped. Then she began to understand that he had stopped moving. Suddenly, his knees buckled, and he fell to the ground. "John!" Jenny shouted as she fought her way through the knee-high snow, reaching him in seconds. She put her arm through his and pulled him up. "Come on, John, you're almost home."

He looked at her as if he were seeing her for the first time, as if he were waking up from a hard sleep. "Jenny? The meat. I need to get it and the gun."

"We'll get it after." Jenny bent down and picked up his gun. "Here is your gun." John took it and the two of them managed to make it back to the house.

His clothes were frozen to him, and his face was frost-bitten. "My God, sweetheart, what happened?" she asked as she led him to the fireplace, stripped off the frozen wet clothes, sat him in the rocking chair, and wrapped him in blankets. She put the teapot on and soon handed him a hot cup of molasses tea. He had not spoken. His body was still shaking so badly that Jenny had to hold the tea for him. After a few sips, the shaking stopped, and he began to talk. He and Mitchel had had a good hunt, but at the end of the day, they spotted a moose. "Jen, it was the biggest one I ever saw, and it was heading out on the lake. We followed it and that darn animal took us up toward the east side of the end of the lake. That moose was running, and we were running after it trying to keep up but staying far enough downwind so he couldn't see or smell us. He began to go toward shore. We knew that once he reached land, we would lose him. We were still too far away for a shot. About ten feet from shore, we heard this loud crack and watched dumbfounded as the moose began sinking into the water; his back feet and legs went in while he clawed at the ice with his front legs trying to get out. We raced to within five feet of him wondering how we would get him out. He was still half in and half out when we reached him. He was huge, Jen. My God, his head would cover that whole wall. John pointed to the fifteen-foot wall of the cabin."

"So, what did you do?"

"Well, it was a dilemma because we couldn't shoot him there. We would lose him for sure, and we couldn't get near him because of the ice breaking on us. Besides, the old boy was so tired from trying to get out and from the freezing water that we figured he didn't have much struggle left in him. We figured that since we were so close to shore, if we could get him even five feet closer, he could reach bottom and walk out, breaking the thinner ice near shore. Mitchel had a rope, but we couldn't get near enough to throw it over him, and then we didn't know if we could drag him in. By now that poor moose was howling and groaning so loud his echo was bouncing off every mountain around us. Soon Frank Plumley appeared at the edge of the lake. He'd heard the bellowing from his place on Plumley Point. At the same time, that old hermit, Fournier, showed up, you know, the one who lives in a shack on Plumley's land?"

Jenny nodded and said, "I can't believe you and Mitchel were trying to haul in a moose."

"Well, better believe it because we were, and you haven't heard the best of it yet, but now there are four of us trying to get this moose. So, we decided to tie ropes to each other and lay prone on the ice, wrapping the last piece of rope around the antlers and try hauling him in. Since Frank was the youngest, he opted to be the one to throw the rope. By now Frank's wife Margaret, hearing the commotion, had come out and yelled at Frank to be careful." "Oh, my goodness, Margaret was there too?"

"Yes, yes, she was. So, Mitchel was on the ice, and the hermit and I were on land with the rope. We held our breath as Frank inched out onto the ice, then lay down flat and tried to lasso the moose. That moose was almost dead by now, and if we didn't get him closer to shore, he would be. Finally, on the fourth throw Frank hooked the moose and began to inch his way back out as did Mitchel. Soon, Mitchel was on land pulling on the rope with Fournier and me. The moose suddenly felt the tug and pulled hard against it, dragging Frank with it. It seemed that because the moose feared humans more than the water, instead of moving toward the pull, he was trying to pull away further out into the lake. Suddenly, in a whisper, Frank was gone! We saw nothing but ice and the animal."

Jenny put her hand to her mouth, "No," she cried.

"Hold on, Jen, just wait until I finish, Anyway, we soon saw Frank's arms and head above the ice. He had broken through the ice and now was pulling Mitchel in with him.

"Cut the rope, Frank!" Mitchel yelled.

Then we all began to yell, "Frank, cut the rope!" The moose was now docile with its front legs in the water since the weight of him thrashing around broke the ice holding his front legs up. Frank found his knife, cut the rope between him and the moose, and we began to pull as hard as we could on the rope. We pulled him in a few feet, breaking ice with his body when he raised his arm and hollered. 'Okay, we're good. I'm on ground.' He continued to walk, breaking the ice on the way. Now, there was a free path for the moose to walk out or at least get to a standing place, but he wasn't moving. We thought he was dead. 'Well, one way to find out,' Mitchel said. He walked back out on the ice standing about ten feet from the animal and shot his rifle in the air. The moose jerked its head toward the sound and quickly began to swim toward shore within a few feet of me. It half stumbled, half walked and fell crashing to the ground right in front of old Fournier's shack.

"'Is he dead?' Mitchel shouted, as we walked in. We all figured its heart had given out. 'I think so,' Frank shouted back, but when we got there Mitchel checked its neck and the old moose was still breathing. 'Tough old critter,' Fournier remarked shaking his head. We all stood around looking at this magnificent animal."

"So, who shot him?" Jenny asked, thinking of all the meat outside in the snow.

"Well, that's the thing. Margaret left for the lodge and returned with blankets to put over Frank and the animal. Mitchel gathered some wood and made a fire in the snow."

"In the snow?"

"I know, but he did it. Mitchel said that we could not take this moose after he had struggled so much to survive. We all knew this in our hearts even though the old hermit did mention how much meat that would be, but after we all glared at him, he quieted down. Anyway, we didn't know if he would die or not, but if he did, it would not be by our hands.

By now Frank had gone in to get warm and thaw out. It was late afternoon, and we still had a long walk back, so

Mitchel and I headed back down the lake. Halfway down to East Bay Landing we heard the shouts. We turned and watched as that big moose struggled to his feet and disappeared into the woods. We were wet, tired, but happy. I left Mitchel off at the landing and crossed over to our place."

"My," Jenny exclaimed, "what a great story. I'm glad you made it home." "Not a story, my love, true."

"Uh huh," Jenny smiled, as she put on her gear to go out and get the meat to bring into the barn before the animals came for it.

"Wait, I'm...."

"No, you are not. You need to rest, old man. You just stay there," and he did. He closed his eyes and fell asleep. The next day, he got up to go out to the barn. The snow had stopped, and the bright sun shone like gold across the snow. His step was slower, he was tired, and when he reached the barn door, he had to rest. That evening, John Scott closed his eyes and never woke again. As Jenny stood by his grave, she knew she would see him soon, and she knew his last day was out in the wilderness where he loved to be.

Ned, Addie, Annie, Ann, Patrick, and both towns of Newcomb and Long Lake attended the Scott funeral. He was dressed in his tartan and buried next to the ridge, his favorite place at the cabin. Jenny Dodds Scott would lie down next to him. She lived for one more week and died of a broken heart. They would be together forever in the mountains that they loved.

# 27

## A New Rice; Another Move

Since Abram Jr's. death, seasons folded in upon each other, with autumn leaves floating to the ground soon covered in white. Spring whisked in with leaf sprouts opening to the summer sun that beat down on Abram as he tilled the soil and cut the hay. When Mary Ann Keller and Abram Rice returned to the farm, Abram continued working for Michael Wright. Mary Ann had been feeling sick lately. One morning, Eliza Wright was watching Mary Ann as she came out of the outhouse and meandered up to the house. Eliza was sitting on the porch spinning, a task she loved. She was watching the new leaves unfold in the warm breeze, when suddenly Mary Ann doubled over and began to vomit. Eliza raced down to her and put her hand on her back. "Mary Ann, what is it?" She felt her head. "No fever." Eliza breathed a sigh of relief. When Mary Ann straightened up, Eliza looked at her chalk-white face. She saw the mask. "You are pregnant," she blurted out.

"What? I can't be. There is something wrong with me. The doc told me; I can't have children."

"Well, believe me, whoever the doc is, he is wrong. How long have you been getting sick?"

"I don't know maybe a couple of months." "Mostly in the morning?"

"Always in the morning."

"Mary Ann, you are going to have a child. I know. When I was pregnant for Leafie, I had morning sickness and Jane Radcliff across the street had morning sickness for all of her children."

"Oh no. What are we going to do? We barely support each other on what Abram makes now. We will have to do something else if we are having a child." "Don't worry. We will help you as much as we can; at least you can have the baby here, and Jane and I can deliver it. I have delivered Jane's last two babies." Mary Ann dreaded telling Abram, and she did not tell him until she was sure, which was two months later. She asked him to come outside and walk with her to the pond where Abram had built a bench. They all went swimming in the swimming hole and cooked supper out there on Sunday nights.

Mary Ann sat on the bench and patted the seat, motioning Abram to sit beside her. "What is it, dear? What do we need to talk about? Are you okay?" "Yes, I am, but, Abram, what I am going to tell you is going to be a shock so...."

"You're pregnant."

Mary Ann's mouth dropped open. "Oh my God, you know. I can't believe Eliza told you."

"She didn't. Mary Ann, I have had several children. Remember? I know the signs."

"But why didn't you say something?"

"Because it was up to you to tell me. I wondered when that was going to be."

"You're not mad."

"Of course not. I love you, and I will love having a child with you." "But the money."

"It's okay. I haven't told you yet, but I got a letter from my friend, Norman Bissell."

"From Newcomb?"

"Yes, originally, but now he lives in a place called Milford and works in an iron mine there and makes good money. He told me they need workers and the company even provides housing for us if we go."

Mary Ann took a deep breath, "Where is this place?

"It is about three hours south of here on a river called The Susquehanna." "Does Michael know?"

"Yes. I talked to him about it, and he is encouraging us to go. We could start a real life, you, me, and the baby."

"Oh, I don't know. I'm scared about having the baby in a strange place." Mary Ann began to pace. She could go by herself out into the deep forest and kill a panther or a bear, but the thought of moving away from here terrified her. She did not want to move even further away from her beloved

Adirondacks to a place where she knew no one. "Do you think they have woods there?"

"There is a lot of farmland like here, but it is surrounded by woods. Besides Mary Ann, you are going to have a baby. You can't be out running around the forest shooting every day. In fact, I think you should start staying closer to the farm. And guess what? Norman's wife is a midwife. She has delivered lots of babies, and the mine has its own doctor, too."

They discussed it several times, and after seeing how set Abram was, Mary Ann stopped protesting.

On a hot day in August, they packed up their meager belongings and began the trek to Milford. As they traveled further south, the air became warmer. The morning sickness had left Mary Ann, but the tension, heat, and constant movement brought back the nausea. They had to stop several times, but on August 30, they arrived at their little bungalow in Milford. The Bissell family came over the next morning with fresh biscuits. Abram greeted them and introduced them to his wife. Norman Bissell knew Abram had married one of the Kellers. He did not know it was not Mary Ann, nor would anyone else in Milford know that secret.

The job at the mines was hard, but the pay was better than farm work. Six months later Martha Ann Rice was born. Soon, Abram and Mary Ann were able to buy their own home and raised their daughter. Though Mary Ann was busy caring for Abram and Martha, sometimes while sitting in her rocker on the back porch, she imagined she was looking out at her giant white pines shimmering in the summer breeze, the small round island in the middle of the lake south of East Bay Landing, or the red mirrored maples looking up at her on an autumn afternoon from the watery depth of the still waters.

While in St. Lawrence County, she and Abram attended the Canton and then Ogdensburg Fair every year. Abram met Bligh Dodds one year while showing horses for Michael Wright. Bligh's father was the younger brother of Thomas Dodds Sr., who settled in the Rossie area after the Doddses came to America. He bought land and helped organize the fairs held in Canton. Now, the fair had moved to the outskirts of Ogdensburg, eighteen miles from Canton. Bligh worked for months getting ready for the big fair.

Mary Ann was tired of her daily routine and missed the excitement of riding through the woods at breakneck speeds. She still shot her gun and bow, but she also missed going to the fair. She loved the smell of peanuts roasting over the fire, the music, and especially the horses and betting on the horse races. There were always several breeds at the fair, including Morgans, Freesias, Appaloosas, and Clydesdales.

The summer that Martha was three years old, they decided to take her to the fair. They stayed with Michael and Eliza, and Abram helped Michael bring his prize pigs and Ayrshire cows to the fair. Mary Ann had clothing for sale, such as men's pants and shirts, women's dresses, and children's clothes, as well as knitted and crocheted items. Martha squealed with delight as she stuffed her mouth with muffins and candy people handed her as she sat by her mother in the tent. Mary Ann was curious about some of the vendors and customers. There was great commotion when the gypsies arrived in the covered wagons smelling of herbs. Unlike Mary Ann's friends and family, where the men usually drove the wagons, the gypsy women raced in with their colorful shawls and skirts billowing in the wind driving their horses to their usual places at the fair. It was wonderful being out and about with people again.

While at the farm, she could ride, which she did for most of the last morning they were there. Michael had bought a beautiful brown Morgan, and Mary Ann climbed on him and did not want to get off. He was fast and attentive, and Mary Ann had tears in her eyes when she kissed him goodbye.

On the way home, sadness seeped through Mary Ann and held on like glue. She thought about the feel, smell, and friendship of the horses. She could still smell the Morgan she had been privileged to ride. She had given all that up because they could not afford a horse. She looked over at Abram and then at Martha, pushed the sadness down into her heart and replaced it with joy for the two people in her life she loved more than anything else in the world. She would be happy with her family. By fall, she was busy preparing items to sell for Christmas. Martha was squealing at the sight of the Christmas tree, and they all looked forward to Christmas morning.

After they had opened their presents and eaten Christmas breakfast, Abram asked Mary Ann to come outside to the barn with him. He said he needed help with something. "But Abram, Martha is just going down for her nap. Can't it wait?"

"No, dear, I am afraid it can't." He lifted Martha and began to put her jacket and hat on. "Now, get your jacket and come outside and help me." Mary Ann was not happy. She grabbed her hat and followed Abram, mumbling that he couldn't do anything by himself. They rounded the corner of the barn. Mary Ann looked up from the ground and standing not fifteen feet from her was the magnificent Morgan she had ridden at the farm. "Wha…. What?" She looked at Abram questioningly.

"He is yours."

"What? What? Mine? What do you mean? He is Michael's horse." "No. He never was. I bought him for you."

"You bought… you bought me a horse?" Mary Ann could barely speak. Pulling herself together for a moment, looking in the horse's eyes, she knew he recognized her. "Oh, Abram, he knows me. He remembers me!" She shouted, and then she raced to him, wrapped her arms around him and cried. Abram smiled, not knowing if the horse could really remember but accepting that Mary Ann knew. He felt that familiar warmth spread through him as he watched her. He smiled as he saw her face shine with joy. He had saddled the Morgan, and she already had her foot in the stirrup swinging her leg over his back to mount him.

Finally, Martha's giggles and screams, "Horsy, horsy," broke through Mary Ann's dream, and she looked at Martha and Abram.

"But, Abram, how? This is a Morgan. I know how much they cost."

"It is impolite to talk about the cost of a Christmas gift."

"Oh my, yes. Well, thank you, Abram, thank you so much."

"You are welcome. I will take Martha in for her nap. Now, off with you, girl. You ride." And she did, every evening when Abram came home. As Martha grew, on many afternoons, neighbors saw the magnificent brown horse carrying the two through the fields, down the dirt road, and along the woods of the Susquehanna River.

One night in early January, much to Abram's protests, Mary Ann attended the town meeting. Abram had gone to a few, but he did not like the bickering and preferred to stay out of politics. When Mary Ann walked through the door at the first meeting, all eyes followed her as she pulled up a chair and sat against the far wall. When the meeting opened, the first item addressed the woman in the room. "Ah, Mary Ann," the chairman said, "this is a meeting for men only."

"I know," she replied, still sitting. "Well, you mean, you want to stay?" "Yes."

There was much murmuring among the men, and finally Norman Bissell spoke, "She wants to stay. I say we let her." There was more murmuring, and then the chairperson ordered them to take a vote. Several men voted no, but the majority voted yes with the stipulation that she could not vote or speak in the meeting. By the third meeting, she was voicing her opinion, and by the sixth meeting, the men were listening to her.

It was after one of these meetings, on the way home, that the idea of opening a business occurred to her. She did well at the fair selling her clothing. Several of those men at the town meeting were in business. Several were well- off. Perhaps they would buy suits instead of having their wives make them. Some of them had several children, and wives did not have the time to make enough clothing for the whole family. That night she and Abram talked over the idea, and so her tailoring and fabric business began the next month out of their home. The business grew, and soon she opened a shop in town.

When Martha was thirteen years old and working in the store with her mother, she asked, "Mom, why don't we ever go see your family? Don't I have grandparents and aunts and uncles like my friends?"

"Yes, Martha, and some day we will meet them. They live so far away in the mountains, and we just haven't had time," Mary Ann lied. She had known this would come up one day. She knew she needed to tell Martha about her relatives, but she did not want her to meet them, so she continued to hide the truth from her.

"Right, but you get letters from a John Rice. Why doesn't he come to visit?"

"He has a family and works hard." "But...."

"That will be enough, Martha."

"Okay, mom, but I'm going to meet my family someday."

"I'm sure you will, sweetheart. I'm sure you will." Martha was a beauty like her mother with dark hair and piercing blue eyes. She was small boned like her dad and was beginning to attract stares and smiles from the local boys. Abram noticed and put a stop to it right away. Martha's best friend was the boy next door, and Abram had the talk with him when he and Martha turned fifteen: There would be no hanky panky with his daughter. Young Bradley Turner nodded, rendered speechless by Abram's deadly stare. He stayed away for a while until Martha complained so vehemently that Abram invited the boy to supper. After that, he was a fixture in the Rice household. Martha and her mother continued to run the business and soon hired Bradley to deliver their products throughout town. Sometimes people came from out of town to be fitted and they had to pick up their own.

One such out of towner was Susan Fenimore Cooper, James Fenimore Cooper's daughter. The Cooper family was wealthy. Susan's grandfather had founded Cooperstown, a town close to Milford, and her father's books were selling well all over the country. He had died; Susan continued to write, becoming locally popular. She also attended university and library events to speak about her father. On this day, Susan and Mary Ann were both at a meeting to discuss the new railroad coming into the area. There were only three women in the meeting. Mary Ann drove her horse and buggy to the meeting. She walked through the door and sat in one of the back rows. A few minutes later, another woman came in and sat beside her. This is how Mary Ann met Susan. After the meeting, they talked, and

Susan requisitioned a fitting from Mary Ann. All the way home as Mary Ann guided her horse down the road, she was elated. Not only did it look like the railway was going to go through, but James Fenimore Cooper's daughter was coming to her home to be fitted. Her business was successful, which was a blessing since a short time later the iron mines closed and Abram lost his job. He began to help in the shop, expanding their delivery business. He also managed their small farm and began making and selling bullets and muskets. Their family was thriving, and though both sometimes felt the prick of pain in their heart for their loved ones, they never stopped loving each other or their decision to leave that night so many years ago.

# 28

## THE WINTER OF 1880

IT HAPPENED IN the dead of winter in 1880, a winter Mary Ann Keller would not see coming. Christmas was always celebrated at the Rice house with the three of them going into the woods to cut the tree. Abram would wait until the two women could decide on just the right tree, and he would chop it down and haul it into the house. Mary Ann and Martha would decorate it with popcorn and cranberries picked from the shores of the river. "You know, Martha, we never had a Christmas tree," Mary Ann remarked one night when they were knitting together and admiring the tree.

"Really."

"Really. I don't know if they do now, but it was not popular back then; besides, no one could afford decorations or even had room for a tree in the house."

"Oh, were you poor?"

"No, not as poor as most of our neighbors, but most of the neighbors that stayed were poor. We all lived off the game we could trap or shoot and whatever we could grow, which was meagre some years. We are blessed to have what we have here. Your father has done well."

"And so have you." Martha admired her mother, who could still take down a bear with a single shot, ride like no one she had seen before, come home, fix dinner, mend socks, and speak like a politician at the town meetings. When Martha was young, Abram would sit in the oak rocker at night and tell her stories of the place called Long Lake. She heard about sugaring, fishing, hunting, and his good friend Lysander Hall who was always in one scrape or the other. He told her about the Abenaki, Mitchel Sabattis. He told her about the Scotts, the Plumleys, and how Mary Ann saved a life one day. "But who did she save, dad? Was it one of your friends' daughters?"

Mary Ann and Abram would glance at each other, and he would move on with the story. Martha knew that meant he did not want to talk about such things, and that happened whenever she asked about his family. She would look at her mother who sat in the other rocker sewing her rag rugs or knitting and interject an "um hmm" or "now, Abram, that is not exactly how it went...."

The years rolled by, and now Martha was in her twenties and had turned down the boy next door and two others for marriage. Instead, she lived at home running the tailor shop full time. She and her mother were spending more and more time in local politics while Mary Ann pursued her right to vote. Though Milford let her participate in the town meeting, they still did not allow her to vote. Mary Ann read newspaper articles like the one about Virginia Monora of Missouri who registered to vote, was denied, and sued the registrar. The registrar had rejected her application, so Virginia sued, charging the registrar with violation of the fourteenth amendment stating that the citizenship had the right to vote. Virginia did not win, but Mary Ann saw it coming. What she did not see coming began in January of 1880.

It was a Tuesday morning during the January thaw that a man who had recently visited relatives in Philadelphia came into the shop. Martha fitted him for a new suit. He was anxious for Martha to finish because he had a head-ache and wanted to leave to take some powder for the pain. She quickly finished up, and by the time the man left, he looked quite ill.

What Martha did not know was that two days later that man was dead from heart failure. Three days later, Martha woke up with a sore throat. She took some powder, but it had no effect. When she came into the kitchen that morning Mary Ann noticed that Martha did not look well. "Martha are you okay?" she asked at breakfast.

"I think so. It's just a sore throat and headache. I guess I caught a cold. I took some powder for it."

"Well, why don't you take today off? Your father and I will run the shop. Go lie down." Martha did not argue. She was more tired than she ever remembered, so she went to her bed immediately and fell asleep. Mary Ann told Abram, so they opened the shop together. At 11:00, he went in to check on his daughter. She was still asleep. "Martha," he whispered in her ear. She turned onto her back and looked at him. Abram's mouth fell open, and then quickly he regained composure and asked, "How are you?"

"Not too good, dad. I think I have a fever."

He put his hand on her forehead. It was so hot he just sat there with his mouth open. Martha's eyes closed. "Uh, honey, I'll get your mom." Martha groaned. Abram rushed out into the kitchen. "Mary Ann, come quick. She is burning up!"

Mary Ann came in, took one look at her daughter, and said to Abram, "She needs a doctor." She had recently read about an illness that had descended upon Philadelphia and New York City. There were no cases of it around Milford, but this was it. It was called Yellow Fever, and it was deadly. Oh Lord, she thought, please don't let it be that; please let it be a bad cold. Abram rode out to the doc's house, but his wife reported that he had gone to Albany to a meeting. He would be back the next afternoon. In the meantime, the doctor's wife assured Abram it was not Yellow Fever since it was the middle of winter and there were no mosquitos in the area. "What are her symptoms?" "She has a sore throat and fever."

"Is there a rash?" "No, don't think so."

"Well, she probably has that grippe that is going around now. Keep her warm. Give her chicken broth, and as soon as he comes in, I will send him over."

By the time the doc came to the house it was early evening the next day. Martha's fever was raging. She had a red tongue and a rash on her stomach, and her throat was worse. Doc examined her and went out to the kitchen where her mother and father were waiting. "What is it, Doc? I know she's worse," Mary Ann said. "I've been putting cold cloths on her head, and I thought the fever was down, but now it is back up."

"I'm afraid she has scarlet fever," Doc said, shaking his head.

"Scarlet fever, but only children get that," Mary Ann replied, her face and eyes scrunched up in worry.

"No, no, that isn't so, Mary Ann. Many adults get it too, and you two need to be careful."

"What can we do?" Mary Ann asked.

"Well, nothing more than you are already doing. Keep her warm. Give her water and pray that her fever breaks."

Abram and Mary Ann took turns throughout the night keeping vigil over their daughter, but it would not be enough. Four days later in the early morning hours, Martha took her last breath. She was only twenty-six years old and had so much to live for. Abram and Mary Ann were devastated. A week ago, they were laughing and tending the shop. Now, she was gone from a disease that many people did not die from; however, some did, but Mary Ann could not understand why it had to take her daughter. They buried her under her favorite tree, the elm at the end of the path coming from the field. Most of the town came for the ceremony, and all the women brought food. Mary Ann felt angry that all these people were coming and going. She wanted to be alone. She wanted to be on Babe in Long Lake. She wanted to ride up Sawmill Road. She wanted to be anyplace but here.

Abram suggested she write home. That would make her feel better. The following week she sat down and wrote to her sister, Sarah, and told her what had happened. Of all her siblings, she wondered why she wrote to Sarah, who would not write back. Then she realized it was because before she fell in love with Abram, and after her mother died, Sarah had been the one she ran to, the one she talked to, the one who took charge. She wished Sarah could take charge now and heal the pain that pierced her heart. Two weeks later, she received a reply. Sarah wrote that she was so sorry for her loss. John and Melvina sent cards and asked her to come for a visit. Sarah did not.

# 29

## THE VISIT

IN APRIL, ABRAM convinced Mary Ann to go home for a visit, so on an overcast Monday with dark dotted snow clinging to the sides of the dirt road, they began their trek back to Long Lake. They drove their surrey to Utica, left it at the livery station, and boarded the train to North Creek. It was a frightening and exciting ride as neither Abram nor Mary Ann had ever been on a train. They couldn't believe how fast it went and how loud the train whistle was when they approached the crossings. The train stopped quite often to take wood from the car behind the engine and feed the furnace. Mary Ann liked the smell of the wood-burning engines. However, the kerosene lamps began making her sick halfway through the trip. She wished they had taken the stage the whole way. The sickness passed, and by the time they pulled into Saratoga she was feeling better.

The next trek took them to North Creek where they bought a ticket for the stage for the last jaunt of the journey. That night, they stayed in Aiden Laird in Minerva. Tomorrow they would be in Long Lake. Mary Ann hoped her sister would receive her. Going home would be good for her because she loved the woods but being shunned would add to her grief. She now wished she had brought Martha home to meet her relatives. They had never told their daughter that the two of them were not married or that Abram was married to someone else. Mary Ann always thought she would tell her later when Martha had children. That was not to be. It seemed like it happened so fast. She was a young woman, laughing and happy, one day and gone a few days later. Tears brimmed her eyes and began rolling down her cheeks. She took out her handkerchief and dotted it off her cheeks before Abram saw. He had held her night after night while she cried. He thought the crying was over, and it mostly was. Mary Ann did not want to burden him anymore and Abram did not want to burden Mary Ann, but for the past two weeks, he had been feeling poorly. He felt tired and strangely dizzy at times. Luckily, it came and went so he could make this trip for Mary Ann. He would see the doctor when they returned.

Instead, both of them focused on the beautiful woods they grew up in. The sound of the Big Brook creek in the spring when it sped down the mountain like an unstoppable freight train. Mary Ann knew, the first place she would go was into the woods. The snow would still be deep up there, and the town would smell like syrup. She wondered if they still had the sugaring party in town. She could still smell the sweet scent of the maple syrup as it cut through the cold mountain air. How had the community changed? She knew that there were now many wood-framed houses, Stephen Lamos had a mill on the Carthage Road, and Mitchel Sabattis now ran a tourist place on the Carthage Road. Mary Ann knew because her sister, Almina, and Abram's children, Melvina and John, wrote to keep them informed about the goings on in town.

Mary Ann thought back to those days when Mitchel and Abram would drink ale instead of work. It did not look like either of them was going anywhere. Now Mitchel owned acres of land around the town, and she and Abram were successful merchants able to afford train travel.

The whole town knew they were coming. As they approached Shaw Pond, their eyes were drawn to the left; perched majestically behind the pond was Robert Shaw's new boarding house. "Oh my, that house is magnificent," Mary Ann gasped. She thought about her friend, Mary Sargent, who had been so enamored by Robert Shaw and wondered whether this would have been her house had she lived.

When Mary Ann and Abram looked out the stagecoach window as they came into town from Newcomb, they saw men digging steps into the dirt bank just past the new house that Benjamin and Lavonia Emerson had built. One of the men was slender with black hair poking out from under his cap. "Oh my gosh, that is John. Abram, look." Mary Ann pointed out the stage window.

"You are right. It is," Abram said as he felt his heart move in his chest. His little boy was now a man.

Mary Ann yelled, "John!" and waved.

John Rice stopped his shoveling, turned around, and seeing the coach, waved back. He dropped his shovel and ran to catch the stage when it stopped at the Long Lake Hotel. As Mary Ann stepped down from the stage, John ran up to her. "John, it is so good to see you."

"You too." Just then Abram stepped down and saw his son. He didn't know whether to shake hands or hug him or just nod his head. John, being John, rushed up to his father and hugged him. Abram breathed a sigh of relief and hugged his son.

Soon Robert and Gitty Shaw came across the street. Robert had built a house across from the hotel. He had rented out the Long Lake Hotel to Henry Austin. "Well, hello," Robert said as he greeted the two.

"Hello," Mary Ann said, "your house on the pond is beautiful."

"Thank you. We heard about your loss and are so sorry," Robert said. "We have been praying for you."

"Thank you," Abram said and then to change the way this was going, he asked, "What are they building back there, John?"

"It's Bill Stanton's house. He built it a couple of years ago. We are helping him shore up the bank because it started crumbling last fall."

"Nice view up on that hill."

"Right, you can see all the way down the lake."

Abram heard the buckboard in the distance. "Oh, here comes Josiah now."

"You are staying over at the Houghton place in Big Brook?" "Yes," Mary Ann replied.

"Hey, you two. I've come to pick you up. Melvina has supper on, so we'd better get you back. John, Robert." Josiah tipped his hat. "Afternoon, Josiah. How's everything up your way?"

"Oh, good. Garden's doing good this year. I noticed on the way over, the Lake House already has guests."

"Ya, some sports came up early to go out fishing with Jeremiah Plumley and Farrand Austin."

"Yup." Josiah stepped down, grabbed Mary Ann's trunk, and loaded it onto the wagon while Abram loaded a second bag. They climbed onto the buckboard seat with Josiah. He clucked to the horses, lifted the reins, and they were headed north for the big hill with the sharp left curve at the bottom.

John Rice turned and began climbing back up the hill where he was digging, back to his job building, repairing, and doing whatever needed to be done around town. He wondered how his father and Mary Ann would be treated this time.

Josiah Houghton stayed silent on the ride across the water on the wooden raft that ferried them from the east bank to the west bank of the river. Once off the raft, they continued hearing only the steady clip clop of the horseshoes on the packed dirt road. The silence was awkward, and Abram was glad when they turned into Josiah's farm and saw Melvina running out to greet them.

"Thanks for coming to get us, Josiah," Abram said. Josiah nodded his head, stepped down, and began unhooking the horses to put them in for the day. Over dinner that night, Mary Ann told them that she would love to ride while she was here. "I know Babe passed, but I understand she had a colt."

"That she did, and we just happen to have her out in the barn." After dinner, Mary Ann ran to the barn and found the colt. They had named her Babe II. Mary Ann approached her and was amazed that she had the same white marking on her forehead as her mother. The next morning Mary Ann saddled up Babe II and led her to the family home on the trail between the barn and Big Brook where old Babe was buried. Sawmill Road was now smooth and well packed. She guided Babe II down the path, watching the dew roll off the river. She breathed in the cool mountain air and felt the old familiar peace flow through her body. She was home. She would always love these mountains. She looked at the large mountain now called Kempshall, the giant dome she had seen every morning on her way to school, sometimes clothed in morning fog, sometimes topped with snow gleaming like a king's crown against the rising sun, sometimes silhouetted in a blazing red sunset. She prayed to God to lift the sorrow that weighed her down. The sorrow of losing her beautiful daughter, the sorrow of never having another child. The sorrow of giving up this place for love. She thought of Abram and their life together. It was good. Even God would have to see that. She would not regret leaving here, only hurting her sister. She looked over at the dark water, so quiet today. This was dawn and dusk water, so smooth it looked like she could step on it. The reflection of the giant pines lay upon the glassy surface. God, she prayed, please forgive me for hurting my sister, and if it be your will, let us one day come together as sisters.

She heard the whisper of the wind shuffling through the pine boughs chasing the scent of balsam into the air. She heard the squirrels and chipmunks scampering among the dry leaves. She envisioned her and Abram building a small house right here at the end of the lake near the hermit on the ridge or on Clear Lake where the Rutherfords lived. Through the years many dinners had turned into their dream talks of moving back home. They both still called it home. Abram missed the mountains too. They sometimes talked into the night about selling the business and their farm and moving back up here. Businesses were coming into the town. Peddlers were making their rounds. Why couldn't they join in the fray opening a small store or delivering items to each house. Of course, they knew this was a dream. The town would not accept them together, and they would never live apart. At first the excitement of being there would outweigh the shunning, but would anyone even come into their business? How long would it be before the pain of seeing the cold stares brought them to a place of sadness?

Mary Ann turned Babe II around and headed back up the road giving her memories, dreams, and prayers over to the great forested mountain behind her.

It was the day after her ride. It was the day Abram had gone to help Isaac Sabattis with some planting. The sun was blanketing the field in front of the Houghton house when two figures crested the hill, turned left, and began walking up the driveway. "We have company coming," Mary Ann announced. Melvina's youngest, John, just home for lunch from school, came running to the door. He always wanted to know who was coming and always wanted to greet them. Mary Ann squinted her eyes and put one hand over them to block the sun, but she still could not see who the two figures were other than they wore dresses. Suddenly, John shouted, "Oh, its Aunt Sarah and Aunt Amelia."

Mary Ann turned to Melvina, "Does Sarah know I am here?" "Of course," Melvina replied.

"Did you know she was coming here?"

"Of course," Melvina replied. By this time, the two women had reached the porch. Melvina and Sarah stepped onto the porch, and Melvina greeted them. Mary Ann felt hot and cold at the same time. She could not move. Fear and shame coated her. She stared at Sarah and tried to read what to do. Almina left Sarah at the bottom of the steps, rushed up the steps, and threw her arms around Mary Ann. "Welcome home, Mary Ann. I am so sorry about Martha."

Tears began to well up in Mary Ann's eyes. She hugged her sister back and whispered, "Thank you. It's good to be home." When Almina pulled away, Mary Ann looked up and was staring straight into Sarah's dark eyes. Sarah had moved up onto the porch and was standing behind Almina.

She looked at Mary Ann and said, "Mary, I am so sorry. So sorry for your loss." She reached out her arms and gathered Mary Ann into them and began hugging her. "Oh, my Lord, Sarah. Thank you. Thank you for that." She began to cry as they hugged, her face buried in her sister's shoulder. It was as if she had never left. She was a child crying on Sarah's shoulder as her big sister comforted her.

Sarah loosened her hug, took a handkerchief out of her pocket, and handed it to Mary Ann. Then she said, "Mary Ann, come with me." The two walked down the road to the Keller homestead heading over to the beautiful gravesite of their mom, dad, young Abram, and Almira, who had passed in the winter of 1869. Sitting on the bench David Keller had made, the two sisters cried and talked. Mary Ann told her sister how sorry she was to have hurt her like that. Sarah looked Mary Ann straight in the face and said, "Mary Ann, I want you to know that I will never forgive Abram. I just cannot, but you are blood, and you were young, so I am beginning to forgive you." It was while sitting on that bench with her sister that Mary Ann revealed her biggest fear. Abram had not fooled her for an instant. She saw how he struggled lifting the suitcases onto the carriage, how he walked bent and slow up the hill on his way home, and how he struggled to breathe at times. "Sarah, I understand how you feel about Abram, but I think he is not well and is hiding it from me. He refuses to go to a doctor and blames it all on getting old."

"Mary Ann, it may well be that. I know I have slowed down as the years go by. You are much younger than us, so it may be hard for you to understand. I am sure he is fine." Mary Ann listened to her sister. She was probably right. Sarah was moving much slower too as they walked back up the hill.

Three days later when Abram and Mary Ann stepped up on their carriage to ride home, the Keller and Rice families were there to see them off. Sarah was not. Several towns-people waved as the stagecoach passed them by. The town was growing not only physically and financially, but also spiritually as echoes of children's laughter and the spirit of the winds dusted the little settlement taming heathens and healing souls.

# 30

## HOTELS, BRIDGES, AND HOMECOMING

THE RIVER STILL divided the settlement, which grew between the Carthage Road on the east side and the road from Zenas Parker's on past the Kellers on the west side of the lake. They used log rafts to transport animals, linens, lumber, and other items from one side of the lake to the other. They also continued to travel by canoe in the warm months and horse and sleigh in the winter months. When the ice froze over, there was more visiting done—more knitting circles, more games such as fox and geese played by children on the lake, and more transporting goods from one side to the other. As the town grew, it became harder to wait until winter to do these tasks.

Isaac Robinson owned the land across from the Lake House down to the road going into Zenas Parker's farm. He built a sawmill on the fast-moving creek that ran down the hill a mile west of the western shore of the lake. During the first ten years of the settlement, the men had thrown large logs across the swamp-like part of the lake to walk from the east to the west side. However, these were only used for walking across the lake and transporting items by pack basket. The logs were not stable enough to drive a cart over, and each year, some logs disappeared beneath the waters or rotted so badly they sank to the bottom of the lake. The new sawmill created a problem for builders and businesses struggling to get across the lake to the sawmill. With a bridge, they could bring their wagons.

Therefore, at the February 1880 town meeting, with Superintendents Benjamin Emerson and Charles Hanmer, the men voted to join the east and west sides of the lake building a real bridge. They voted to raise $3,000 to build the bridge from the east shore of the Kellogg Lake House to Pine Island and from there to the west shore of the Robinson property.

Figure 4 First log bridge

Figure 5 First float bridge and Lake House around 1870

In the Adirondacks. Kellogg's Lake House, Long Lake.

Figure 6 Plank Bridge 1880

Figure 7 Robinson Mill and farm. Sawmill Road that
continued past the Keller farm, on the left.

The town did not have the money to improve the roads;
however, the community was moving away from farming
and into serving the sports, so all eyes began to focus on
transportation. They traveled by water in boats made by
Alba Cole, Mitchel Sabattis, Caleb Chase, Ransom Palmer,
and newcomer George Smith.

One day while paddling with his brother-in-law, Mitchel
Sabattis, Henry Dornburgh began looking at the bluff on
the east side of the lake behind Mitchel's boarding house
called Sabattis House and Garden. "You know, Mitchel,
that is one beautiful spot." He pointed over to the piece of
land that jutted out into the lake.

"Yes, I know. Kind of wish I had built my place there, but
thought I needed it to be on the Carthage Road."

"I know, makes sense," Henry replied. That night he
lay awake all-night thinking about that view and what he

could do with that property. The next day Henry called his wife Phoebe and son William into a meeting. After they were all seated around the kitchen table, Henry began to tell them what he had been thinking all night. He was a builder, and he told them about the property and now that tourists were coming to the Adirondacks, he could build a beautiful place for them to stay with golf, swimming, boating, and even skiing across the road in the winter. They questioned whether he could afford to build what he was talking about; when he assured him that he could, Phoebe set up a meeting with her father, Robert Shaw, Henry, and Mitchel. By now, Robert Shaw had legal as well as medical and religious knowledge.

"You know, Henry, this project looks expensive," Robert cautioned, "your plans show it will be fancier than anything around here." Granted, tourists and sports were now coming into town. Mitchel and Caleb Chase could barely keep up with the boat building. Even with the Austins and Coles also building boats, they were all kept busy. However, most of the people coming were men wanting to hunt and fish. They did not care about a grand hotel. They wanted to be out in the woods sleeping under the trees and eating the day's catch.

"Yes, I know it will be expensive. That is my intent—to have the fanciest summer hotel in these parts. We will advertise down in the city to bring those rich folks up here."

Mitchel stepped back, thought for a moment, and said, "But Henry, most of the people that come here are men who hunt and fish. They don't care about fancy. They have fancy in their homes. They want to sleep under the balsams, eat their catch of the day over a campfire, or take a deer rack back to the city to show their friends."

"Right, Mitchel, but times are changing, and you aren't keeping up. The women are starting to come. The wives could stay here while their husbands hunt."

"Uh huh," Mitchel thought about the sports he guided, and most of them did not want their wives with them when they came out of the woods smelling as they did; they wanted to spend the night drinking ale at the bar, but he said no more. He sold the land and watched as Phoebe halfway through the project began fretting over money. They ran out of money before it was built and finally sold it to a man named Edmund Butler.

Soon, the building of the great Sagamore Hotel sprang into action. Edmund Butler was a shrewd businessman who teamed up with guides such as Jeremiah and John Plumley, Jerome Woods, the Austins, and the Sabattis sons to cater to sports and the wealthy clients from the city. He built several cabins to house the help and built a barn at the bottom of the hill on Sagamore Road next to Calvin Towns. It housed the horses that clients could ride for a fee. He hired young people from town to work at the hotel. Addie Scott and Maryann Houghton began working at the hotel along with Henry Duane, son of Alex, and two of the Cole girls.

The help was to always call him Mr. Butler, and they were required to wear uniforms. At first, the hotel struggled.

Calvin Towns recalled the travel past his house the first summer. There were few surreys or stagecoaches traveling the road. The Lake House, The Long Lake Hotel, Palmers,' Mitchel's hotel up the road, and John Plumley's new place between Mitchel's and old William Helms's hotel past the falls on Carthage Road were beginning to boom, but the Sagamore remained quiet. However, soon the carriages rumbled along Carthage Road, guide boats toted guests to the village, and the Sagamore was bustling with business. The new golf course provided ample exercise for its guests as the course ran up the steep hill across from the Sagamore and back down the other side. Guests blanketed the beach, and the church offered ice cream socials. There was plenty of work, and the great hotel employed half the town. It became the pride of the village and beyond. Soon even winter visitors were arriving by sleigh with their fur blankets and hot coal foot warmers. They began skiing on the hill, and the hotels cleared the lake for skating. Christmas was a joyful time to spend in Long Lake with mammoth Christmas trees adorning the large rooms in the hotels and boarding houses.

Adolphus LeBlanc, newcomer from Canada, bustled in, opening the first barber shop. Young Orville Cole, his brother Melvin, their cousin Irving, Earl Plumley, and Arthur and Inez Cary gathered across from the Hanmer Store to play fox and geese in the winter snow and stickball in the summer. Three-year- old Hamor Houghton, son of Josiah and new wife Lydia Parker, made snowballs outside his home, and Hampton LaPelle laughed and screamed as he slid down the hill across from Joe Sullivan's on Maple Avenue. Life was improving in the little town as more people began to stay and send their children to school. Places began to pop up on the north end of the lake, and tourists were delighted to stay at Plumley Point in the new lodge that faced Buck Mountain.

On this day, fourteen-year-old Annie Scott paddled her canoe past the Sagamore Hotel, under the bridge, to a tiny sand beach two miles north of the bridge on the east side where the Lamoses lived. Since the Tarbell family moved in and built on the big hill, people began calling it Tarbell Hill Road. Annie had agreed to meet Wallace Plumley here. She got out of her boat and looked around. Her heart was racing. She waited. He did not show. She called quietly, "Wallace." No one answered. She waited another ten minutes, but still Wallace Plumley did not come. She decided that she would never agree to meet him again. After calling out one more time, she crawled back into her canoe and started to sit down. Suddenly, a twig cracked, loud in the silent air. She looked up, expecting to see Wallace and give him a piece of her mind. Instead, she saw Mary Ann Keller.

"Mary Ann, what are you doing here? "Oh, I come here sometimes to think." "But I didn't even know you were home."

"I came home two days ago. I'm staying at Melvina's until I get a place." "But, where, where is Abram?" Annie didn't know whether to get out of the boat and join her or say goodbye and paddle away. She had not known Mary Ann well. She knew the gossip, and she knew about her riding and shooting skills.

"He is gone."

"Gone where?" Annie was trying to understand. Did she mean gone hunting or gone away for a while?

"Annie, Abram died a month ago."

"What? Oh, I am so sorry. I didn't know." She stepped out of the boat and reached out to Mary Ann, giving her a short hug.

"Thank you."

"You two were just here not that long ago."

"I know, Annie, It was sudden. He had been having trouble breathing and feeling tired. I had made an appointment with the doctor, but he got up on a Tuesday morning, went out to the barn to feed the horse and didn't come back. I went out and found him lying in the meadow. The doctor said it was a massive heart attack and he would have died instantly. "Oh my Lord, Mary Ann, how awful. I have heard nothing. When is the service?

He wanted to be buried down there. He always felt ashamed of what he did to his family. You know?" "Yes, but…."

"That is what he wanted. He is buried with our daughter."

"So sorry, Mary Ann."

"I guess some people would say it is payback for what I did."

"Oh my, I don't believe that. God wouldn't kill innocent people like your daughter."

"Guess you are right," Mary Ann said.

"So, is this your favorite spot?" Annie asked.

"No, my favorite spot is at the end of the lake by the old Bowen shack on that beach."

"Oh, right, down past Frank Plumley's property." "Yes."

Annie thought for a moment and then said, "Hey, if you aren't doing anything, want to come with me down to the beach in a couple of hours?"

Mary Ann hesitated and then realized that she needed a friend in this town. "Uh, sure."

"Okay. Meet me on the shore of Keller Bay."

"Okay, I'll be there. They waved goodbye as each of them paddled to their home. They did meet, and Annie being Annie had a reason for the trip besides getting to know Mary Ann better. Just before they reached the Plumley property halfway to the beach on the east side of the lake, Annie said to Mary Ann, "I need to stop off here for minute. Is that okay with you?"

"Sure." She had heard that young Wallace Plumley had been sweet on Annie since they were children. The path between the house of her grandparents, John and Jenny Scott, and the old cabin of his parents, John and Zebedia Plumley, was well worn from the children meeting to play cowboys and Indians in the woods, go fishing, or climb a favorite tree. On several occasions, Mary Ann, her sisters, and brothers had traveled that path to meet up with one another. She also knew that Wallace's older brother, Frank, owned this place, so Wallace would surely be here. When they arrived, they pulled the boat up on shore. Wallace came running out of the thicket, his black hair blowing straight up in the air. "Saw you coming. Annie, I'm sorry. Frank wouldn't let me go. I had to do chores. I tried."

"And I waited. Wallace, don't make plans with me any- more if you won't come."

"But I tried...uh, Mary Ann, haven't seen you in a long while. So sorry to hear about your daughter."

"Thank you, Wallace. I'll leave you two alone and go up and see Margaret. Annie don't be too hard on him. There is something to be said for a young man doing chores and helping his ma."

"Right, Annie. Come on, forgive me?" Wallace put his arm around her shoulders.

Annie looked up at him, smiled, and said, "This time, Wallace, but just this time."

Mary Ann went up to the lodge and said hello to Mrs. Plumley. Luckily, Frank was out delivering a lodge guest back to Kellogg's Lake Hotel.

A few minutes later, Annie came up to the lodge, "Mary Ann, you ready?"

She said goodbye to Margaret and ambled on down the path toward the lake. She remembered the numerous times she and Abram had come down here fishing. She remembered his laughter and the way he moved about in the canoe almost tipping it over several times. She smiled and thought, Abram was never fit for this land. He wasn't a great hunter, trapper, or fisherman. She was thinking that moving away was the best thing that happened to him because he was able to have the store and do what he did best, which was business.

"Okay," Mary Ann replied. They hopped in the boat, turned northwest, and landed on Bowen's beach thirty minutes later. "Wow, Annie, do you remember old Mr. Bowen?

"No, I don't. I was too young."

"He was a kind man, kind of knew things that were going to happen and would listen to people."

"Did he know about you and Abram?" Annie hesitated to ask such a question since she didn't know how Mary Ann would respond, but Annie Scott was a girl who needed to know things. "Oh, I am sorry. Maybe that was too personal."

"No, not at all. I went through all that humiliation when I came for Abram Jr.'s funeral and then when I came back after my daughter died. I am beyond that now. Besides, I promised Abram I would be myself and face whatever comes my way like the hunter that I am, and, yes, Mr. Bowen knew about us. He let me share my pain and frustration with him. He was a kind man. I wish he were still here." They investigated the little shack he had built on the shore of this great river. It was big enough for two people, and Mary Ann remembered sitting on the log that served as a bench for the table. They would drink tea and talk, and she always felt happy when she left. So many people in her life were gone. She felt a sadness seep through her that hurt to the bone.

Annie saw it, put her hand on Mary Ann's arm, and pulled her away from the place. "Let's explore the woods, Mary Ann. I heard there are ponds here, three they say, but I have never seen them."

Mary Ann looked up at this kind young girl. "Sure, let's go, Annie. There are three lakes here. They are called Anthony Ponds after the first man that came here to live in the summer, and I have something else I want to show you. She started off into the woods."

"Hey, hold up," Annie shouted as she tried to keep up. Mary Ann stopped on the old military road that ran through the woods between Anthony Pond and the Bowen cabin. She turned, waiting for Annie to catch up, and then began pulling branches off the side of the road.

"What are you doing?" Annie gasped trying to catch her breath.

"I want to show you something the hermit showed me. Annie finally made it to Mary Ann. She looked down and there sitting in the muck was an old black cannon.

"Is that what I think it is?"

"A cannon. Yup. Mr. Bowen showed it to me many years ago. He didn't want anyone knowing it was here. He thought it would bring people down here invading his privacy."

"But what would a cannon be doing here?" Why would soldiers of the

Civil War bring a canon into the Adirondacks. It didn't make sense.

"Want to hear the story?"

"Sure. Let's sit down." They sat down on the old log next to the cannon. "Well, supposedly, after the Revolutionary War, a man named Sir John Johnson, a loyalist from Johnstown, was being tracked by General Schuyler, a Patriot. Sir John had fought against the Revolutionists. Now, after the Patriots' victory, Loyalists were tracked down, jailed, tarred, and feathered and their land confiscated. The news spread that John was being targeted. He gathered several men and headed for Canada as did many other Loyalists. The usual route to Canada was down the Hudson, into Lake George to Lake Champlain, and then into Canada. However, he did not take that well-known route for obvious reasons.

"Right," Annie was completely spellbound by this story. "So, what time of year was it?"

"They started in May of 1776." "Oh, so at least good weather."

"Usually other than mud, but not this May. Anyway, they decided to go through the lakes, ponds, and rivers of the Adirondack forest. They would go down the Indian trail from Johnstown to the Sacandaga River where John's father had a summer place. They would rest there then follow the trails along the Sacandaga River into uncharted wilderness. The week before, they had a terrible snowstorm so they would have to travel on snowshoes over melting snow. They brought two small cannons. These cannons were called Patteroes, and the men carried them on sleds following their Mohawk guides. By the end of May, they had made it to Raquette Lake where they left their snowshoes. They were now a burden since the snow had melted away. They left them in a pile in that little settlement.

"Oh, so Raquette Lake. I get it."

"Right, from there, of course, they came up the river. The journey was long, and the forests were thick with blow down. They were not used to traveling over such rugged territory. Some turned back. Some starved, and some staggered on. They built rafts and loaded their equipment onto the rafts floating them up this part of the river. No one knows why they left the cannons except that they figured they were close enough to the Canadian border that it made more sense to move quickly, so they buried the cannons in case anyone came through looking for them.

"So, from here, they went north to where?"

According to old Peter Sabattis, Mitchel's father, who said his father was one of the guides tracking Johnson for the colonel, they found these cannons and continued tracking Johnson north up the St. Lawrence, and then he disappeared into Canada."

"So, Johnson escaped?"

"That is the story." Annie looked at her new friend who not long ago looked pale and drawn. Now her dark eyes sparkled, and she was smiling. Annie Scott realized that Mary Ann Keller was back and there would be no stopping her. Annie and Mary Ann became close friends. Annie never became the marksman, guide, and frontier woman Mary Ann was. Instead, she married Wallace Plumley, and they built a tourist business that would coincide with the tailoring business that Mary Ann Keller would soon begin in Long Lake.

# 31

---

## Fire and the Buttercup

No sooner had the Kellogg's Lake House been built than Cyrus Kellogg died, leaving his wife Christine to run it. The Kellogg boys all ran off doing their own things, leaving their mom to fend for herself. Danny Kellogg was moving slowly these days, and only one of Jeff Rutherford's kids was available to help. That was Sadie, who had married one of the Cole boys; she helped when she could. Her brothers Jeff, Isaac, and Ernie had all gone away to school and just came home to visit during the holidays.

This crisis of Cyrus's death that left the management of the hotel solely with Christine Kellogg was solved one fateful summer night by some out-of- town men who were hired to help the locals build the new plank bridge. One night, one of the men who was staying at the hotel called another a liar because he said he hunted with old Michael Wright and shot a deer after Michael had missed it. The other man shouted, "Then you didn't hunt with Michael Wright because he never misses."

"Well, he did this time."

"Right, and just where were you hunting?" Isaac Sabattis yelled.

"Oh, ah, you know, up there on that mountain. Sabattis. Right. It was Sabattis Mountain."

Now Isaac knew the man was lying. Nobody hunted on Sabattis mountain except a Sabattis and someone who had been invited. Wright would not be up there without one of them. "You're lying. I know you're lying."

"Why you," the man growled and took a swing at Isaac. Isaac ducked, then pulled back, doubled his right fist, and punched the man in the eye. He howled for a couple minutes, and then another man jumped in. Within five minutes, the whole place was in the brawl. No one knows how the lantern got knocked over or who knocked it over, but the fire began while the fight was going on, and no one noticed until flames were shooting up to the ceiling. They tried to put it out, but it was too late. The fire fed on the dry wood beams, and within an hour the Lake Hotel was no more.

Luckily, by now the larger, newer Sagamore Hotel was taking in sports. In the meantime, the Adirondacks had caught the eye of some wealthy people like the Vanderbilts, Whitneys, and Durants.

Thomas Durant had made his money in the railroads and built several lodges in the Adirondacks, two being in the neighboring hamlet of Raquette Lake. He saw how bringing the elite from eastern cities to the Adirondack wilderness could mean profits for him. He pulled his son, William, into the project, and William built several residences in Raquette Lake for seasonal tourists. He also began development on a parcel of land on a long point jutting out into the river. He established a post office, named it Durant, and placed himself there as the postmaster. His neighbor Charlie Bennett, who was already there when William arrived, had been Durant's guide. Charlie's brother Ed opened a hotel on the north shore of what he called Long Point. William Durant had stayed there several times, and, like his father, saw the Adirondacks as a potential money-making resort, though travel to the resort was difficult. Many city people would not endure the stage ride up to these mountains, so hotels such as Bennett's remained small and unprofitable.

One morning, William Durant was sitting on his porch at Camp Pine Knot watching the old guide, Alva Dunning, paddle a couple of sports down the river. The water was calm, flowing like a gentle breeze. It was there in the tranquility of the morning sunrise on Raquette Lake that he began to form an idea that would transform these struggling hamlets into busy towns with wealthy women and men spending their money in the hotels and stores. He would put steamboats on all the lakes so the tourists could travel by train to the first lake and then ride the boats to the hotels and lodges in the Adirondacks.

That winter, William began bringing steamboats in over the ice. Soon, the boats were transporting guests as far north as Blue Mountain Lake; when that was finished, William turned his sights to Long Lake. He named a steamboat the Buttercup and decided to moor it at the magnificent Sagamore Hotel. He knew that as soon as the elite saw photos of this building, they would swarm to pay for transportation to the resort.

In 1884, William Durant strutted into the Long Lake town meeting announcing that for a mere $1,000.00 he would dam up the north end of the lake and put his steamship on Long Lake. He went on to say that this ship would transport wealthy people to the stores and hotels on the lake, increasing the businessmen's wealth. One problem with this plan was that it would destroy the guides' livelihood, and several guides were at the meeting.

Charlie Sabattis listened to the rhetoric of the man wearing a fancy suit, tie, and expensive hat; then he spoke up, "And what are us guides supposed to do while your steamboats are cruising down the lake taking our business away?"

William's reply was, "Times are changing, and you need to go along or get left behind. I'm offering you a good deal."

"For you," Robert Shaw snapped as he stood up, "but there is no guarantee we will get that money back because it may not work. Why would people want to travel way up here?"

"Because they are rich, they want adventure, and some of them want to hunt so they would still employ guides."

"But not the tourists, which are more profitable than the sports right now. So, you already have the steamboat ready, I take it?"

"That is correct. I'm docking her at the Sagamore on Monday."

"You can't do that," said Mary Ann Keller, who was sitting next to her brother. She recalled her first meeting in Long Lake soon after she had returned years ago. They let her in, but the men formed a circle after the meeting. She knew they were discussing the best way to exclude her. She marched over and stated, "I live in this town too. I can't legally vote, but there is nothing in the records that says I can't attend the town meetings. I run a business just like the rest of you, and I am not married, so I have no representative; therefore, I'm coming to the meetings." Mary Ann was the only tailor in town. She made their Sunday best suits. She said her piece, turned, and ambled on home. At the next meeting, the men welcomed her, and business went on as usual. Soon, she was able to offer a few words, and then they began listening to her. Much to Mary Ann's delight, this year, her nephew's wife, Pauline Houghton Rice, had attended with her husband James a few times.

William Durant responded to Mary Ann's comment, "Why can't I do that, and who are you?"

"Because we ain't said so," Lysander Hall butted in. "Simple as that." "Right, well I don't really need your money to do it."

"But you do need our vote," Lyman Russell replied. "Maybe."

"Well then maybe we just put it to a vote," Warren Cole managed to interject, thinking of his boatbuilding and guiding business. The vote was a unanimous no.

Durant slammed his fist on the table and stormed out murmuring, "Imbeciles, savages, and ignorant idiots."

Lysander was right behind him saying, "Come here and say that, fancy man."

"Lysander, stop. It isn't worth going to jail. He can't do it so come on back," Warren Cole patted him on the back and led him back to the meeting.

After the meeting, Durant was more determined than ever to do exactly what he wanted to do, and he did. He ordered his men to dam up the north end of the lake, and his steamboat began transporting tourists. Durant had won; however, he failed to consider how these pioneers had fought through hard winters and mud-soaked springs to feed their families and that they would not be coerced into anything by an outsider.

At first, they watched the steamboat, cursed it, and saw their guiding and boatbuilding businesses rapidly decline. Lysander, now sixty-one years old, John and Wallace Plumley, Charles Hanmer, Charlie Sabattis, Edwin Stanton, Farrand Austin, and old Isaac Robinson were among the many who seethed every time that boat skimmed down the lake.

One night in early spring when the channel had freed up its ice and the syrup season was at its close, Lysander Hall secretly met with Charlie Sabattis, Wallace Plumley, and several other men. That night they formed a plan to get rid of the Buttercup. As Wallace walked home with Annie Scott, she knew something was wrong. He was unusually quiet and tight-lipped. "What are you up to, Wallace? I know that look."

"Oh, just had a meeting with the men." "What men?"

"Oh, some other guides." "Who?"

"Can't say."

"Oh." She thought a moment. "Okay, when are you doing this?" They had discussed the financial ramifications of the steamboats, and Wallace had threatened that the men would act. She figured that was the topic of the meeting.

"In late spring. That is all I can say, Annie." "Okay."

"Except that Durant shouldn't mess with us."

They hugged at Annie's cabin, and she watched Wallace walk down the path into the woods. Lord, please don't let him get hurt, she thought to herself.

That same night, Lyman Russell talked to his wife, Angie Henderson Russell, about his concern over the welfare of his work. "Angie, if Durant, comes in here and puts steamships on the lake, I don't know how we will survive." He watched as his baby daughter Harriet nursed at her mother's breast.

"Oh, Lyman, we will be fine. We will be fine," she patted him on the shoulder, handed him the baby, and began gathering up their few dishes. She knew from her brother Henry that the guides were furious at the thought of losing their livelihood. It frightened her, too.

One morning after a warm June evening in 1885, Jerome Woods came to get the Buttercup ready, and she was gone. He contacted Durant who in turn notified the constable and threatened to put an even bigger boat on Long Lake, but it would be ten years before another boat of that size graced the shores of Long Lake. The Buttercup had simply disappeared into a watery grave beneath the white capped waters of Long Lake. The men who did it never told. The town folks secretly knew and never told. Besides the guides, the only people who knew for sure were Harriet Hall and Annie Plumley until they told their best friend, Angie Russell, and swore her to secrecy.

# 32

## DUNCAN DODDS AND
## LEAFIE WRIGHT

SECRECY REIGNED IN the late 1800s from the Adirondacks to the Scottish settlements in Rossie and Crary Mills, secrets Leafie Wright carried about the new boy working at the Ostranders' farm down the road and secrets about her cousin, Duncan Dodds. One spring morning just after the fog lifted, while Leafie was walking past Ostranders' farm on her way to the blueberry patches, she noticed a man coming out of the big blue barn. He waved and hollered, "Morning."

Leafie stopped, "Hello." She continued down the road.

"Hold up," the man yelled as he turned and secured the latch on the sliding barn door. Leafie watched as he made his way toward her. His hair gleamed gold in the morning sun. When he was within two feet of her, he said, "I'm Almeron Huntley, and who might you be?"

"I'm, ah...." Leafie found herself looking into the bluest eyes she had ever seen. She forgot her name. She forgot where she was. She forgot everything except shiny blonde hair and piercing blue eyes staring at her like arrows into her soul. "Leafie, Leafie is my name."

"Well nice to meet you, Leafie. What an odd name."

"Yes, like Almeron," she quipped. She finally pulled herself together enough to discover words.

He laughed, "Yes, I hate my name, but it's an old family name." "Same here. So where are you from?"

"Waddington, but I'm working here for the summer to pay for college." "College?"

"Yes, I'm going to St. Lawrence University." "Wow. Expensive."

"Yes, but my uncle who also has a strange name, Columbus Huntley, is helping me through."

"That is wonderful. What a generous family.

"Yes, and you, what about you?"

"Oh, we have the gray farm on the right down there." She turned and pointed to the farm.

"Oh, I think I met your dad. Big hunter and fisherman, I hear."

"That's him." She moved from one foot to another, not wanting to pull herself away from this handsome man who towered over her. "Uh, well, I'm on my way to pick blueberries, so I uh will just be on my way."

"Oh, yes," Almeron stammered as if coming out of a deep sleep. "Good to meet you, neighbor."

"You, too." Leafie turned and continued down the road stealing a glance back at Almeron as he meandered down the path and disappear into the house. That morning picking berries was a fast affair. On the way back, she found herself looking for the young man in bib overalls with the shock of hair falling over his right eye. Though she did not expect to see him, her heart beat a little slower because he was nowhere in sight. The next morning, Leafie went down that dirt road again. Soon, she was walking down the road specifically to meet the handsome boy, and he was watching for her so they could meet.

In summer of that year, Leafie received a letter from her cousin, Duncan Dodds. He wrote about wanting to go to school in Scotland but that he was hesitant to tell his parents. He did not think they would let him go even though he had a scholarship. Almeron was finishing his schooling at St. Lawrence and was spending a year in Scotland at the University of Edinburgh. Leafie sat down on a hot June evening and wrote to Duncan Dodds about Almeron.

Duncan had a limp from the stone boat accident years earlier. Though he attended the local school and did well, his parents kept him home much of the time. Thomas taught him carpentry and farming. They assumed he would grow up and stay on or close to the farm. Instead, he had written Leafie that he was unhappy and wanted to pursue his education and become an attorney. He loved his Uncle Wright and was fascinated with stories of the law and how it could harm or help people.

When his cousin James Dodds, now a political attorney in Scotland, was visiting the farm, he had talked to Duncan about the law and his hometown of St Boswell, Scotland. Duncan was fascinated, reading everything he could get his hands on. Now that his cousin was in the political scene, he offered to finance a loan for Duncan's education, more out of guilt for falsely accusing Duncan's uncle of horse thievery than of true altruism, but the offer was there.

Leafie wrote that he needed to tell his parents and go, but it would not be so easy. Henrietta was dead set on his staying on the farm, and Thomas was dead set against James Dodds being involved with his family in any capacity. Duncan had approached his parents once about the idea.

Thomas shook his head, "You are not to have anything to do with that traitor."

"But, dad, he apologized. He really thought uncle stole those horses." "Makes no difference. It's family." His father turned and marched out, slamming the door.

"Mom, can't you talk to him? I want to study. I don't want to be a farmer."

"But, Duncan, how would you manage with your leg, getting on the buggy and then the train?"

"Just like I manage here. With my brace and my crutch if I need it. Please, mom, talk to him."

"But we don't want you to go. We don't...."

"Everything is don't, can't, or something else negative. I will find another way." Duncan slammed the door and rushed out onto the porch without his cane. He hobbled to the steps, determined to get away from his parents. His good leg moved down to the first step; his body leaned in to take the next step, but his bad leg did not move. Duncan tumbled down to the ground.

"Duncan, Duncan, are you hurt?" Henrietta screamed as she rushed down to help him.

"I'm fine, fine. Mom just leave me alone. Please." His mother backed away. Duncan got up and hobbled into the woods to his favorite tree. He sat there thinking, knowing they would never let him go. He had applied to the university months ago and learned last week that he was accepted. He was going. He formulated a plan.

After his accident, he had spent months in bed. He was fascinated with writing, so he practiced copying his family's handwriting. His mother laughed when he showed her his exact copy of a letter she had written and remarked that this skill would be useful for a thief, not a farmer. The family viewed his skill with amazement, happy that he had found something to occupy his time.

He now wrote to James in his mother's handwriting and asked him to pick him up at the Edinberg train station on a certain day and time. Within a week, he received a letter from James saying he would pick him up. Then, he forged a letter to Michael and Eliza Wright from his mother asking if Duncan could spend the night and get a ride to the train station. He signed the letters Henrietta Dodds. His best friend gave him a ride to Michael and Eliza's farm.

In the meantime, Leafie had written to Henrietta telling her about Almeron's plans to attend school in Scotland. Thomas and Henrietta had met Almeron several times. Almeron's grandfather Joseph Huntley was the local Methodist minister in Waddington. The Ostranders sometimes came out to his church. At one point they had mentioned that they had no help. The reverend had seven children, so he had plenty of help. He knew that Almeron was smart and wanted to go to school, but there was no money.

"I'll tell you what," the reverend said, "Almeron is a worker. He could work for you." Bill Ostrander agreed, and Almeron came the very next day. After learning that Almeron was also going to Edinburgh University, Thomas changed his mind about Duncan going to Scotland.

The morning that Duncan was setting his plan in motion, Henrietta rushed out to the barn to tell Duncan the good news. He was not there. "Thomas, have you seen Duncan?"

"He's in the barn milking."

"No, he isn't."

"Well then he must have gone out to the field. I'll find him." Thomas went to all three fields, but Duncan was not there.

"I don't understand it. Where could he be?" Henrietta cried as she went to his room in the attic. As soon as she poked her head in the alcove at the top of the stairs, she knew. The bed was made, and his hanging hooks were empty. "Thomas, he has gone. Everything is gone!"

"What?"

"He is gone, Thomas. He has taken everything." "But...."

"He wanted to go to that university. I bet he has found a way." "But we were going to...."

"I know. Say yes, help him pack, and take him to the train station. Oh, Lord, how could he have gotten there? Who would have taken him?" "Well, Henrietta, the boy is nineteen years old."

"I know. I know. You don't suppose George Dodds took him?" Duncan spent a lot of time over at the youngest Dodds's house in Waddington. He was helping George build a new house. Henrietta had introduced George Dodds to Ann Walton, her friend's daughter from the same Canadian village Henrietta grew up in. George and Ann fell in love, married, and were building a large brick home overlooking the St. Lawrence.

"I am going to ride to Waddington and see if he is there," Henrietta sighed.

"I would go with you, but the vet is coming to look at that sick cow."

"I know. Well then, I'll be off." Thomas hooked up the surrey, and she sped down the path.

When Henrietta entered the little town on the St. Lawrence, the island house in the middle of the river always caught her eye. This morning the river was swallowing shards of light from the morning sun as it bubbled its way down past the budding town. Henrietta saw the turrets of the Dodds's house to her left as she ambled down the path.

George was certainly building a grand house for his bride. The white veranda with Tuscan columns across the front and around the sides until it was stopped by the wings seemed mammoth. They now had the low-pitched gable up and the broad ornate cornice. Red peonies, cowslips, and red roses lined the front entrance with the peonies hanging onto the last vestiges of a summer bloom. George was on a ladder doing something to the windows on the second floor as Henrietta pulled to a stop in front of the porch. Ann Dodds, black shoulder length hair flying in the wind, came out and greeted her, "Henrietta, what a surprise." She put her hands up to her hair pushing the sides to the back. "I look a sight. I haven't had time to do my hair. George, Henrietta has come to visit." He began to climb down the ladder.

Henrietta put up her hand, "George, please stay there. Ann don't worry about your hair. I am sorry to come so early. I am not coming for a visit. I am looking for Duncan. Is he here?"

By now George was halfway down the ladder. "No, he isn't here. Haven't seen him in a few days. Is something wrong?" Henrietta explained his disappearance and began to say her goodbyes so she could get over to the Wrights and see if he was there.

"Henrietta, please come in. Come in for tea first. You need to rest a few minutes before going on," Ann chided.

"Well, I am in a hurry but perhaps for a moment. George, the house is beautiful. Looks like you are almost finished."

"Yes, just touching up here and there. I'm sure Duncan is fine, Henrietta. Now, I will get back to work while you girls have your tea."

Upon entering the house, Henrietta's mouth dropped open. The last time she had been here George had just finished the framing. Now it was almost finished.

"Oh my, what a large kitchen, and you have a cooking stove."

"Yes. I love it." Ann guided Henrietta to the large mahogany table. "Oh, I have always loved this table. I knew Thomas and Helen wanted George to have it. It is perfect in this large room."

"Yes, I love that the wood came from Scotland and George's dad built it. So, about Duncan...."

Henrietta explained that he wanted to go to school, and Ann listened. When Henrietta finished her tea, she stood up. "Ann, I really must go now." Soon she was on the road bound for the Wright farm. Henrietta pulled into the farm a little after noon.

Leafie met her with a hug. "What a wonderful surprise. Come on in. Mom, Henrietta's here."

Eliza came out of the kitchen into the dining room wearing a white apron covered with flour. "Henrietta, come in. I'll put some coffee on. So nice to see you."

"Well, I'm here looking for Duncan. Have you seen him?"

Eliza and Leafie looked questioningly at each other. "Well, of course we have seen him. You know Michael is giving him a ride to the train station. Did you come to say a final goodbye?" "What? Duncan is here?"

"Why, of course, he came last night after supper. Wait. You seem surprised. You asked us in the letter to take him."

"Letter? What letter?"

Henrietta went to the mahogany buffet, pulled open a drawer, grabbed a paper, and handed it to Henrietta. She looked it over. Her eyes went to the bottom of the page where she saw her signature.

By now Eliza realized what had happened. She put her hand to her mouth, "Oh no, Henrietta. You didn't write this, did you?"

"No, I didn't. Oh, I am furious at Duncan. I am so sorry he lied to you." "Well, not really lied," Leafie piped up. Eliza gave her the be quiet scowl and Leafie looked down.

"Well, he is here now, so at least I know he is okay." "That is true," Eliza added.

"Last night when we found out Almeron was going too, we decided to give him our blessing to go, but he will still get a piece of my mind for forging my signature. When he was so sick and confined to his bed as a boy, he started copying signatures. He was fascinated and became quite good at it."

"I have many letters from you, and I certainly was fooled, but if you want to catch him you had better hurry out to the barn because Duncan, Almeron, and dad are hitching up the wagon right now. Dad is taking him into the station on his way to the feed store."

"Oh my gosh. Oh no. Leafie, please, run out there and stop them." Leafie began running to the barn with Henrietta and Eliza following. Just before they reached the door, Michael met them with the horses and wagon. Sure enough, Duncan was perched between Michael and Almeron ready to go to Scotland.

"Duncan, get down from there right now!" Henrietta hollered. "Oh no," Duncan groaned as he crawled down from the wagon.

"What on earth? Your father and I were so worried. We had no idea what happened to you, sneaking off in the middle of the night."

"Ma, it was the only way; I have to go. I am going."

"I know, Duncan; I know. Your father and I have agreed to let you go." "You're kidding."

"No, I am not. You are a man now, and I feel much better about the trip since Almeron will be there too. I just wish you had told your father."

"Me too, but we have to go, Ma; the train...." Duncan wrapped his arms around his mother. "Tell dad I will write him and apologize. I am sorry I worried you."

On that mid-summer day, Henrietta said goodbye to her boy, and Leafie said goodbye to her fiancé. Scotland was waiting for these two men. One would come back for his wedding and one would never come back to live on his homeplace.

# 33

## CLOUDS ON THE HORIZON

LUCKILY, FOR DUNCAN and Almeron, they left before the black cloud of plague came down upon upstate New York like a giant wind sweeping up anyone who got in its path. It waited until the men came home from war. It waited until children were rumbling through the Adirondacks. It waited then pounced like a panther upon those people.

Five years before the giant cloud descended, Mary Sabattis was walking home from school, kicking up the autumn leaves and breathing in the first smoke of the season. She looked up at the Shaw house on the corner across from the Long Lake Hotel and saw the smoke curling out of the chimney into the chilly afternoon air. It was a sunny day but not hot enough to melt away the winter cold fast approaching the little town. She had almost reached the hotel when she heard the rumble of horses' hooves. She looked up the hill toward the Wesleyan Church and was amazed as two brown horses pulling a surrey came barreling over the hill at top speed. She could hear the driver shouting, and before she knew it, they were upon her. She looked around and ran into the trees as far as she could go. It seemed as if the contraption was following her because soon the driver had pulled on the reins and forced the animals off the road and onto the flat lot used by the store for carriage parking. She ran further into the woods, now to the water, looking back as she ran, her legs trembling. She knew they couldn't get through the trees unless the horses got free. She prayed and ran and listened to the driver yelling "stop, whoa," and profanity she knew she shouldn't be hearing. Finally, the noises stopped, so she stopped. She walked back a few feet and saw that the horses were still, but something was on the ground. She ran over and saw a young man lying face up. His eyes were closed. She was terrified, but she kneeled next to him, listened to his chest, and was relieved that at least he was breathing.

"Hey mister. Mister. Wake up," He remained motionless. By this time Henry Austin and Robert Shaw were approaching the man. Mary backed away and let them help. She knew Robert was a sort of doctor. "Will he be okay? Who is he?" Mary cried.

"It's Calvin, Calvin Towns," Robert replied. "Came in a couple of weeks ago." He checked his pulse and heart. Then he slapped his face. "Hey, Calvin, wake up. Come on, open your eyes." Mary was surprised that Robert knew him, but then again, he knew everybody that came into town.

"What. What happened?" the man mumbled as he started to get up.

"No, stay there. Calvin, you have had an accident, but you're going to be ok," Robert comforted. Then he looked up at Mary, "You okay?" "Oh, yes; quite scary, though."

"Yes, I saw some of it through my window; at least the part where you were running into the woods and the horses were following."

Calvin looked at Mary, "Oh ma'am, I am so sorry. Something spooked my horses at the top of the hill, and they would not stop. This is only the second time I've had them out, but I never...."

"Best to take them out several times away from town before using the town as a test run," Henry chided as he turned and walked back into his store mumbling about idiot kids.

Calvin picked up his hat and began to get up. He reached his full height and then began to waver. Robert and Mary steadied him. After a few minutes, he said, "I'm okay now. I got it."

"Well, don't know that you should be taking that thing home right now," Robert said.

"Uh, well, I can...."

"Nope. No, you don't. My son Ai just came in. I'll have him drive your outfit home. He can tie his horse on the back and ride home. Not that far anyway, right? You still staying at Mitchel's place down the road?"

"Yup, I'll be staying there working for him until I can get my own place." Robert told him to wait there while he walked across the street to get Ai.

"Really. You are staying at our place?" "Your place?"

"Well, my dad's place, Mitchel Sabattis." "Mitchel is your dad?"

"Yes, but where...."

"I'm staying in the cabin across the road. You know, across from you?" "Wait a minute, I have seen you. Aren't you building my brother Isaac's house?"

"Your brother... uh, yes." Just then Ai Shaw came across the road leading his great black Shire horse. "Wow! That is some horse." He was breathtakingly beautiful; the largest horse Calvin had ever seen. His coat gleamed in the sun, and he stood heads above his owner. "Where did he come from?"

"Got him from a farmer up in Canton."

"What? Thought those horses were only found in England and Scotland." "Not anymore. They are being shipped over here, and they can pull like oxen. Good animal," Ai said as he patted the giant beast on his neck. He walked over and began tying the horse to the back of the surrey.

Calvin turned to Mary, "Will I see you again?"

"I'm sure you will since we live across the street." And they did. Every chance Mary got, she was bringing Calvin lemonade or water or fresh baked biscuits. It was not long before he popped the question. They were married a year later moving into a house he built just down the road on the corner of where the Newcomb Road joined Carthage Road. Soon, Mary discovered she was pregnant, and in 1882 they had little George, named after Calvin's father. Two years later they had Paul. Calvin continued to build houses and guide. Mary stayed home and helped her mother and father at the Sabattis House. This business brought in sports for Calvin and Mitchel to guide and kept Elizabeth and Mary busy with lodging. Mitchel hired John Brown Jr. from Big Brook to take care of the maintenance and lawn at the hotel. He was smitten with another of Mitchel's children, but Elizabeth Sabattis would have no part of that. John could barely speak English, and though her daughter could understand him, Elizabeth could not. She was always leery of the Canadians especially after word had spread about encounters with pirates. Jenny Scott had told her what had happened on their journey down from Canada. Pirates had robbed them and killed Fergus, her husband. They were saved by a tribe of Abenakis who were related to Mitchel and another new family in town, the Josephs.

Calvin and Mary had a hard but good life. Many suppers were held at the Sabattis house with all nine children, now mostly grown, around the table. At the Christmas and Easter service, the Sabattis family filled two rows in church, and Mitchel played his violin. George and Paul loved their grandfather and grandmother and spent days doing chores around the house while their father sometimes worked away.

When Paul was five and George was seven, they attended the little school next to the Wesleyan Church. One Friday on a balmy November day, the town hosted a harvest party held at the back lot of the Long Lake Hotel. All the stores had treats for the children. Since Mary relished any alone time, she agreed to let the children go with Simeon and Almina Cole and their children (cousins by marriage). The stores had pumpkin bread, maple candy, venison jerky, and games for the children. That night George and Paul stayed at Big Brook Village with Simeon and Almina. After work, John Brown headed home with two passengers in his wagon, George and Paul Towns. Late that afternoon, Simeon took them fishing off the Big Brook bridge and Almina cooked the trout for dinner. Around 8:00 that night she tucked the children in their beds with their cousins.

One of the reasons Mary Towns wanted the time alone was to gather the black walnuts from the tree to store for winter. It was a time-consuming task, and she never had time. Mary went out around 8:00 am and began to gather. She had to climb up the old wooden ladder and shake some of the branches to get them down. She was so absorbed in her task that she hardly noticed the wind picking up and dark clouds gathering above Owls Head Mountain. As she started up the ladder one more time, she heard it coming. A loud blasting wind that almost blew her off the ladder. She steadied herself, looked up, and saw huge rolling black clouds straight over her head. Suddenly, another burst of wind tore her scarf off and blew some of the walnuts out of her basket. She wrapped her arms around her basket and began the trek to the house. Fall leaves holding on with a last shred of strength gave way and flew by her face. She passed the rope swing set between two maples and turned left to go to the house. She heard the roar, looked up, and knew no more. This was November of 1887 and Mary Towns lay within fifteen feet of her front porch until Simeon came upon her. The children screamed and began crying, "Mommy, Mommy!" Simeon knelt next to her.

"Mommy, wake up," young Paul cried as Simeon lifted her and carried her to the bed. She opened her eyes, looked up questioningly at Simeon.

"Mary, what happened?" "Uh."

"I found you outside."

Just then Calvin came through the door. "Mary, I'm home."

The boys raced to their father. "Daddy, daddy. Something is wrong with mommy!" He followed them into the room and saw her on the bed.

"Oh my God. What?" He looked at Simeon.

"I don't know. Found her outside unconscious. I'm glad you're here. She is trying to talk but isn't making any sense. I'll run and get Doc."

"Ok, thanks." He looked at Mary. He took her hand. "I love you."

Mary moved her mouth. Calvin put his ear down to her and heard her whisper, "I love you too." Then she shut her eyes and was silent again.

Doc Parker came and checked her over. He didn't know if there was brain injury or not; only time would tell. After he left, Calvin calmed the boys down, fixed dinner, and put them to bed while continuing to check on Mary. Later, Calvin went outside with his jack light, and what he saw took his breath away.

He knew that Mary was picking walnuts that morning. He knew that a terrible storm had come up quickly. He followed her trail, found where she lay, and looked all around. About ten feet from where she had fallen was the whole bottom limb of the maple tree. His heart dropped when he figured out that the limb had become a projectile in the wind and had hit his wife full force in the head. He feared for Mary. He feared her not awakening. That night in November of 1887 Mary Sabattis Towns died.

# 34

---

## THE SCOURGE

IT WAITED UNTIL a blustery autumn night in 1888 in Long Lake to come upon young George Towns in his bed in the wee hours of the morning. It left its mark on him, a high fever and a red rash. Six months after Mary's passing, Calvin Towns had remarried. Her name was Emaline, and she was Jeff Rutherford's daughter. Her husband had died of tuberculosis the year before. Calvin and Emaline met when Jeff came to town with her to get supplies and hired Calvin to help with the sugaring. It would be Jeff's last sugaring year. He was an old man, and his sons had married and moved away. The Kelloggs, his cousins, were scattered throughout the country though Henry had returned home and now helped his mother in the post office she ran after her hotel burned down. He had become a surveyor with a new baby named Oliver, and Danny Kellogg who came over from Scotland had moved to Vermont a few years ago. The Rutherfords still lived on Clear Lake, and Jeff still walked his woods, now with a cane, now a little bent, now with an air of gratitude to his parents for sailing across the Atlantic to give him this life. Jeff introduced his daughter to Calvin Towns. Calvin needed a mother for his children, and Emaline was looking for a new husband. It was perfect, and so they were married.

That week in November had been a busy week for Emaline Towns. She had been canning corn and venison, collecting walnuts, which reminded her of why she was here, and taking care of the children. She had Paul and George, and a baby on the way. She knew she had married Calvin so her parents would not be responsible for her, and she knew he had married her to give his children a mother. Calvin was a good man. Though her heart still beat faster when she heard her first husband's name, she cared about Calvin and loved him in a different way.

At 3:00, when six-year-old George (Baby) Towns arrived home from school, Emaline noticed he was a little flushed. On the way home, George had raced Clara Sabattis all the way to his house. Clara lived a little way beyond George on the Carthage Road across from her grandfather, Mitchel Sabattis. As they all sat down to supper that evening, George seemed tired and asked to be excused to go to his room.

"What?" Calvin, asked, "you're turning down your mother's chicken and dumplings? That is your favorite. Are you sick?"

"No, I just feel tired."

Emaline leaned over and put her hand on her son's forehead. "He is not feverish." Emaline knew he didn't look right, but she remembered that he had done extra chores for his sister that morning because she had burned her hand while putting wood on the fire. "Okay, Baby, let's get you to bed." She took him up the ladder to his bed, tucked him in, and kissed him good night, thinking he would feel better in the morning. Usually, he protested her using the name his brother had christened him with when he was born, "Baby." Emaline knew her little boy was sick when she heard no protests.

Before dawn the next day, Emaline woke up to the sound of growling. She thought there must be a wolf or bear outside. As she became fully awake, she realized it was coming from the loft. She jumped out of bed and started climbing the ladder; she heard Paul yelling frantically, "Mom, dad, something is wrong with George!" By the time Emaline reached the boy, Calvin was climbing the ladder behind her. Emaline did not have to put her hand on George's forehead to feel the heat.

"Momma," he cried hoarsely.

"I'm here and so is your dad. It will be okay."

"Baby, I'm going now to get the doc. He'll get you fixed up in a hurry." Calvin grabbed his boots, coat, and hat, rushed out the door, jumped on his horse, and galloped down Carthage Road to old William Helms's place to get Captain Parker. As he flew down the road, he thought about the doc who not that long ago had come and looked at his poor Mary. He knew Doc Parker had gone to medical school and the story was that he had a degree and had practiced in the city for a few years until he lost a patient due to a misdiagnosis. Shortly thereafter, he slid into the Adirondacks, melting into the hush of the forested mountains like other suffering souls who hid among the spruce and balsam. The doc did not want to practice medicine, but he was forced to in this little town with no real doctor.

It was bitter cold that morning. By the time Calvin reached doc's house, the snow was pelting his face so hard he could barely look up to guide his old horse along the white path marked by the tree line on both sides.

Calvin finally reached the house and banged on the door. Nothing. He banged again shouting frantically, "Doc. Doc, wake up. My boy is really sick." Finally, he heard rustling inside. The old wooden door squeaked open, and a white beard flew into Calvin Town's face.

"What, what's the matter, Cal?"

"It's George, Doc. He's real sick. Please come." "But...."

"I know. Hurry!" Captain put on his jacket, grabbed his bag, and took off out the door. They soon pulled up in front of the big gray house with the wide front porch.

Emaline met them at the door. "Oh, thank God, Doc. He's real sick. Come this way." She led him into the room where George lay pale as a sheet of ice and hot as an ember.

Doc examined him, shook his head, and said, "Calvin, Emaline, I'm just not sure what he has. You are right. He has a fever. I would say it is a bad cold, but we need to watch him closely, give him plenty of water, and keep cold compresses on his forehead to keep the fever down."

"Okay, Doc. Thanks, but could you stay here tonight?" Emaline asked.

Doc looked out the window and looked back down at Baby. "Well, looks like I just might have to. Don't want your husband to have to go back up that road to take me home in this storm. We'll set up an all-night vigil on George, so someone is with him all the time."

Just then the big door opened and in walked Robert Shaw. He had heard the news and brought his famous salve made from echinacea leaves and other ingredients. This medicine helped with colds and sore throats. He rubbed it on George's chest and told the family he thought the boy had the grippe and his fever would break in the night.

The next morning brought out the clear winter sun creating a mirror of the new snow. Mitchel Sabattis stopped to get Calvin to help him shovel only to find the little Towns boy sick with fever. Mitchel knelt and looked at him. "I think George is extremely sick," he said, looking down at the tiny figure in the bed.

"I know, Mitchel, do you have any medicine that can help him?"

"No, Emaline, I don't know this illness," but he made a poultice of mud and herbs and lay it on his head. He did this to calm Emaline down, not because he thought it would help. It did not help. Nothing helped. George fell into unconsciousness that afternoon, and on November 18 he died. The family was devastated, and the whole town came to the funeral in the new cemetery on the hill that the Stantons had dedicated only months before. Calvin walked over to Mary's grave and looked out over the hill. The sun bore down on the blue strip of river as if a spotlight were shining on the little town below. Calvin knew Mary and Baby were safe and at peace now, but the town was far from safe. The worst was yet to come, and it came to Mitchel Sabattis' nine-year-old granddaughter, Clara Rose.

When Clara came down with the fever, Mitchel tried to treat her with old recipes he knew from his grandfather, but they failed, so he called on Doc Parker again. After looking at Clara, Doc stated, "This is not the flu or grippe. It is something else, and since George was with Clara just before he became ill, we have to assume it is very contagious." Two days later, Clara Sabattis joined George Towns up on the great hill, as did her mother two weeks later.

From the day George got sick, it worked on Mitchel's mind that this could be something contagious. He knew it was not consumption or pneumonia and feared for the town because winter was upon them. The Towns and Sabattis families stayed to themselves as instructed by Doc Parker, and as spring began to blossom, and snow melted away so did the disease. There were no more cases that winter. Everyone came out to sugaring in the March thaw, and the children gathered in the schoolhouse next to the Wesleyan Church, the one in Big Brook, and the new one at the end of Tarbell Hill. The deaths were behind them. Farmers began to plant their crops, and the business owners began to prepare for the new tourists arriving for great adventures in the wilds of Long Lake.

However, one man did not participate in the sugaring or prepare for tourists. That man was Captain Doc Parker. Last summer he had joined William Helms, John Lapelle, Thomas Cary, and Manning Sutton to play music on the steps of the Long Lake Hotel during the sugaring party. At times Lyman and Angie Russell joined them as they sang into the early evening sunsets creating a fire show over Owls Head Mountain. Even the Russell children sang with the adults in church and at the outdoor jams set up by the doc.

Hattie Russell was a middle child of eight living in Big Brook with her siblings and friends. Her family lived at what people began to call Watch Rock because you could watch all the goings on both north and south of the lake while standing on this rock that jutted several feet out from the shoreline.

While not playing his saxophone or participating in the many activities, Doc Parker hid away in his cabin studying his medical books and talking with Robert Shaw and Mitchel Sabattis. By late spring, the three had concluded that the two children had contracted a disease called Diphtheria.

Mysteriously and surprisingly for the doc, throughout the winter, the plague disappeared. It had been an exceptionally cold winter and to save on wood, they closed the school until spring. However, on March 11 and 12 of that year, over fifty feet of snow fell during the Great Blizzard. Though the worst devastation from this storm was south of the Adirondacks and in the city, it did impact Long Lake in that many were forced to stay home, and schools were still closed.

When the spring thaw came, people flew out of their homes like butterflies. Neighbors chatted over clotheslines, children played in the schoolyard, and men gathered on the hotel porch on Sunday afternoons talking about the terrible winter. They smoked their pipes and drank their beer.

In June of that year, eight-year-old Harriet Russell, daughter of Lyman and Angie, had her friend Charlotte Cole over to play. They played outside while their mothers planted and weeded the garden. That evening, Hattie complained of a sore throat. Angie put her to bed early, thinking it was the spring pollen. Hattie had a sore throat and sneezes every spring. During the night, Angie heard her coughing, went to her room, and immediately woke her husband.

"Oh my God, Lyman; she has it. She has the disease."

"No. It can't be that. It's gone. There hasn't been a case since last fall, and it's June for God's sake."

"Lyman, we need a doctor! We need a doctor now! Maybe it isn't what killed the others, but I know she is burning up!"

Once again, Doc came. He looked in her mouth and saw the gray coating covering the roof of her mouth. Diphtheria was back. On June 27, it killed Hattie Russell. Two days later, it took her sisters, Carrie and Pearl.

That same day, Caroline Cole, age 51, succumbed to the disease, followed by her children Charlotte, and Emory. Meanwhile, the shadow of death hung over the Henderson home, where Delia, fourteen, died on July 2, Edward, twenty, the following day, and John Henderson, seven, on July 13.

There seemed to be no end to the epidemic. In September of 1889, Charlie Parker and six-year-old Julius Parker, grandsons of Zenas Parker, awoke in the night coughing. Their parents, Diana and Richard, heard the dreaded sound, "Oh my Lord, no!" Diana cried as she ran to their bed.

Richard took one look at Julius and wept. He knew. By now, the other children were out of their beds. "Stay where you are. Do not come in here," Richard ordered. Julius died on September 28, along with two-year-old Charlie. Willard, fifteen, succumbed to the illness on October 1, and thirteen-year-old Flora died ten days later. Richard, Diana, and their four other children were spared.

Then the disease went after the Houghtons, killing eleven-year-old Hattie Belle and then Melvina Rice Houghton who had been watching the Hanmer children. The cemetery on the hill was growing. The town was dying.

When the illness ended the following year, it left terrible devastation in its wake. Alba Cole and Richard Parker, who had fought and survived the horrible Civil War, had lost half of their family. Alba was seen wandering along the lake staring vacantly as if in a trance. He sought out Richard Parker, and they hunted and talked, but the tragedy had changed him forever. Richard's wife, Diana, was in shock. Thirteen-year-old Durward and eleven-year-old Robert Parker stayed silent and close, as if waiting for the hammer of the illness to fall upon them. On top of having huge losses, these families were isolated from the others. All through that summer, no one would come near them except to leave food and wood at their doorstep. Amid this sickness, Lysander Hall became ill. In 1890, the tough pioneer took his last breath. He had been a town icon, and young boys looked up to him. A sadness swept through the community like a strong wind seeping through the cracks of the little houses surrounding the lake. Throughout that winter, families kept their children close. Fear flew through the community, but no more cases came, and that spring ushered in a season of joy. People gathered at James Rice's store and smoked their pipes while discussing the prospects of getting a real doctor. Women gathered in quilting circles at each other's houses.

Porch talks mushroomed into a serious discussion at the town meeting. Farrand Austin, his son Merlin, Walt Jennings, Warren Cole, John Plumley, James Rice, John Lapelle, George Palmer, Robert Shaw, and Ed Stanton were there. Charles Hanmer attended in his capacity as constable. He sat with Mary Ann Keller and Emaline Towns. John Plumley suggested they offer $500.00 to bring a doctor into the town.

"No doctor is going to come here for $500.00," argued Walt.

"Walt, $500.00 is a lot of money, and you heard the treasurer's report. After all the money we have given for the new roads and...."

"Which did not get completed because of so many of us with that damn disease," Warren added.

"Right, but if we had had a doctor, maybe we would have gotten rid of it earlier."

"Indian Lake has a doctor, and it got quite a few of them," Ferrand offered.

Old John LaPelle spoke up, "Well, the church could probably donate a little. I think we need to offer a good amount, so we don't get somebody unqualified. Charlie and Robert could check them out, right?"

Charlie Hanmer looked at Robert. "Sure, we can do that," Robert agreed. Charlie nodded.

Mary Ann spoke up, "How about $800.00?"

In the end, they voted to offer a doctor $1,000 to come, and in November 1894, Dr. Burch accepted the offer. He became Long Lake's first doctor just in time: Scarlet Fever hit the town right after he arrived. The Parker family lost eighteen-year-old Etta, Richard, Diana Parker's daughter, and Zenas Parker's granddaughter.

One thing Doctor Burch did differently was to have Charlie Hanmer put quarantine notices on a known ill house; all those living inside were not to mingle with the population. Neighbors went into action securing groceries and medicine for the ill families, cutting and piling wood outside the houses, and helping in other ways. Later, at another town meeting headed by Henry Kellogg, they proposed that in times of serious illness, quarantine would mean moving the ill to a "pest house." The town purchased two empty houses located a distance from any other houses. They fixed them up to shelter the sick. One such house was the old Dickenson house in a clearing along the Carthage Road. The Dickensons had moved in thinking they would build a large farm. They lasted one winter. That spring they packed up everything and headed west.

Another pest house was on the west side of Long Lake along Rice Road. Dr. Burch did not last long in this uncivilized community where no one locked their doors and many paid him with rabbits, turnips, and whatever else they had to give. Dr. Burch escaped after less than a year. Eventually, the town hired Dr. Decker who was greeted his first night with a coonskin cap and a venison pot roast. He loved the town and the people, and they persuaded him to stay a while. The town was on its way to becoming a thriving community with grand hotels, barbershops, blacksmith shops, and grocery stores.

# 35

## THE WEDDING

D AY BROKE ACROSS the horizon as Michael Wright came
through the clearing heading to Frank Plumley's Inn
on the Hill on Carthage Road in Long Lake. He thought
about the night before last, which he had spent in John
Scott's old campsite on the banks of the Hudson River in
Newcomb. He loved waking to the familiar sound of the
Hudson River rippling over the rocks and roots, stopping
for nothing. The next morning, Michael had headed east on
foot to Ann and Patrick Parker's place. Even before reaching it, he could smell the bacon frying and see the flapjacks
piled up on his plate doused with rich maple syrup given
by those brilliant colorful trees scattered among the pines.
He was not disappointed. He had breakfast with Ann and
Patrick and then began the trek to Long Lake.

Now, he was anticipating another delightful breakfast in
Long Lake at this large, wooded house on the hill looking
over the ribbon-like lake. Suddenly, Michael heard a crack

behind him, turned expecting to see an animal, and there stood Duncan Dodds, red hair glistening in the morning sun with a smile as big as the crescent moon.

"Uncle, it's me. I'm back."

"For God's sake, boy; I know it's you; still haven't learned anything about creeping up on an old codger like me. Liable to get yourself shot doing that in these parts." He walked over and put his arms around Duncan.

"I know, Uncle. I just forgot. I've been studying for so long and only went a few times hunting in Scotland."

"So, you back to stay?" Michael looked around and looked back at Duncan. "Are you going down to the farm or did you move here?"

"I came here. I got a job in Tupper Lake as a logging lawyer. I'm over here to see a client new on the logging scene."

"Oh, and who would that be?"

"His name is Roy Hosley, and he is interested in forming a company." "Well, congratulations. You did well, son. I'm proud of you. I just left Almeron Huntley all starry-eyed waiting for...."

"I know, the wedding day, but we're going to get some hunting in first, right?"

"Yup, but I could sure use a hot cup of coffee and some bacon and eggs. If I remember right, Mrs. Plumley puts on quite a spread." The two of them stepped up onto the front porch of the large white inn, walked in, and sat down with the rest of the guests. They would stay there the next two nights and then head down to the wedding.

It was a glorious day for a wedding. Sunlight fell across the front yard of the farm. It was in full decoration with white ribbons hanging from the trees and the ladies in their best dresses and bonnets. The men wore top hats. Leafie even persuaded her uncle to wear a black top hat. The Doddses, Rules, Ostranders, and all their friends from Rossie to Newcomb and Long Lake attended. Old friends, John Huntley, Wheaton Huntley, Almeron's uncles, and Michael Wright were telling stories of Long Lake and Newcomb. John laughed when they talked about farming in Long Lake. "Oh yes, seems the only one that grew anything there was old Dave Keller. I got out of there right after my second harvest."

"Dad told us about you and your adventures," Uncle John Wheaton added.

"Yup, Wright, that young man's grandfather, Joel Plumley," pointing to Wallace Plumley at the end of the porch with his wife Annie Scott, Ned Scott's daughter, "we had some run ins with all kinds of game." Soon, Ann and Patrick Parker, their son Sam, and daughter Isabelle joined the gathering. Ned Scott's other daughter Addie had married and moved away.

Patrick jumped in with, "Oh, you're John Huntley. I met you when Ann and I first came to Newcomb. You lived in Long Lake and came to the mill with my uncle Mitchel Sabattis."

"Well, I'll be. Mitchel's your uncle?"

"Sure is." Just then Leafie's mother, Eliza, motioned for Wright to come forward. The wedding was starting.

Duncan Dodds played the wedding march on the old organ his grandfather had brought with him from Scotland in 1819. Michael and Leafie Wright began on the porch and walked the path to the beautiful elm tree on the corner. It was under the canopy of that majestic elm that Leafie and Almeron Huntley began their journey.

They found a house in Waddington that sat close to the St. Lawrence near George and Ann Dodds's place. Almeron taught school and worked with his wife's distant cousin, Jack Rule, making harnesses in his barn. Eventually Jack opened a harness shop on Main Street next to the cobbler. Leafie, Henrietta Dodds, and her daughter Mary Helen quilted and canned together. Joseph Dalzell, a cousin of John Rule, occupied an office off the harness shop where he served as Justice of the Peace for Hammond and Waddington.

In December of 1888, while quilting with Henrietta, Leafie told her that she was not feeling well.

"Oh, and what seems to be the problem?" Henrietta said as she looked up from her knitting."

"I am sick in the morning." "Ahh, only in the morning?" "Mostly. Sometimes at night."

"Leafie, you ninny, you are probably pregnant." "What?"

"Are your breasts sore?" "Yes."

"You better make an appointment with the doctor." Leafie did, and to the delight of Almeron and Leafie, the doctor confirmed that she was pregnant.

Nine months later, on July 29, 1989, Wright Huntley was born at home. Leafie was devoted to her son and took him on walks through the little growing town.

It was autumn. The winds were streaking across the St. Lawrence carrying the great northern chill that brought in September. Leafie parked the big black carriage at the foot of the stairs while she gathered the flour she had purchased from the store on the corner next to the church. She took the bag out of the carriage, turned, and put it on the step; when she turned back, the carriage was careening backwards straight toward the river. "Oh, my God!" she screamed as she raced toward the carriage. The carriage went over the bank and was now close to shore. She saw a man digging a trench next to the dirt road opposite the river. "Help!" She shouted as she ran toward the carriage. The man turned, saw the black pram, and began running. He reached it just before the river took it. "Oh, my Lord, thank you. Thank you so much," Leafie puffed as she caught up with them. When she caught her breath, she said, "I am Leafie, Leafie Huntley, and this is my baby, Wright."

"You're welcome. Whew, that was a close one," he said as he put his hands just above his knees, bent over, and breathed heavily. After a few seconds, he stood up and introduced himself.

Leafie looked up at him, "Oh, my goodness, John Rule, it's you. I didn't recognize you at first. Your brother runs the harness shop where Almeron works."

"That's right."

"And I think your wife is a Dodds, right?"

"Yup, George's daughter. Most of the Doddses, Rules, and Martins come from those settlers who came from Scotland in the 1800s. We're all related somehow." He took a couple steps to the right, bent down, and picked up his hat.

Leafie laughed, "I know, but I've been to your house for the quilting bee, so I know Mary Helen, but I have never met you. I did hear though that you are about to have one of these." She pointed to the baby.

"That's true. Just found out."

"Have you picked out names yet?"

"Mary said if it's a girl, it will be Annie, and if a boy, another John. Don't know as I like that much, but Mary wants him named after the long line of Johns in the Rule family. Well, nice seeing you. I have to get back to work." John turned and began walking back to where he had been working.

"Yes, yes, of course, and once again, thank you," Leafie offered as she began pushing the carriage up the hill toward home.

That night Leafie shared with Almeron what happened. She did not want to tell him about her carelessness, but Waddington was so small, the whole town knew about it an hour after it happened.

"Almeron, it was so fast, and the wheel lock did not hold."

"I'll look at it in the morning. I can fix it. So, John Rule came to the rescue. I'll have to thank him."

"Yes, seems like a nice enough fellow. They are going to name their baby after his father and grandfather. You know, Almeron, I was thinking, when we have our next one, I'd like to...."

"Name him Almeron? Never."

"But that is what I was wondering. What was your father's name?" Almeron looked away not speaking. "You never talk about your parents. You were raised by your grandparents. Why?"

Almeron turned back, "Do you really need to know that Leafie?"

"Well, I just wondered; you know I would like our children to know their grandparents."

"They will. Michael and Eliza."

"Almeron. You know I don't mean my parents." She looked up at him, exasperated.

"All I know is that my mother's name was Clarissa, Grandpa and Grandma's daughter."

"You don't know who your father is?"

"No. Grandpa and Grandma Huntley raised me and would never talk about it."

"But where is your mother?" "Don't know that either."

"You mean she just disappeared or maybe died?"

"Leafie, I told you. I don't know. That is it. It doesn't matter. All I know is my great grandma and grandpa came here from the highlands in Scotland. All that matters is us. I'm going to sleep now." He put his arm around her, kissed her, and soon was fast asleep. Leafie was not. Her mind was churning. Who would know? Only Reverend Joseph Huntley, and he was not willing to talk about it. Why was there no father at all? She suspected Clarissa had a baby when she was young, and her parents raised him as their own. He did not even know they were not his parents until he was eighteen. Duncan! Duncan Dodds could find out. A trip to visit Duncan was in order. But could he keep her secret investigation from Almeron? She rolled over and put her arm around Almeron. He is right, she thought; it doesn't matter. All that matters is my family right here right now. She pushed the thoughts of asking Duncan into the dark recesses of her mind and basked in the comfort of her husband lying next to her and her baby in the next room all nestled in the bosom of the budding village of Waddington.

# 36

## SMOKE ON THE HORIZON

O N JANUARY 16, 1893, two guests of the Sagamore Hotel in Long Lake had spent several hours in the bar drinking and talking with Calvin Towns and the bartender, John Rice. The two brothers, Jerry and Byron, had rented a room and at one point told Calvin that they might only sleep a couple of hours and head for home instead of waiting until morning. One of the men was anxious to see his girlfriend; he wanted to cancel the room and leave for home. Calvin suggested that they not leave in the state they were in. The brothers went up to their room; Calvin and John Rice closed and left. The last thing John Rice did was empty the ashtray into the trash can next to the laundry room behind the bar and empty a glass of water on top of it.

Isaac Sabattis woke up around 3:00 am. He put on his boots to begin the cold trek to the outhouse. When he opened the door, he smelled smoke. He turned around and looked across at his father's place, the Sabattis House and

Gardens. The smoke was so thick he could barely see the building. He quickly dressed, ran over toward Mitchel's, and was met by his brother and several other people running toward the hotel. "Dad, are you all right?"

"Me, sure son, just worried about all the guests at that hotel."

Halfway to his father's place, he realized the fire was west of his father's on Bluff Point. The Shaws, Austins, and several others had gathered, and Isaac could hear them trying to comprehend that their beautiful hotel was on fire. Now he knew it was the Sagamore Hotel. Someone at the Long Lake Hotel rang the fire bell. Robert and Ai Shaw, young Walter Jennings, Orren Lapelle, Richard Parker, and the Plumley boys rushed into the hotel screaming, "Fire!" They formed a bucket brigade, but there was no stopping this fire.

Calvin Towns soon arrived, frantically looking for the two friends he had met that night. He spotted John Rice in the bucket line standing by Richard Parker. Calvin rushed over, "John, I can't find Jerry and Byron."

"Who?" Richard Parker asked as he stepped out of the line.

"Two men. Two men we were talking to last night. I don't see them." "Oh, Lord, that's right. They were still there," John gasped.

"I think we got everybody out; if we didn't, it's too late now." Richard remarked. The three of them heard another loud crack, looked up and saw the smoke turn into flames shooting up past the trees. By now, the brigade had stopped, and Orren had ordered the men to water down the houses next door. In the meantime, some of the people had managed to enter the hotel and were pulling everything out they could salvage. Edmund Butler and several men had managed to get some of the beds out of the hotel, but most of the contents burned up in the flames.

"Oh my God," Calvin gasped. "They were drunk. They probably passed out." Calvin paced back and forth not knowing what to do. "Probably didn't get out," Richard replied.

Calvin looked at this man. Richard's round face remained stoic. He stood there staring at the flames as still as the huge maple that loomed over him. The man never got riled about anything, and since Diphtheria had taken half his family, he had become even more detached.

As the three of them stood in the cold night, the grand hotel burned to the ground. John and Stephen Lamos, undertakers for the town, Constable Hanmer, and Calvin Towns came back the next morning and searched for remains. They found none. Calvin always hoped that the two men got up in the night and traveled back home.

Ed Butler was frantic. He had sunk a fortune into this hotel, and he had hired many who were now out of jobs. Among them were Lewis Joseph, cousin to Patrick Parker, Ann Dodds's husband in Newcomb; Richard Parker's son Robert; and young James Ovitt, who had helped build the cottages. Diana Parker and Eunice Helms did laundry.

Whispers spread like wildfire through the town about what Edmund Butler and all of them would do.

Desperate for help, Edmund called on Robert Shaw the next day. He knocked on the door and Gitty Shaw opened it. "Robert home?"

"Yes, Edmund. I am so sorry. I can't believe it."

"Me neither, and I was so careful about the lamps. I just don't know how...." He shook his head and looked down. Just then Robert came to the door.

"Ed, been expecting you. Come on in." Edmund walked in and sat down opposite Robert while Gitty made them tea. "Lord, so sorry, Ed. What happened?"

"I don't know. Just don't know. Everything was fine when I left around midnight. The Lamoses and Charlie Hanmer are up there now looking around."

"Right. Do they think it might be arson?"

"I guess they have to investigate. I just know that a lot of people are out of work, including me. I just can't believe it. We were so careful."

"Terrible thing. I know. It will affect the whole town. Even Ai will feel the hit. He cuts and delivers a lot of wood from the mill for that hotel."

"I know," Edmund shook his head, "which is why I've come to ask for your help with something. Robert, do you think the town can help me rebuild?"

"Well, as you know, the town never has money to spare, but all you can do is go to the town meeting and ask. Would be good of you to go to the meetings anyway."

"I know. I know. Just too busy."

Robert nodded his head, "Right, right except there are more reasons to get involved in the town when you own a business. More reasons, indeed, like when your business gets burned down and you have no friends on the board." Edmund listened to this man, quietly fuming as he usually did when trying to speak to this town powerhouse. He checked his temper and said, "Robert, I know I have not been involved in the past, but if you can persuade the town to help me, I will go to every meeting, and I will make sure I only use your sawmill. I figure I need a loan of $15,000 to get it rebuilt and running." "Hmmm and attend church. Also, attend church?"

"What? Why?"

"Because that is also being part of the town, and the good Lord wants us all to spend Sunday morning worshiping him." "Okay, Okay, Robert, I'll go."

"Good then," Robert said as he stood up. "Board meeting is next Wednesday night. I'll see you there if not before." They shook hands. Robert walked him to the door and ushered him out. He shut the door and said, "Fifteen thousand. Well, Lord, I think we can pare that down to $12,000 and still get the job done. Amen."

In the past, Robert Shaw had accused Edmund Butler of running a brothel. Edmund had denied it, but it had spread about town, so neither Edmund nor Robert knew how the town would react to the request. A hotel of ill repute was an unsightly blight on the town, but the town needed the hotel for business and jobs. They called an emergency meeting at Edmund's request, and that night Butler made his plea, "Folks, I only need $15,000, and I could rebuild. It is just as good for the town as for me." There was much conversation about the brothel accusation; Edmund swore it was all rumors. Some people complained that he served too much alcohol. Edmund shouted at Robert Shaw, "You were wrong about the brothel, and I had a legal right to serve alcohol." Robert had not said a word.

"Except when they are so drunk it causes a place to go up in flames," Willard Sutton chided.

"Nobody knows how the fire started." Edmund looked at Constable Hanmer who was standing in the back of the room, arms crossed staring at Edmund.

"Nope, not yet, but I think it was a cigarette, and we know it began in one of the rooms upstairs."

"See. Could have been anything. No reason to assume it was because someone was doing something wrong."

Robert Shaw finally jumped in, "Well, folks, it doesn't look like we are getting anywhere with this. I know some of you think that is too much money, so what if we drop it down to $12,000? Let's table it and have another meeting in two weeks. You can go home and think about it." There was much murmuring; finally, Reuben Cary seconded it, and they voted to meet again in two weeks.

When Edmund arrived at his home, which had almost gone up with the fire, he was hot with anger at this ridiculous town and its idiot leader Robert Shaw. He felt that they were a bunch of crooks, but he knew how to handle them. His ten-year-old niece, Maggie Rafferty, and his wife Margaret greeted him at the door. They were still cleaning up from the smoke. "The house looks good. You two okay?" Edmund asked.

"Yes, Uncle, but that fire was sure scary."

"Yes, indeed, I know." He put his arm around her. He had heard Margaret calming her down after a nightmare about the fire. Edmund and Margaret had taken in his niece when she was eight years old. Her father died when she was three, and this year his sister, Maggie's mother, had to move to Newcomb with her cousin to help her while she battled Tuberculosis.

He would never forget the night of the fire. It was a bitter cold night and he had been shoveling snow that afternoon. He came in, warmed himself, ate dinner, checked in with his bartender John Rice, had a couple of drinks, walked next door to his house, and fell into a deep sleep. In the middle of the night, a crackling snapping sound woke him. Then he smelled the smoke. He shook Margaret. "Margaret, Margaret, wake up. Wake up. I think there is a fire."

"What?"

"Get up. Get out of here now!" He jumped out of bed and ran down the hall yelling "Maggie, get up. Fire!" He opened her door just as she was crawling out of bed. "Just grab your coat and get outside!"

By the time the three of them managed to tumble down the steps, they saw smoke billowing from the hotel.

Their faces were black with soot; Maggie was coughing while Margaret patted her on the back and cried. Edmund hugged his family and sent them to Calvin Towns's house. As they were running across the lawn, there was a loud boom. The women looked back and saw massive flames shooting into the sky. Flames had already licked the huge white pines between the hotel and their house. God, please save our house, Margaret prayed. By the time they reached the Towns's house, Emaline Towns was up and opened the door as Calvin ran out. She brought the two shaken women inside. Margaret would not stay. She returned home and grabbed a bucket to help her husband water down their house. "But Marg...." Edmund started to object.

"Stop. I'm doing this." Edmund did not say another word. By now several other townspeople had come with their buckets. They knew the hotel was gone. They would try to save the Butler home, and they did.

The next day, the Butler home was still standing but filled with black smoke. Margaret, Maggie, and several of the men, women, and children gathered to clean out the house. Margaret was glad she had helped the other women with the soapmaking that spring. Now, there would be plenty of ashes to mix with the fat for more soap. Several townspeople had arrived at the blackened hole where the hotel had stood to gather up barrels of ashes.

After the town meeting, Edmund drew up a petition, went to each man on the town board, promised money or favors, and had him sign the petition in his favor deftly avoiding

Constable Hanmer. Next, he went to the sawmill owners. He talked with William Wilson but made a deal with Boyden Robinson who quoted him the lowest price in town while offering to buy a circular saw Butler had been trying to sell.

The Bissells, who owned Centennial House southwest of the Sagamore, voted against it since their business had increased due to the loss of the hotel. Orren Lapelle and Stephen Lamos, who now owned a sawmill and shingle mill, were for it because their business had dropped since the fire. As with their ancestors before them, these men had to prioritize providing for their family. They saw the new hotel as insurance of the survival of the town. The only flaw in this offer was that he had already promised Robert Shaw he would only use his sawmill for the rebuilding. The next part of Butler's plan involved meeting Robert Shaw late one night in the freight room of his store.

"And to what do I owe this visit?" asked Shaw.

"I have come to ask for your vote on the issue of $15,000 for building the hotel. If you do that, I will guarantee that all my guests will come to your store and your store only to purchase supplies.

"Well, Mr. Butler, I am surprised. I will say to you right now that you cannot stir me one bit by offers of any kind other than the agreement we already made. What you are doing is illegal, and you know it; just where will your guests go if I do not vote your way?"

"I will send them to James Cole's and Hanmer's stores."

"So, a bit of blackmail, I see."

"Yes, but you did not help me at the town meeting like you promised."

"I did not promise you anything but bringing it to the board, and that I did. They would not even have heard it if it came from you. I will not vote for it because you are breaking our verbal agreement, and worse yet, you have no remorse about it."

"Fine. I don't need your signature because enough have already signed my petition, so you can't stand in my way. The rest of the town is against you. I only need your vote to go forward, and if you vote against me, you vote against the jobs of a lot of people."

Because the town was so small, Robert already knew about the petition, but he acted surprised. "My, my Mr. Butler, I see you have been busy. Let me have twenty-four hours to investigate, then meet me back here, and I will tell you whether I will sign it too." He went to each man Butler mentioned and asked if he had signed the petition. Most men had signed it. Later, he met with his brother William who told him that the people were blaming him for not having a grand hotel in town. He suggested that Robert go along with the petition and let people learn from their own mistakes. Next, Robert met with John Lapelle and David Keller Jr., the most spiritual men he knew. They too advised him to walk away from the matter. That evening, Robert met with Ed Butler and told him, "Ed, this is the first time I ever took my hands off an undertaking, but I am afraid for my sanity. I am against the whole idea, but since Supervisor Boyden has also signed the petition, I will step down and vote to give you the money. I want to state to you that I am opposed to it, but I will not be the only man in town to stop it."

"Good show," Butler remarked; "knew you'd see it my way." He marched out the door proud of what he had accomplished. He had won.

The next day, the Town of Long Lake voted to give Edmund Butler $12,000 to rebuild the hotel. This time, he decided to make the veranda even wider and added many luxuries to attract the wealthy people in the southern part of the state who were now coming in droves to the Adirondacks for holidays. Months went by, and the $12,000 was spent; however, the hotel was not finished. Because Mr. Butler had no credibility, he could not get the funds to complete it. The town was now out $12,000 and still had no hotel. In the meantime, Butler became sick. At first, he thought it was grippe. He continued to work hard on the hotel. Finally, it became so acute that he could barely get out of bed. He knew he was dying.

One Sunday after church, Robert Shaw walked down the road and knocked on Ed Butler's door. When Margaret opened the door, she was surprised to see Robert standing there in his black suit, white shirt, and top hat. "Hello Margaret. I heard Ed is sick."

"Yes, he is."

"Can I see him?"

"Yes, yes, of course. Please come in." Margaret ushered Robert up the stairs to the first bedroom on the right.

Robert stood in the doorway looking at the man on the bed. Edmund's face was thinner and whiter. His blonde hair hung lank over his ears. It was a larger room than most and the quilt was red, blue, and white. The curtains were drawn, and Edmund looked like he was sleeping. Robert coughed and Edmund opened his eyes.

"Well, I'll be. What are you doing here?"

"Checking up on you. Heard you were sick. What is it?" Robert asked as he sat down in the quilted chair next to the bed.

"I don't know. My stomach mostly," Ed put his hands on his stomach. "Well, we said prayers for you in church today, and I brought you my salve. It has helped others, but maybe you should see the new doc."

"Oh, well. Thanks Robert. Uh...." Edmund felt shame slide through his body as he knew he had not stepped foot in the church after promising Robert he would if he helped him get the money. He had also bought most of his lumber for the hotel from Robinsons' mill because it was a few cents cheaper, and he had made some deals with Isaac. He also feared doctors.

"I don't know about a doctor. Think it's just something I ate. I'll give it a few more days."

"Yes," Robert replied, knowing it was more than something he ate. "Well, good luck then, and hope the salve helps." Mrs. Butler ushered him to the door and whispered thanks to him before he left.

A few weeks later, Butler asked to see Robert again. This time he told him what was going on. He confessed that he could not finish the hotel, had given up hope of ever getting the money to complete it, and thought it was making him sick.

"Well, really, that is too bad. There is so much money in the country; it seems as though you ought to find enough to complete this project. I will see what I can do to help you if you like."

Butler was stunned to think that this man would offer to help him. "Why, thank you, Robert; I am in your debt."

"No, I do this not only for you, but for our town. I have come to believe that we need the hotel, but you are not in my debt."

True to his word, Robert traveled from New York City to Plattsburgh trying to procure the money, but no one would entrust the money to Mr. Butler. He had to come home and tell Ed that he could not get the funds. Mr. Butler took to his bed again becoming more ill each day. One morning he awoke and remembered an investor he had forgotten about. He summoned Robert again and asked him one more time to go to New York City. The next day Robert left for the city, once again traveling over rough roads, finally arriving, and being ushered in to see a Mr. Hoe. Robert told him of the investment opportunity, which he knew was a long shot. Who would want to invest in a hotel in some out-of-the-way place called Long Lake forty-two miles from a railroad? He explained the situation.

"And who am I doing this to please?" asked Mr. Hoe.

"Mr. Edmund Butler."

"I do not care for Mr. Butler."

"Then, do it for me." Mr. Hoe agreed to the deal but only if Robert Shaw would receive the check for $5,000.00. When Edmund had spent that money, Mr. Hoe would send Robert another check. Robert Shaw returned with the good news, and within a few days, Butler was out of bed and organizing the continuing construction, this time using the Shaw sawmill. When it was finished, the Sagamore Hotel stood five stories high, was 112 feet long and fifty feet wide. It commanded a view of the whole lake and was the most magnificent structure in the Adirondacks.

# 37

## FREEDOM

B Y NOW OTHER wealthy men were purchasing the wooded
lands in the Adirondacks and building great lodges
they called camps on the water's edge. Before the turn of
the century, the towns south of Long Lake were bustling
with newcomers as steamboats and then trains roared into
these towns carrying within them wealthy tourists willing
to spend their money.

One such man, Dr. Seward Webb, was son-in-law to
William Vanderbilt who now owned land throughout the
Adirondacks. He looked at the land west of Long Lake
between David Smith's old property and the town called
Tupper Lake. It was there that he formed the Adirondack
& St. Lawrence Railroad Company, which became the
Mohawk & Malone Railway Company. He commissioned a
train station deep in the woods only accessible by a crude
road carved through the thick web of pines, spruce, and
hardwood trees. Webb's lodge was built on the edge of

Smith Lake where the loons called out at the break of dawn and the wolves howled in the cold night air. Dr. Webb and his wife Lila would sit out on his porch and enjoy the peace and quiet far north of New York City. This lake that David Smith claimed so many years ago was renamed Lake Lila by Dr. Webb.

Figure 8 Nehasane Lodge, Lake Lila

Seward Webb came before another wealthy man, William Whitney, who bought a large swath of land just north of Webb's property. Both men employed several Long Lakers such as Lulu Ames who became postmistress at Nehasane, the name for Dr. Webb's lodge. William Whitney hired Isaac Clement to caretake his place in the winter.

Isaac Clement left his mark throughout Long Lake with his rock walls. At times he brought his young son Edgar with him. "Son," he said, "the best wall is one that you see most of the rock and little of the mortar."

Toward the end of the nineteenth century more stores popped up in the little town including one run by Judge Timothy Sullivan and his wife Bridget. He built it east of the Lake House on a small rise above the lake. Isaac Clement became friends with him, and the judge let Isaac run up grocery bills for his family of four children. Along with the store, the judge built a magnificent house with a wide porch. It faced another new building called Foresters Hall where the Loyal Order of the Foresters held their meetings.

Beth Clement, the oldest child in the Clement family, had her hands full helping her mother with the younger children, helping with the wash, canning, planting, harvesting, and feeding the chickens and pigs. Beth was two years older than Edgar Clement, but at ten years old, she looked out for her brother. Because Isaac had to take any job he could, he was often away from the family building stone walls and doing carpentry work. One of his recent jobs was at a place called Bog River near the Whitney property toward Tupper Lake. The man who sought Isaac out was Augusta Low who wanted a large rock wall built on his property. He came to Isaac's house and after discussing it with him pulled a piece of paper out of the pocket of the inside of his coat. "Now, Mr. Clement, here is the contract. You just need to sign it and we will be ready to start."

Isaac stared at the paper then looked up at Augusta and replied, "Well Mr. Low, I don't do anything too quick, so I'll just take this contract here, read through it, and let you know what I decide."

Augusta was surprised since it was a large job, and most men would have signed immediately, but he could wait. Isaac was the best in the business. "Okay, but I don't want to wait too long because I would like it finished before the next snow."

It was spring. Isaac stuck the paper in his pocket. The next day, he had to go to Tupper Lake to the lumber mill. He drove his horse and wagon up early in the morning and arrived right after it opened. They unloaded the lumber and Isaac sat outside waiting. Soon, another man drove up with a wagon of cut logs to be hewn. Isaac watched the young man as he came toward him. He noticed he had a slight limp. Before the man reached the bench next to Isaac, he said, "Morning."

"Morning," Isaac replied, glancing at this man with curly red hair and glasses.

"Great morning. Looks like a clear day. You got a project going?" "Yup, always do. How about you?"

"Oh, I'm a lawyer here in town and I'm building my house. I'm Duncan, Duncan Dodds"

"A lawyer, huh? Well, I think I'm going to be building a rock wall down toward Long Lake, but I'm not sure. Guess if you're a lawyer, you can read."

"I can."

"I'm thinking since you're waiting here anyway, would you read this over for me with your legal eyes and tell me what it says? I don't quite understand it."

Duncan looked at the man as Isaac pulled the paper out of his pocket, opened it up, looked at it, and handed it to Duncan upside-down. "The man who gave me this said it was a contract. Ain't never had one of these before," Isaac grumbled to Duncan. "Been building these things all around Long Lake and Newcomb with a man's handshake."

"I know, Isaac, but times are changing."

"Yup, and now you lawyers are taking the place of a handshake for money."

"No, mister, we earn our money because we protect people who may hire someone who doesn't complete the job or by reading legal documents for people."

"Like me. Okay then." Isaac reached out to take the paper back from Duncan, but Duncan pulled it away from his reach.

"Wait a minute. I didn't say I wouldn't read it for you." "I know, but I ain't got the money to pay you."

"That's okay, I'm bored right now. I'll read it if you tell me your name." "Oh, Isaac. Isaac Clement is my name."

"Do you live here?" "No."

"Where?"

"Long Lake. Okay, is that enough? What does the paper say?"

"Well, it says that he will pay you half to start the job and the other half when you are finished, and he won't pay if you get hurt. That is the gist of it. Looks normal. Oh, and it is Augusta Low. I know him. He's a good man." "So, it's mostly the same deal we all make by saying it."

"Yes, it looks good. You want to sign it now?" "Sign it?"

"Yes, see this line? You just make an X on it." He would not let this proud man know that an X was not a usual signature.

"Isaac put his X on the paper and the next day began the job but with thoughts of leaving it because this man, Low, had made him sign the paper. It meant nothing to Isaac because he was a man of his word, and the wall was completed not because of the X on the paper, but because he said he would complete it.

In the meantime, Isaac's wife Jane sewed for Mary Ann Keller who ran her tailor shop from the Keller farm. She was in her sixties and no longer raced her horse down Sawmill Road, but she still traveled the dusty road many mornings looking out at the dew rising off her beloved lake, watching a nuthatch inch up a yellow pine, or watching the leaves unfold into points of glory on a late spring morning. Memories sprang up as she passed the clearing where Abram gave her that first kiss. She remembered every bend in the road, every sound of the woodpecker, and every smell of this ancient, forested land. She had traveled these woods from the farm to the shore of Buck Mountain. She had survived encounters with bears, panthers, and even being stuck out in the lake in a heavy snow, but nothing had compared to the loss of her daughter and her love.

She did what tough Adirondack women did. She picked herself up, dusted herself off, and moved forward watching, always watching the goings on surrounding her. She recalled what her sister told her before she died. "Mary Ann,

I forgive you for what you did. Abram and I were thrown together day after day and what we thought was love was not. We cared for each other like friends, not two people in love. Don't feel sad or guilty. I am happy that you lived. You lived fully. You rode your horse, wild, unafraid, and you did it full speed ahead, no brakes." Sarah was right. Mary Ann had lived a good life among the whippoorwills that flittered around the dark branches and the squirrels that scampered up and down the trees in an endless search for food, much like the families who arrived with bitter winter winds at their backs searching for something not found elsewhere. Freedom. Freedom to look out at the gentle morning waters of this beautiful lake knowing that at any moment it could become a white-capped rolling menace ready to strike anything in its path. Yes, this was the land the Kellers came to, and this is the land they would die on, and all was well with Mary Ann Keller as she rode down Sawmill Road one more time.

# ACKNOWLEDGMENTS

A huge thanks to my editor, Martha Francis, for keeping me focused on dates and names, which proved difficult in this book. Thank you to my many readers who continually ask me when my next book will be out and give me their feedback on the latest book. Gratitude to Hilary LeBlanc for photos and newspaper help and Jim Swedberg who continues to beautifully photograph covers for my books. Thank you to Louisa Wright for portraying the woodswoman on the cover. I appreciate those historians, Jessie Stone and Francis Seaman who came before me and left vital information in our archives. Thank you, Helen Kentile, for taking my calls and for all those who gave me their histories or turned them over to our archives. Brian Castler and Joan Burke, thank you for getting me information I needed from the archives. Thank you to my Aunt Ann Huntley who gathered, stored, and then turned over to me all the data on our family in St. Lawrence County, and to my cousin, Charles Dalzell, who died many years ago but documented the journey of my ancestors to this country, and thanks to my dad who inherited the journal and my brother, Larry, who made copies of it for us. Thank you, Grandpa and Grandma Huntley, for being role models for me always.

# REFERENCES

Albert, T. & King, S. (1965) *The History of Hamilton County*. Lake Pleasant, NY: Wilderness Books.

Auclair, H. (2000) *French-Canadian Lineage of Emily Bertha Disotell*. Unpublished manuscript.

Benedict, D. & Roy, C. (2009, June 7) Abenaki People in the Adirondacks. *Adirondack Journal*. Blue Mountain, NY: Blue Mountain Museum.

Bufo, A. (1973, Fall) Workhorse of the Woods. *Adirondack Life*. 20-24.

Cedar Point Road Map. (2017) From the archives of the Newcomb, NY, Historical Museum.

Clement, E. (1888) History of Clement Family. Long Lake, NY.

Dalzell, C. & Dodd, A. (1877) Certified copy of marriage certificate. Waddington, NY.

Dalzell, G. (1937) *Immigration of the Dodds Family to America*. Canton, NY. Donaldson, A. (1921) *History of the Adirondacks* (Book 1). New York: The Century Co.

Eildon Hills Melrose, Scottish Borders UK. (2016). Retrieved December 2016. http://www.touristnetuk.com/scotland/borders. Emerson, L. (1840-1928). Early Life at Long Lake. Long Lake, NY: Lavonia Stanton Emerson.

Fennessy, L. (1996). History of Newcomb. Newcomb, NY: Lana Fennessy. Hammond Historical Museum (2018) https://www.hammondmuseum.com

Hochschild, H. (1952). *Township 34. A History with Digression of an Adirondack Township in Hamilton County in the State of New York*. New York.

Huntley, G. (2013) *Conquering the Wild*. Morgan Hill, CA: Bookstand Publishing.

Huntley, G. (2015) *Long Lake, Adirondack Heartland*. Morgan Hill, CA: Bookstand Publishing.

Huntley, G. (2018). *So Proudly They Hailed*. Morgan Hill, CA: Bookstand Publishing.

Huntley, V. (1978) *John Huntley of Lyme Connecticut*. Moodus, CT: Moodus Printing.

Rule, J. & Dodds, M. (1882) Certified copy of marriage certificate. Waddington, NY.

Rule, J.S. 81, of Waddington dies on Tuesday. (1928) *Commercial Advertiser*. Canton, NY.

Rule-Huntley. (1914). A very pretty home wedding. *The Madrid Harold*. Madrid, NY.

Scott, P. (2003) *The History of Strathbogie*. Tiverton, England: XL Publishing. Seaman, F. & Stone J. Notes from Long Lake Archives. Retrieved 2012-2015. Shaw, G. & Shaw, R. (1842-1900) *Tahawus-Newcomb and Long Lake*. Blue Mountain Lake, NY: Adirondack Experience.

Stoddard, R. (1874). Mitchel Sabattis of Long Lake. *The Adirondacks: Illustrated*. In a list by the proprietor of Long Lake Hotel, C.H. Kellogg. Retrieved 2016. www.hamilton.nygenweb.net/bios/sabattis.html.

The Quarterly. (1987) St. Lawrence County Historical Society. https://www.slcha.org/quarterly/issues/v032no3.pdf

Retrieved 2020. Todd, J. (1845). *Long Lake*. Fleischmanns, New York. Purple Mountain Publishing.

Town of Chester. Town of Chester.org. Historical Society. Retrieved December 2017. http://www.townofchesterny. org/

Town of Newcomb. Retrieved January 2018. http://www. newcombny.com/about/history.

Ike Robinson's shotgun, used from the mid 1840's to the mid 1870's courtesy of James Swedberg.

# BACKGROUND NOTE

The author has visited Scotland, Long Lake, Newcomb, Chestertown, Hammond, Rossie, Crary Mills, Canton, Waddington, and Ogdensburg researching graveyards and history in those areas. While visiting Waddington several times, the author interviewed people who knew the Dodds, Rule, and Huntley families and remembered the harness making shop run by the author's relatives. The author saw the shop and entered the house built in the early 1800s by Thomas Dodds. "The farm" in this book in Crary Mills is still active and owned by the Huntley family. This author tries to walk the ground she writes about, so she has walked throughout the area called Sawmill Road and Big Brook Village in the book. She grew up in this area and has camped, hiked, and canoed throughout the region.

www.gailhuntley.com
Gailhuntley01@yahoo.com